FINAN

RSMC NEXT GENERATION

AMY DAVIES

CONTENTS

This book is for anyone who thinks it is wrong to be different. Being who you are is NOT wrong. You are perfect the way you are.

Be Strong. Be You.

CHAPTER ONE

FINAN

My feet hit the rocky path in time with every heartbeat with each mile I run. Sweat is covering my body as I run up the hike trail I enjoy just thirty minutes away from the clubhouse.

I have long lost my t-shirt, which is tucked into the back of my shorts, and some AWOL is blasting through my earbuds, drowning out everything around me, as well as my inner thoughts.

Thoughts I don't want to think about right now. Pain tries to slice through me, but I push it down, not wanting to deal with it right now.

Now is the time for me to beat my thoughts, get to the top, enjoy the scenery, and then head home to deal with what has happened.

My heart beats against my ribcage, and my lungs scream at me to stop, but I bask in the feeling that running gives me. The need to focus on my breathing helps keep my thoughts away.

I get to the top of the trail and see other hikers up here. Some are taking their time to enjoy the view, while others, like me, are here to get lost in the exercise. Running helps keep me sane. I have always struggled with talking to people, which some people find strange, since I had a great childhood, and grew up in the club. The best parents anyone could ask for.

I have a blood brother who is truly my best friend and is always at my side, and I have many club brothers, who are cousins and uncles. Then there are the old ladies, who are my aunties.

I walk over to a large rock and climb up, sitting on the rough edge, where I watch the people below. My heart pounds as I pull in deep breaths, filling my lungs with fresh oxygen.

Dropping my backpack to my side, I pull my legs up and rest my forearms on my knees, taking in the serene moment.

A moment before all hell breaks loose when I get back home.

Before I left, my father and mom, Rookie and Della, broke the news to my brother, Calder, and me, that our mom has breast cancer. They caught it early, and the doctors believe she has a good chance of making a full recovery.

Mom will have the lump cut out, then they will decide once more tests are done if she needs chemo or radiation.

Letting my legs fall flat in front of me, I lean back on my palms, watching the clouds move across the sky. There may be clouds, but fuck me, it is hot. Tipping my head back, I point my face to the sky, close my eyes, and soak in the rays.

I tune into the sounds around me: kids laughing, some whining that they're tired; men talking work or sports. I hear couples talking about future plans, and I feel that familiar pang in my chest.

Royal is in that planning stage of his life after he got married in Vegas, after drinking himself to an almost blackout stage, but I think Tree is good for him. She calls him on his bullshit, so she also fits in with the club.

Her family have joined ours, and it feels right. The Rugged Skulls are always looking at ways of expanding, whether it be family or business. The Winslow's are like family now, maybe even more if my brother pulls his head out of his ass, but I know he doesn't see things like I do.

He seems to be blind to what is in front of him most of the time—well, unless he's looking in the mirror.

We're close in age, which is one of the reasons he's my best friend as well as my blood brother. There are just under eleven months between us; Irish twins we're known as. When I was born, my parents gave me an Irish name, then when my mom got pregnant with Calder, they hunted down for the right name that would flow with mine and also had an Irish theme. So they chose well.

Bringing my head back up, I click my neck before reaching for the backpack to get a bottle of water and some snacks. Twisting the cap off my water, I down half of it in one, soothing my dry throat.

Pulling open a container of fruit salad, I start eating the fruit, still people-watching.

A woman walks past me, her trim body partly covered in lycra shorts and matching sports bra. Her legs are tanned and toned, leading up to a flat stomach. Her hair is dark brown, almost black, short, and pulled back into a low and very tiny ponytail. I can't see her eyes because she's wearing sports sunglasses, similar to the ones I own, but today I'm in my aviators.

She throws a glance my way, offering me a small smile, before she carries on past. I dip my head in greeting but that's it, even as my gaze follows her and her perfect bubble ass in those shorts, until she's out of sight.

My dick takes note, twitching at the sight. Fuck, I can't be getting a hard-on out here where there are kids. I stay for a little while longer, cooling down before the trek back down to my truck.

Finishing off my water, I drop the bottle and the fruit back into my backpack, before throwing it over my shoulders and making my way off the rock.

Jumping down, I collide with someone. A small, warm person, that feeling soft beneath my hands.

Looking down, I see it's the woman who walked past me not so long ago.

"Oh my God, I am so sorry. I wasn't looking where I was going."

I smile down at her. "No problem. I should have made sure there was no one close when I jumped down. You okay? I didn't hurt you, did I?" My hands rest on her shoulders, and her skin is soft yet clammy beneath my callused palms.

She shivers, making me grin, then backs away a step, before she answers while taking her sunglasses off.

"No, I'm fine."

"That you are," slips from my mouth, and in inwardly groan.

Fucking lame as shit.

Because of being a club brat, I never had to try with women. They were there when I needed the release. It was the same in high school. All the girls wanted to get on their knees for me, and I took on the attention.

Her eyes are a deep brown, and they pull me in, so much I actually step forward, making her frown and step back.

I catch myself and back away. Licking my lips, I take in her face. She looks older than my twenty-four, maybe in her early thirties. My parents and the guys from the club say that I'm an old soul, because I act older than my actual age.

She smiles at me, her eyes crinkling in that genuine smile way.

"A flirt, I see."

I shrug at her comment, smiling.

Flirting is something my brothers are good at. I would rather watch people and take cues from them. It's something I've always done; sitting back, watching what makes people tick, what makes them happy. Facial expression and body language is something I've studied in my own time.

6

This woman likes what she sees, but I also see a guard in place, because she clearly sees that I'm younger than her.

"Possibly," is all I say.

"You going back down?" she asks, pointing down the trail, and I nod.

"Yeah. I need to get back. I have work to deal with."

"Can I walk with you, or do you plan to run back down?" she asks me.

"I can do with a walk," I answer.

We walk side by side, not saying much, but I can feel the heat coming off her body. The way her arm brushes against mine every few steps. Each time, the hairs on my body stand on end, and my dick twitches. Thankfully, it has the sense to not chub out in a public place.

"So, what do you do for work?" her breathy voice comes from next to me.

I'm not ashamed of the club, far from it, but most women only want my cock because I'm in the club.

"I find things," is all I say.

When we started the Rugged Hunters, we kept it on the downlow, mainly because the police hate us getting involved, but when their hands are tied, there is only so much they can do. That is why civilians come to us.

But we mostly work with MC's, or people not of the friendly kind.

"Sounds ominous," she says, and I give her a smile.

"It really isn't. But it pays the bills."

She simply nods and looks away, and I know I've fucked up by not elaborating, but I don't want her to know about me and the club. I want her to want me. Finan Price, not Finan, member of the Rugged Skulls MC.

That is, if she wants to know me at all.

Fuck, I hate feeling like this. No fucker would guess that a member of an MC would be socially awkward, but here I am. Like I've said, I didn't need to chase girls. They came to me.

Watching my brothers in the club flirt and fuck, I've picked up on plenty, so I know what I'm doing, but I've never had to make an extra effort to get a chick into bed.

I think this woman next to me would need a lot of effort, and I think she would be worth it.

We hit the bottom of the trail that leads out onto the large open parking lot, where some RVs are parked, with families sitting on the picnic benches enjoying their day.

"This is me," she says, pointing to a red SUV.

"Impressive," I state, walking her over to her vehicle.

"Thanks. I work hard, so I get to spend my money on adult things." She throws me a cheeky smile, and I chuckle.

The car beeps, so I pull open the driver's door for her, moving back so she can step closer.

"So what do you do for work?" I ask her the same question.

Her laugh makes my body sing, which has never happened before. She's getting under my skin, and we haven't even known each other for an hour. What the fuck is happening to me?

"Oh, you know, I design stuff."

"Sounds ominous," I reply, and her laughter gets louder.

The sounds smooths over my skin, making every nerve ending come alive. Her smile is wide, showing rows of straight white teeth; teeth I want to feel scrape along my cock.

Shit.

Her brown eyes are bright with laughter, and her hands go to her belly, holding it tight as she laughs at me. I grin, loving seeing her looking so carefree, and it's because of me. I lean against the car, watching her laugh, getting it out of her system.

"Oh, God, I needed that. More than you know." That gets my attention.

I straighten up, my gaze fixed on her, while she dries her eyes from laughing.

"Everything okay?"

She waves my question off.

"Yeah, just some family things going on." My question catches her off guard, because her laughing stops almost instantly.

She bites her lip as the air around us shifts.

This never happens to any other women I talk to, so why is this static between is building.

I stand stock still as her gaze drifts over my body, taking in the tribal tattoos on my biceps and shoulders, plus the scripture that runs across my collarbone. I work hard for my body, so I like that she is showing her appreciation. My cock jerks again, loving the feel of her taking in her fill of me.

Hell, I can see her on her knees, sucking my cock with those lips of hers. See her large tits bounce as I fuck her into the bed. They look like more than a handful, and I am more than fucking happy with that.

I look over her body up close, since she's doing it to me, and by the looks of her nipples pebbling in her sports bra, I think she approves, just like my cock does in my shorts.

"Like what you see, babe?" I ask her, breaking the silence between us.

Her gaze snaps to mine, and she bites her lip again, before smiling and climbing into the car, but she doesn't close the door.

Stepping forward, I lean one hand on top of the door and one on the car. I edge in, closing the distance between us.

This isn't my usual style, but she seems to make me want to be a cocky bastard. She clearly likes what she sees, and damn, it's me she sees and not the cut.

Taking a page out of my brother's book, I lean in further, taking her mouth in a sweet kiss, but it quicky heats up when I deepen it. My hand finds the back of her head, holding her to me. Her gasps lets my tongue inside her mouth, licking my way around the warm cavern.

God, she tastes fucking good. I bet she tastes good everywhere.

I pull back before I get us arrested for public indecency.

"Fuck. We need to stop before I take you right here on the seat, right here for everyone to see." Her cheeks flush at my words. Her lips are swollen from my kiss, and fuck me, I like that.

She's my first kiss in over eight years. I fell in love, or I thought I did. Then she bolted with some cunt in a BMW and a polo shirt. I haven't kissed anyone else since her. Never wanted that intimacy from another woman until now, with this woman.

How the hell did she get under my skin so quickly?

She also makes me not be me. If that makes sense? I'm awkward when it comes to talking to people I don't know. In the club, I'm fine, but outside, I feel out of my comfort zone.

My mom says it's because I'm always deep in thought, an old soul, watching and waiting for when people need me. I have been like this from a very young age, always watching the kids play. I did join in, but mostly I would watch them learn something, then when they couldn't do it the right way, I would see where they were going wrong and show them.

She says I'm her little 'Watcher.' I'm there for when anyone needs me. That I am loyal and fierce, not only in body but in mind too.

Licking my lips, I can taste this woman on me, and I groan, stepping back more, making her frown. If I don't go now, I know I will do something that will get us in trouble or scare her away.

"I need to go." I spin on my heel, heading to my own truck.

I hear her calling to me, but she doesn't know my name.

"Hey, tattoo boy." That makes me chuckle, and I look over my shoulder at her, cocking an eyebrow.

She shrugs, leaning out of her car.

"I don't know your name. I'm Joss, by the way."

"Finan."

"Maybe I'll see you here on another day, Finan," she says, and closes the door.

I stand still, watching her drive away. Shaking my head, I let out a small laugh, get into my truck, and head back to the clubhouse. I need to shower and clean up so I can go and see my mom.

Meeting Joss seems to have come at the right time. Being around her made me completely forget the shit that is swirling in my life right now.

Bring on the day I see her again.

CHAPTER TWO

JOSS

Sucking the jelly from my fingers, I place the plate in my other hand down on the kitchen island and call out to my daughter.

"Juni. Breakfast is ready. Get your butt down here."

I hear her stomping around upstairs and sigh, knowing I'm in for another argument with her. Leaning back against the counter, I pick up my coffee mug, savoring the deep, earthy taste of the black liquid.

My phone beeps next to me, I inwardly groan knowing who it is that is texting me this early. My mother-in-law. She loves to torment me. Hell, she has for going on sixteen years.

The day my late husband brought me home to meet his folks was the day she decided to hate on me. From the get-go, she disliked me, never thought I was good enough for her son. And do not get me started on when we got married, or even when I got pregnant with Juni.

When Owen was alive, I believed I was a princess. I never wanted for anything, and he worshiped the ground I walked on, just like I did him. He was my world. So you can imagine how delighted I was when he proposed to me.

We had a small, intimate wedding, with just our immediate family and some friends. We didn't want anything big; just wanted it done because he was going to be deployed. I used to hate it when he left, but he lived for the Army, so I stood by him and supported him through it.

We may have been young, very young but we loved each other and wanted to be man and wife before he left.

I was and am still a proud Army wife, even though Owen has been dead for fourteen years. On his first tour, his convoy was hit, and he was killed, along with two other men and one female. I was seven months pregnant with our only baby. Being a teenage widow was devastating but I got through it.

It devastated me; my world crumbled around me. My in-laws hated that I was carrying a piece of their dead son. They demanded that I have an abortion.

Juni coming into the room breaks me from my thoughts, then has me looking at my phone.

"Eat something this morning, please."

Juni sighs, rolling her eyes at me, and I grit my teeth to stop from starting yet another screaming match, which I know is inevitable.

Ines: I want to see Juni this weekend. Make it happen.

Sighing, I look up at my fourteen-year-old daughter, who is eating a pancake, smothering it with peanut butter and jelly. I smile because that's what her father liked.

Looking back down at my phone, I type out a quick, sharp response.

Me: Not this weekend. She has plans. Not changing them.

My phone dings but I ignore it, placing it back on the counter. I join Juni at the island.

"What's the plans in school today?" I ask, before popping some fruit into my mouth.

The burst of orange flavor hits my taste buds, making my mouth water. I eat more because I know I have a full day of work, and I often forget to eat, so I eat when I remember.

"Was that Grandma texting?" Juni asks me, before taking a sip of her orange juice.

"Yeah. She wants to see you this weekend. I told her you had plans."

She nods. "Good. She knows I'm going to Nicole's party. I told her when I saw her last. Why can't she ever think of me, Mom?"

I walk around the island and kiss the top of her head. Since Juni was born, Owen's parents have always been in her life, always trying to dictate how I bring her up. Trying to take over when they don't like the things I do.

We have been just fine the two of us. We click. We are a mother and daughter team. My own parents respect boundaries and our relationship, and never try to sabotage it, unlike Owen's family.

They believe that since Owen died, and Juni is their only connection to him, they deserve her more than me, because I work too much and never have time for my daughter.

I work while she is in school, or when she goes to bed. Nothing and no one gets in the way of our time together. Plus, Juni loves my work. More often than not, she actually helps me design what my client wants and offers a teenage opinion.

"I know, baby. She won't listen. You're at the right age to decide if you want to see them. This is your choice. We've talked about this before. You are a very intelligent young lady, who I love to the moon and back, plus a million times round the world."

That gets me a giggle and a wide smile.

She reminds me so much of Owen. She has his bright blue eyes, his dirty blond hair, but my stubbornness and attitude.

It hits me right in the chest, seeing her looking so much like her dad, who I know would have loved his baby girl just as much as me. Owen had always wanted kids. We had long talks about starting a family, even as young as we were. If you ask his family, he never wanted any.

The only member of my in-laws that have supported me through it all has been Owen's sister, Olivia. She has always called me her sister, and always had my back when it came to her parents. They like to throw their money and high social standing around to get what they want.

Juni looks down at her plate, pushing the pancake around with her fork, thinking deeply before she replies. This is one of the things that reminds me of Owen. He always thought things through, never dived in headfirst, unlike me. Well, that was the old me. Now that I have Juni to think about, I always tend to overthink things.

Looking up at me, I see that her heart is torn. "I'll tell her that I will see her next week. The weekend with Nicole is all planned out and I don't want to be the only one not there. This is the party of the summer," she rushes out, and I smile at her. "I know. We went shopping for the perfect outfit and swimwear, didn't we?" Her smile brightens, and it's like all the sad stuff is forgotten for this moment in time.

"Oh, speaking of meeting up." Again, she looks toward her phone, then back to me. "I've been talking to this girl online. We like the same things: music, clothes, things like that. She is really cool, Mom. She wants to meet up this week. I told her I would ask you."

I stand there staring at her, not sure what to say.

You hear all kinds of horror stories of girls being groomed over the internet, perverted men kidnapping them, doing horrific things too hard to comprehend, even selling the girls.

My heart skips as I take in her hopeful face. I know that look will fall right off when I give her my answer, and she will explode, telling me that I don't love her, that I hate her, that this is why I'm ruining her life.

"I can't allow that, baby. I'm sorry. There are all kinds of people on the internet that use false profiles to drag girls in, giving them a sense of false friendship. You are only fourteen, Juni, I'm sorry, but no. You should be getting excited for Nicole's party, not some girl you met online."

I start picking up the dirty dishes, waiting for the gasket to get blown off before she stomps out of here to catch the school bus. With her getting older and getting close to her period starting, she is full of bubbling emotions that are hard to get a read on sometimes.

Placing the dishes in the sink, I turn around to look at her. Tears fill her eyes. It would break my heart if the tears were for something meaningful, but to meet someone online, no way.

She sucks in a breath, and I count.

Three, two, one...

"Why do you hate me so much? Just because you don't have a social life does not mean you can ruin mine."

"Ruin yours? I do believe I just spent over three-hundred dollars on a new outfit for one freaking day, Juni. I am leaving you at Nicole's house all day, so you can be with your friends. Do not push me on this."

She gets off the stool and rounds the island, coming closer to me. I know she would never dare hit me, but lately, she has been pushing my buttons more and more, and at times, I can't help but think she will snap one day.

"You need to get laid, Mom. Get someone to pull that stick out of your ass and force you to have some fun.

Being with Nicole is not the same as meeting Chloe. I want to meet her. She gets me," she screams, her hair whipping around her face.

Tears rush over her cheeks, and it almost gets me to soften toward her in this situation, but I refuse to, instead thinking back to a job I did last year for a counselling team that helped young girls who were kidnap and rape victims.

I steel my spine, shifting into full mom mode.

"You can walk out that door now and think about what you have said, and still go to Nicole's party this weekend. Or you can keep screaming at me, saying nasty things, and get your skinny ass grounded, so you miss the party. Up to you, kid."

Her eyes widen in shock, her mouth slams shut, and I inwardly jump for joy at the small triumph.

With one more glare, she runs from the kitchen, up to her room to collect her things for school. Once she is out of my sight, I close my eyes, pulling in a deep, fortifying breath to calm my shot nerves.

I hear her stomping back down, then she runs past me.

"I hate you," she calls to me.

"Yeah, well, I hate you too," I call after her in a cheery tone, just so she I don't mean it, just as the door slams.

We have been down this road before. I am not one of those mothers that gives in because my child threw a tantrum. She will learn respect and manners.

Being a hormonal teenager, with a dead father and shitty grandparents, does not give her the right to be a brat.

Once the dishes are rinsed and placed in the dishwasher, I get to making tonight's dinner in the slow cooker. I love to cook, but when I have a busy day, I like to be prepared. Making sure we have food without the fuss of making it from scratch.

When I'm done with that, I fill up my coffee mug and make my way down the hall that leads to my office.

Setting my mug down on the coaster, I hit the switch to turn my computer on. I flick through my social media while my computer boots up, smiling when I see my friends and family posting their happy memories.

I quickly upload an image of the photo I took at the top of the trail I hiked this weekend. It was stunningly beautiful. The sun was high in the sky, very little clouds, and the temperature was hot, perfect for a hike to sweat out any stress.

Images of the guy, Finan, pop into my head as I think of that day. He was something else. All tall, packed with muscles and tattoos. His skin glistened in the sun from the sweat, and damn if I didn't want to lick him.

I have no doubt he has women falling to their knees by just flashing them a smile, because believe me, he almost had me dropping to the ground.

His smile lit up his face, and the short stubble framed his jaw perfectly, like he keeps it in shape. I didn't get to see his eyes because they were hidden behind expensive-looking aviators. What I wouldn't have given to see his eyes.

A thought pops into my head, so I listen, even though I'm not sure I want to know.

I type in his first name—if that's his real name, not that he had any reason to lie to me. Nothing pops up on the social platforms I use. I go to type his name into Google, even though it's a long shot, but my phone rings, pulling me from any desires to find this man.

Pushing thoughts of Juni and Finan out of my head, I get to work. I run my own business, with three other women beneath me. We are freelance writers. We mostly work on taglines and scripts for companies that want to renew their TV and social media commercials.

We have also worked with a sports team, and a boy band.

I do well for myself; enough to support both Juni and me comfortably.

Like I said, she likes to help, especially if my client is targeting teenagers. When she does help, I do up her allowance that week, which she saves for something she really wants.

I brought Juni up with values in all aspects. Like money is not everything, but you must work hard for it. Work hard, play hard, as they say. Also, you won't get anything for nothing.

My phone dings with a text, and I roll my eyes when I see my ex-mother-in-law's name. Clearing the notification, I notice the time and get up to have some lunch.

I always knew she was good for something, I think, and giggle to myself, as I make myself a sandwich before I dive back into work.

CHAPTER THREE

FINAN

I finish off my coffee, before yawning for the millionth time. I enjoy sitting around waiting, if there's something to watch, but staring at a fucking brick building is not my idea of fun.

I'm in the truck with Maverick while we watch to see if this punk-ass turns up. He robbed a pawn shop and stole the owner's gun as well. We're packing because we don't know if the little shit still has the weapon or if he has sold it.

"You want one?" Mav asks from his seat.

Looking down at the cheesy chicken bite shit he's eating, I shake my head.

"Nah, man, I'm good. Thanks though."

He shrugs and munches on a bite, before speaking again.

"You okay? You've been extra quiet the last few days."

Bringing my gaze up to him, I take in how much he looks like Sarge and his brother, Zeb. Olive skin and dark hair. Estelle never got a look in with him.

Thinking over his question, I think back to Joss and the hike. She has been in my dreams, making me wake up sticky because I fucking came all over myself.

The dream was beyond hot, something I don't experience much.

I am not a virgin, not by a long shot. I mean, I'm a club member. But I'm not one to have meaningless sex anymore. I get blowjobs from some of the Rugged Regs when they come around, but usually, I take care of myself. I have also never eaten a pussy before. It was just never my thing; seemed too intimate.

Is it better with a woman? Fuck yes. I just want something more.

When I think of more, I see Joss: the way she smiled at me, her stunning dark eyes as she bit her lip while taking my body inside of her.

I have no doubt that I could fuck her for days and never get bored. Mapping her body with my tongue, my fingers, memorizing every inch of her. I knew I should have asked for her number. Fuck knows if I will see her again. Typical that I make a connection with someone, finally feel like I could get some on the regular with a chick I like, and I forget to ask the most mundane thing.

"Dude, where the fuck did you go?" Mav nudges me.

I blink, not realizing I zoned out. Sitting up straight, sniffing, I shrug my shoulders. I look at him, seeing his brow turned down.

"Sorry, thinking about a dream I had," I explain.

"Must have been fucking hot going by the color on your cheeks, brother." Mav winks at me, and I can't help but smile back at him.

Maverick is the biggest man slut I have ever known. He will fuck anything that smiles at him, or he smiles at. He's bisexual and isn't afraid to hide it. He is proud as fuck of his sexuality, as should everyone be.

"Yeah, it was," is all I say.

I tend to keep things to myself, work shit out on my own, but I have been known to ask for help from time to time.

Maverick goes to say something, but I see the guy's car pulling up.

"There." I point over to where he's parking.

Maverick, puffs out his chest, opening the door. "Let's get this prick. I have a pussy to fuck."

Shaking my head, I should be surprised but I'm not. This is Maverick, after all.

As quietly as we can, we get out, watching the guy's every move.

Stepping closer, I pull my gun out from the waistband of my jeans, aiming at him in case he decides to shoot at us first. Believe me, it will be him before us.

Maverick gets my attention, pointing to the side door, letting me know he's going in that way, while I go in the front. I nod, then look back to the door I'm sneaking through.

Careful twisting the round doorknob, I pull the door open, pointing my gun in first, so I'm not caught off guard. I look both ways as I move further into the room, my gaze scanning the area.

Hearing a man's voice, I quickly move in that direction. I'm only hearing one side of a conversation, so I assume he's talking on his cell phone.

Closing in, I'm very aware of my surroundings. After what happened to Calder a few weeks ago, I am extra vigilant when on a hunt. The fucker loved being shot because he gets to brag about his new scar.

Rounding a corner, I check before moving closer, as the guy sits on a scruffy-looking chair. A coffee table is in front of him, littered with all sorts of drug paraphernalia, beer cans and pizza boxes. The fucker is using this has a hide out or meet up point.

"Yeah, man. I got everything. It was easy as fuck. The old dude cowered like a pussy," the prick says into the phone, then laughs.

I silently walk up behind the chair, seeing Maverick close in next to me. He nods, and I make my move, stepping closer and placing the gun flush against the guy's head, just as Mav pulls the phone away and hangs up the call.

"What the fuck?" the cunt spits out.

"You thought you wouldn't be caught, huh, fucker," Maverick says, while he punches the bastard in the face.

He calls out in pain, looking between the two of us with a wide-eyed, stunned expression on his face.

"Who the fuck are you?" He gets to his feet, and Maverick closes in before pulling his hands behind his back, using zip ties to tie him up.

Pointing to my cut, I grin at him, and his eyes go wide

"We are the Rugged Skulls MC, fuckface. You picked the wrong pawn shop to rob."

I drag the cunt out of the warehouse, while Maverick collects the items that were stolen from the pawn shop, plus some other items. By items, I mean guns, and some electronics.

Mav lights the place up, letting it burn to the ground. It's known for its drug dealing and junkies hanging around, giving people shit in nearby neighborhoods.

I pop open the trunk and throw the fucker in, ready to turn him over to the people who hired the Rugged Hunters.

I don't ask questions; I just do the jobs and collect the cash. The boys would never steer me wrong; I trust them with my life. Being the quiet one of the club, people think I'm a push over, but they would be wrong. I'm the most calculated out of us, seeing things that can be done a different way to cause more damage.

"Let's get this fucker dropped off. My pussy for the night is waiting for me back at the motel room." Maverick rubs his hand over his cock. I shake my head at him, making him laugh.

"Brother, you need to get laid." He winks at me.

"How the fuck can I get laid when you fuck every pussy out there, man?" I joke back, and he laughs harder.

We drive to the place that hired us, hand over the scummy thief, and leave. Maverick drives us to the motel we booked for the night. My eyes are starting to burn from being so tired, my body feels heavy, and my stomach growls from being so hungry.

I usually eat healthily, but right now, a big, huge, greasy burger with onion rings and fries sounds like it would hit the spot.

"You need sleep, brother," Mav says from his seat as he parks the truck. I nod.

"Yeah, but I need food first. You coming to the diner for something to eat?"

"Nah. My food is already here, man." He nods to the girl leaning against the wall next to our motel room door.

I sigh and climb out of the truck. She smiles when she sees us, no doubt thinking she is going to be fucked by us both, but I'm not into that shit. I hate sharing. Once I get my woman, no bastard will see her coming apart from me fucking her with my fingers, tongue, or my cock.

Some of my brothers like to share, mainly Maverick, but not me.

"Hey, honey," Maverick purrs from my side, and I force myself not to roll my eyes.

"You guys look beat; I hope you're not too tired to take care of me," she says in a sexy, smooth voice, and I have to admit, my cock twitches at the sound of it. She's hot, and her voice is one that belongs on one of those sex phone lines.

Mav chuckles as he steps up to her, laying his hands on her hips, moving in to kiss her neck. She giggles, and I cringe at the sound because she all of a sudden sounds fake as fuck.

Shaking my head, I move past them, pulling the key out of my pocket and opening the door. I faintly hear Mav say 'thanks,' but I ignore him. I didn't do this for him. I want my fucking wallet because I never take it on a hunt with me.

They fall onto the bed, tearing each other's clothes off, and I make a quick dash for the door, not wanting to see Maverick's dick yet again. That has happened way too many times for me to count. Tucking my wallet into the back pocket of my jeans, I head for the door.

"I thought he was joining us," the chick calls out with a pout on her face.

Maverick winks, then grabs her tit, making her moan.

"No, honey. You're only here for me. Finan doesn't like to share. Plus, my cock will put his to shame. Ain't that right, brother." He grins at me, and I shake my head at him, smiling.

"In your dreams. My cock is way fucking bigger and better than yours." With that, I leave, feeling my stomach tightening at having a conversation about my dick with a complete stranger.

We joke around as brothers, but that's okay. In front of strangers, no fucking way. Only my woman gets to discuss my cock. I would say she's the only one to see it, but I do get it sucked from time to time by one of the Regs around the clubhouse.

After walking the short distance to the local diner, I push through the door, looking around and taking it all in. Some people are sitting at the tables, some at the long counter that covers most of the room. Booths sit to one side, where some customers are eating and talking.

"Sit where you like, honey. I'll be right with ya." The woman walking around with a tray filled with plates of food says.

I nod and take a seat at one of the back booths, making sure I can see the entrance and the other people in the room. There's a young couple huddled in their booth, kissing and smiling. Young love: that will get you every time.

I smile, then look down at my menu. Once I know what I want, I look up, taking in the room again, just as the waitress comes over, smiling at me.

She looks to be in her late fifties maybe, but still looks put together.

"Hi, doll. What can I get you?" she asks as she places a glass of water on my table.

"I'll have the double cheeseburger and fries, with onion rings. Actually, make that extra fries and a milkshake. Thanks." I smile at her.

"Growing boy, I see," she states, looking over my body.

Grinning, I nod. "Yeah," is all I say.

She expects me to say more, and when I don't, she shrugs and walks away to put my order in. I've always respected the people who do manual and physical work for long hours, but seeing what Royal's wife, Tree, does, when she works, my appreciation for the people who work in diners has grown so fucking much. They are on their feet for up to nine to twelve hours a day, and fuck me, the shit they take from customers is crazy.

Don't get me wrong, Crossroads staff don't get much shit anymore, since Tree married a Rugged Skulls member.

Royal has changed so much since marrying Tree. Albeit it was a drunk as fuck wedding, but they fell in love and are happy.

Thinking of them being happy... Images of Joss pop into my head again. Damn, that woman has plagued my mind since that day at the trail.

I've wondered what she's been doing, who she's been with, like a fucking stalker. I even checked online but didn't get much, since I didn't know her surname. No clue why the fuck I didn't ask.

I sound like a teenage boy meeting a girl for the first time, but she made me feel things no other woman has before, and that got my body and mind intrigued.

My food is brought over to me, breaking my thoughts of the woman who made an impact on me.

"You in town for work, doll?" the waitress asks me, as I add ketchup to my burger and salt to my fries. I like salty fries, when I do actually eat them.

"You could say that." I leave it at that.

"Not very chatty, are you? I mean, when a guy looks like you, he flirts and lays on the charm, but you seem to be playing the quiet, shy type."

"Not playing," I state, my voice harsher than it was. "Can I eat my food now?" I don't look at her when I say this.

"Well, alrighty then," she mutters, and leaves me be.

Fuck. I close my eyes, and my fists clench on top of the table. I didn't want to snap at her, but fuck me, I hate talking about myself to people I don't know.

I eat my food in no time at all, being that hungry.

Sliding out of my booth, I head over to the register to pay. The woman looks up at me.

"I'm sorry for snapping earlier. My work is hard to talk about and it gets to me sometimes." Pulling out my wallet, I hand her a fifty, knowing it's way more than what my meal came to, but it's an apology of sorts. I know she can't make much working here.

"Oh, honey I didn't take it to heart. I've worked here for long enough to know when someone doesn't mean when they lash out." The smile she gives me makes the knot in my stomach lessen.

I nod and head for the door, dreading getting back to the motel. The walk back is peaceful, something I need to clear my head and work out where the fuck I'm sleeping tonight, because I know Maverick can fuck for hours.

As I get closer to where I am supposed to sleep tonight, I see some people sitting around, enjoying the evening. They all laugh and snigger, looking to my room.

I don't have to guess what they're laughing at; I can hear the banshee sounds that are coming from behind the door. Sighing, I head for the office to see if they have another room as far away from my brother as possible.

Once settled into my new room, I strip and jump into the shower, making a quick work of washing the day off my skin. Before I know it, I'm falling into my bed for the night, my dick hard, thinking of how Joss' ass looked in her running shorts; how sexy as hell her tits looked.

I grip my dick, jerking slow and steady, paying close attention to the head, which is turning purple from the pressure. I like slow and steady, slow licks from a chick's tongue. Will Joss do that for me?

36

With my other hand, I tweak my nipples, and before I know it, I'm coming all over my hand and abs. I chuckle to myself, because I should have done this in the shower, or before. Now, I'm all sticky and need another shower.

When I've done all that, I chill in the bed, watching some random old movie until I fall asleep.

CHAPTER FOUR

JOSS

I hit send, sending a text to Juni, letting her know I'm leaving the store and will be home in time to make her some dinner before she goes over to Nicole's house to work on their school project.

I tuck my phone into my back pocket, before loading all the groceries into the trunk of the car. Usually, Juni gets back within minutes, so once I've loaded up the car, I check my phone, but there's nothing. I frown down at the little device in my hand. Nothing.

Pulling up her contact, I tap the call button, which goes to voicemail straight away. My heart skips a beat because this has never happened before. She knows to answer me on the first call. She knows I worry about her.

Deciding to wait until I get home and wait for her, I get into my car and start it up, then drive in the direction of my house. The entire drive, my nerves build, and a sinking feeling in the pit of my stomach gets deeper and deeper.

It's been four days since we had the verbal sparring session about her meeting that girl Chloe, she met online. She has been distant, only giving one-word answers, leaving for school without saying goodbye, or that she loves me.

Clearly me not letting her meet this girl really did do a number on our relationship. This has never been what we have been about. We are always done things together, we talk things out, and we never go to bed angry, but her meeting this Chloe girl really has made Juni's personality change.

For that, I'm scared. Worried.

Pulling up at the house, I check my phone before I even leave the car. Still nothing.

I climb out and try calling her again, yet it goes to voice-mail once more. Now I'm really getting scared.

Once may be a mistake, but not a second or a third time. I hang up again and let out a frustrated sigh, then go to the trunk to unload everything I got at the store.

Carrying everything into the house, I put the groceries away, before getting started on something for us to eat when she gets here. She has to come home.

Another hour goes by and still nothing from Juni.

Another hour.

Food is ready. I look at the clock on the kitchen wall and still no Juni. I call Nicole and speak to her, then her parents. Nicole says Juni was in school, and she saw her walk toward the bus, but after that, she never seen or heard from her.

My panic starts to build. She is never this late home from school.

I call around her other friends, but none have seen or heard from her since school.

It suddenly hits me that I can track her phone.

I pull up the tracker app.

"Come on. Come on. Come on," I mutter as the map loads, then stops on her last known location.

The school. It says she has been offline since school finished.

"What the fuck?" I mutter.

Pulling up my mom's contact, I call her. It rings three times before she answers.

"Hey, baby girl."

"Hey, Mama, is Juni there with you?" I rush out, unable to keep the panic out of my voice.

"No. She said she had plans today. Is she not home yet?"

I pinch the bridge of my nose and close my eyes, feeling a tension headache building.

"No, Mom. She hasn't come home. She isn't returning my texts, answering my calls, or calling me back. Her location is off. It says it was turned off by the school. That was hours ago, Mom. Where is she?"

Tears burn my eyes. I can hear my mom calling my father.

"Baby, meet us at the police station. This needs to be reported. An Amber Alert needs to be put out."

"Oh, my God, Mom. She has to be okay. I can't lose her too," I cry.

My mom's soothing voice comes through the phone. "She is strong and stubborn like her mom. Quick witted. So she will do what she can to get herself home. You have to believe that she is perfectly fine and is just acting like a raging hormonal teenager, okay."

I nod but don't speak. I have to believe that she is okay, that she'll walk through the door any second now. My gaze drifts to the door, praying with all my might that it swings open, and Juni comes charging in. I will take a raging daughter right now rather than a possible missing one. One that could be hurt, or worse.

"I will meet you there, baby, okay. Drive carefully."

"Yes, Mom." We hang up, and I gather my things, hurriedly getting to my car and driving to the police station.

It takes me nearly twenty minutes to get to the police station, and as I park, I see my parents already waiting for me. When I get out of the car, I rush to them, sobbing. My chest constricts from the pressure of worry.

My dad rubs my back as my mom holds me against her body. She soothes me, and it reminds me of when I was younger and sick. She would let me stay home from school and spoil me rotten. Both me and my brother, Matt, got away with murder when we were younger, but we all grew up with principles and respect.

"Come on, sweetie. Let's get this done," my dad says, and I nod.

They lead me inside, and we all walk up to the admin front desk. There is an older guy there in a police uniform, but he looks like he would rather be anywhere but here.

My dad speaks first, breaking the man's concentration from the newspaper in front of him.

"Excuse me, we want to report a missing teenager. My granddaughter." My father's voice carries authority, but the officer looks like he couldn't care less.

"Let me guess you had a fight with her, she ran off, and now you want to report her missing."

I am gob-smacked by the flat tone of his voice. He genuinely sounds bored.

"No, we didn't have an argument. She was fine going to school this morning. School ended five hours ago, and she is still not home. She hasn't called or text. I even tracked her phone, and it says she's offline, but her last location recorded was at the school. I am telling you now, something is wrong," I cry.

He waves his hand in the air at me, like he's blowing off my panicked explanation. Asshole.

"She'll come home when she's hungry. Five hours is nothing."

"She is fourteen years old. An Amber Alert needs to be put out," my dad snaps.

That gets the officer's attention. He leans on the desk, thinking he can intimidate John Samuels. I almost snort at seeing how my father's eyes get that hard look as he stares at the officer. My dad is ex-army, and he does not take shit from anyone.

"Listen here, you fat waste of space in an officer's uniform. Get me your chief. We won't be dealing with you any longer," my dad snaps.

"Now you listen, you piece of shit, you don't get to talk to me that way. Get on out of here. I'm sure the brat will turn up when she's ready to come home," he bellows at my dad, gaining the attention of some other officers.

He looks to me, still pissed off. "Maybe if you were a better mom, and removed that stick from up your ass, your daughter wouldn't run away from you, huh."

I gasp in shock.

How can this person promise to serve and protect, and then act like this when there is a missing fourteen-year-old girl out there?

Before any of us can say anything, a stern voice comes from behind the shitty officer. The man looks like he's in charge, all big and sporting a higher officer look, if you know what I mean. He oozes authority.

"That is enough. Go take a walk," he tells the officer.

"Yes, sir."

I snigger at the sudden childlike voice he's now using. He looks at me with a face like he sucked on a lemon, and I poke my tongue out at him, because yeah, I am in that kind of mood.

This piece of fuck doesn't care for my daughter. He doesn't deserve to wear the uniform.

"I am Chief Raymond. What can I help you folks with?"

My dad explains everything that I had already said. The chief nods as my father speaks. With every word he says, my heart shrinks, my stomach knots, and tears run down my face.

My fear for Juni coming home is building every second she is not with me. I need her home with me. I want to smell her hair, and breathe in her bubblegum scent that she loves so much.

She is never leaving my sight again when we get her home. I may ground her for all of eternity, so I won't lose her again.

I'm pushing down images of her lost, hurt, and scared. I can't let myself believe that this is happening to her, yet I feel it in my gut. We have this connection that can't be described. She is the other half to my soul. I used to think it was Owen, but when he left me, Juni took over.

She is what I live for.

I dry my face of the fresh tears that are coating my skin and look to the Chief. He gives me a sad smile

"Have you and your daughter had a fight lately; anything that could make her run away?"

I nod. "Four days ago. She hasn't spoken to me much since."

He nods, noting some things down, then looking to me again.

"You are not going to like what I am about to say, but it sounds like your daughter is just blowing off steam or making you feel bad for the fight. She'll come home. She's a typical teenager and punishing you. Unfortunately, we see it all the time. There is no reason to issue an Amber Alert. I'm sorry. If she hasn't returned home in twenty-four hours, then we can get the ball rolling."

He genuinely looks sad that there isn't much he can do.

I sob, and my mother pulls me to her. I cry against her body, my own shaking with the fear that something is wrong, but I know the police can't go on a gut feeling.

"I will keep my notes on file and keep an eye out for anything that links to your daughter in the next twenty-four hours. In the meantime, if you genuinely think some-thing is wrong," he looks round, before pulling a small brown business card from his pocket, "contact these guys." With that, he turns and leaves.

My parents thank the Chief and pull me out of the building and over to my car. I can't drive in the state I'm in, so my mom helps me into the passenger seat. She's going to drive my car while my father follows behind us.

I cry all the way home. With puffy eyes, I stare out the window, hoping to catch a glimpse of my daughter. Every teenage girl with dirty blond hair reminds me of Juni.

"She might be at home." My mom sounds hopeful, but I know in my heart she isn't.

We pull up outside. Before my mom can turn the car off, I run to the door and unlock it, rushing inside to make sure.

"JUNI. Juni, are you here?" I call out.

I dart up the stairs to her room and let out a sob when it sinks in that she's not here.

"Oh God, where are you, baby girl," I cry, my knees giving out.

A mother knows when her baby needs her; she knows when something is wrong. And I believe that something is wrong.

I feel my father's arms go around me, holding me tight to him as I fall apart.

Once my tears slow and my breathing calms down, I look down at the brown business card in my hand, which is now slightly rumpled from my tight fists.

RUGGED HUNTERS.

They help people when the police can't, so why does the Chief of Police have their card? Are they into illegal stuff? My chest blooms with hope. They will help find Juni, since the police are making me wait, though I don't think they will do much anyway.

Pulling back from my father, I look up at him then back down to the card.

"Whatever it takes, baby. Give them a call or go to the clubhouse. The club is known, and not for the bad stuff. They seem to be on the good side of the law with a hint of bad ass." I give him a small smile and nod.

"Yeah, I have heard of them. I've only seen them on their bikes, never interacted. I will go now. Will you and Mom stay here in case she comes back? Call me right away if she does."

"We will, baby girl. Are you sure you're okay to drive?" he asks me, and I nod.

Pulling in a deep breath, I steady my heart and climb to my feet. My dad follows.

"I have to do this, Daddy," I say with conviction.

I will get my girl home, come hell or high water. I will bring Juni home.

I look down at the card. Or the Rugged Hunters will I think as I leave the house.

CHAPTER FIVE

FINAN

Lining up my shot on the pool table in the main room, I look up and see my brother, Calder, doing some weird hip shaking thing, trying to distract me from making my shot.

Prick knows it takes a lot to make me fuck up, but he tries anyway. I can hear my father, Rookie, chuckle, before he takes a sip of his beer.

"You will never grow out of that, will you, son?" he asks Calder, who shakes his head, smirking at me.

We have always gone against each other in everyday things, but it never got nasty between us; always fun and filled with sweet triumph when I beat the little shit.

"Where is the fun in that, Pop? I mean, one day the fucker will break." He winks at me, and I shake my head at him.

Looking back down the long thin wood of my pool cue, I take my shot. The white ball bounces off the side, moves across the red felt covering and slams into the solid green ball, which falls into the corner pocket.

"Fucker," Calder mutters, before downing the rest of his drink.

"Boy, you will never learn. Now, pay your brother," Dad says.

Calder pulls his wallet out, slamming a fifty in my hand, and I tip my head at him.

"Thanks, bro." I look at my dad and see how tired he looks.

The worry for my mom is clear on his face. Mom is booked in for her operation next week. She's not overly concerned about it, but my dad's world is my mom, so losing her would make us lose him too.

My father is watching my mom like a hawk. He has been since they broke the news to us. It's hard watching my mom and knowing she's sick, and there is fuck all any of us can do about it. It's in the hands of her doctors and her body to fight it.

Della Price may be sweet and reserved, but damn, she is a fighter and stubborn to boot.

Placing my hand on my dad's shoulder, he drags his gaze from my mom to look at me.

"She'll be fine, Pop. She is one tough broad." I smile. Calder closes in also, all of us now looking at my mom as she laughs with Synclare, Farrah and Astrid.

"She is too stubborn to leave us, Dad. You know that. She'll know that we'll starve to death if she isn't here to feed us," Calder adds.

We try to make light of things, but we know that if they can't cut all the cancer out, then she will need chemotherapy. It's a waiting game now, but still worrying, nonetheless.

"I know, boys. I just fucking hate waiting. It's not my strong suit, you know. When your grandparents went, that was hard enough for Lee and me, then Anthony passed, and it fucked with my head. I know we're getting older, but I can't go on without her. I had always planned to go before her. She's stronger than me. She will survive without me." My dad's voice breaks.

The broody Irish fucker, known as Rookie, looks like he is ready to break. In that split second, my mom turns her head, like she senses our upset, and fuck me, her smile widens as she looks at the three men in her life.

My brother and I standing side by side with our dad is the only place we want to be. That's why we always knew we would prospect into the club. Do anything that was needed to be at our dad's and uncles' sides. To always have their back and offer our loyalty.

"My boys," my mom says as she walks slowly over to us.

She kisses my cheek, then Calder's, before kissing Dad on the mouth.

"There are kids here, you know. Gross as fuck." Calder fake gags, making my parents smile against each other's lips.

Fuck me, this is what I want. This is how I want to feel when I find my old lady.

Joss.

Her name flashes through my head, like it has done for days now.

One of the new prospects comes into the room, calling my brother's and my name.

"Finan, Calder, there's a chick at the gate asking about the Rugged Hunters. Should I let her in?"

"Yeah, man," I say.

"Let's see what this is about," my father states, helping my mom back over to the other women.

He kisses her on the head once she's settled into her chair. We go to walk towards the door, when the prospect comes back inside, followed by someone I never thought I would see again.

Joss.

My breath stutters in my chest, and my cock twitches in my pants at the sight of her. She's wearing simple blue jean shorts with a pair of Vans, and a plain V-neck t-shirt that hugs her juicy tits perfectly.

The top half of her hair is pulled back into a tight, short ponytail, and her face is make-up free. Shit, her eyes look puffy, like she's been crying.

Without thinking, I march forward, my hands going to her shoulders. I bend my knees slightly so I'm at eye level with her, and I can see close up that she has in fact been crying.

"What's happened? Are you okay?"

She breaks down, falling into my arms. I hold her to me, her arms wrapping around my neck as she clings to me. I slide my arm under the knees, carrying her bridal style over to the couch, sitting down with her in my lap.

The women of the club, including my mom, come and sit around, and my dad, brother, and club members close in.

"Joss, what's happened?"

My gaze slides over her body, checking for injuries.

"Son, let her catch her breath," Opal says, as he sits on the table in front of us, touching her calf.

A growl unexpectedly breaks free, making some people chuckle around me.

"Welcome to the club, brother." My gaze snaps up to Edge, seeing him grin down at me.

Joss's breathing evens out. She hiccups and then sits up, never climbing off my lap. One arm stays around my neck, the other settles on my chest as she looks me in the eyes.

"What are you doing here? This is the Rugged Skulls clubhouse," she states, and I nod.

"I'm a patched member, babe. This here is my father, Rookie, my mom, Della, and my blood brother, Calder. We're all members. This here is the club's President, Magnum, and his VP, Opal."

She pulls in a harsh breath, but stays seated on my thighs, and even with her crying and upset, my dick takes note that her lush ass is sitting right on top of him.

Needing to change the subject of her ass and my cock, I ask her, "What are you doing here, Joss?"

She looks around at everyone standing there, then looks back to me.

"I'm looking for the Rugged Hunters. I need to hire them." Once again, she looks around the room, waiting for one of them to say something, but my brothers know that this is on me. I will handle this.

That gets my attention even more. Tucking my forefinger under her chin, I make her look at me.

"I am the Rugged Hunters, as is Calder and a few more of our brothers," I explain.

"Brothers? I thought you only had the one." She looks to Calder, and he smiles at her.

"I'm his blood brother. Everyone standing here are his club brothers," he tells her.

Joss nods in understanding, looking back to me. The sadness in her eyes intensifies, before she speaks.

"My daughter is missing. She's fourteen and didn't come home from school today," she tells me.

"Maybe she's with a friend and forgot to tell you," Calder speaks up. That makes Joss shake her head rapidly.

"No, I called all her friends. They said she left school, walked to the bus stop, but that was the last time she was seen. Her phone's location was turned off at the school."

I look up at Calder, silently talking to him. He nods and pulls out his phone, no doubt calling Maverick.

"I need your phone, baby. My brother Maverick is a tech wiz. He'll find out what's happening, okay? We will find out what has happened."

She gives it to me, and I hand it off to Calder, who leaves the room. I pull her to me, tucking her head in the crook of my neck.

She breathes me in, and I sigh in contentment. Fuck me, is this what my father felt when he met Mom? The way the other members met their old lady? My gaze flicks over to them, and I see Mom looking at me with Joss in my lap with a soft smile on her face.

"Have you been to the police?" my dad asks. He sits on the chair next to me. "I'm Rookie, Finan's father."

"Nice to meet you." Joss greets him back. "My parents took me, but the Chief said that because we had a fight a few days ago, that it could be that Juni—that's my daughter—is cooling off somewhere, punishing me for the argument. It's not true. I can feel it in my heart, in my bones; something is wrong."

"She's right. A mom knows," Risky says, stepping closer to us, sitting on the arm of the chair next to Magnum.

Joss looks too Risky, who nods and smiles.

"How did you know about us?" I ask her, gaining her attention again.

When she looks back to me, her nose skims mine. Our lips almost touch, just a breath away from each other, and I want nothing more than to pull her mouth to mine, to feel and taste her again, but my family is watching, and her kid is missing.

Her head moves back a fraction, before she speaks.

"After the Chief explained that he couldn't technically do anything for twenty-four hours, because we don't have a reason to believe that Juni is in danger, he gave me this card." She pulls out the brown card from her front pocket.

Her breathing has picked up again. I can feel her body starting to coil. She's getting herself into a frenzy again. My arms soothe up and down her back as I look at the card she's holding. It's one of the cards Royal had made up so people who didn't want the police involved in their shit knew how to contact us.

Thank you Royal, and thank you Chief, I think.

"You came straight here?" Opal asks her, touching her calf again because he could sense she was getting worked up again.

My skin prickles at the sight of him touching her. Shit, this has never happened before, not ever. I usually don't give a fuck about seeing my brothers touch one of the Regs that have sucked me off, but seeing my VP touch Joss, my woman... Fuck, that sends me into a frenzy also.

Mine.

"Brother." I growl his name. Seeing another man touch her, even though I know he loves my Aunt Jodie... I don't like him touching her.

The smile he flashes me tells me he knows how I'm feeling. He removes his hand, then switches his gaze back to Joss.

"My parents took me home. My dad convinced me to come here. He said he's heard good things about the club, and that a friend of his hired the club to help track down something. You guys did it," Joss explains.

"I got information, Prez," Maverick booms as he walks into the room.

I'm expecting Magnum to call church, or leave us guys to deal with it, but he looks to Joss, then to me. We stare at each other for a second or ten, then he nods, before looking over to Mav.

"She's with Finan. We can discuss it here. I believe the women will want to offer Joss support too."

A look around and all of the women that are here, nod.

Royal, Jack, Lennox and Travis are all out on a hunt. They've been gone two days already, but I know they will come back if we need them.

Joss sits up and tries to climb off my lap, but my hand on her thigh stops her. She looks at me with wide eyes, her lips parted as my fingers flex, giving her a squeeze.

"Stay. I like you here," I say low enough so that only she hears me. My own words causing a surprised reaction in my head.

"Why?" she asks in an equally low tone.

I go to speak, but Maverick speaks up with the information he found.

"Joss, does Juni have a laptop?"

"Yeah. It's in her bedroom," she replies to him, with a frown on her face.

"I can access a lot on her phone. She used it a lot to talk to some chick called Chloe. But I want to see her laptop, to get into her drive, and see if she has other things saved there."

"My parents are at my house right now," she says.

"PROSPECT," Magnum calls, and the guy comes running. "Go to Joss's house. Her parents will know why you are there. Bring the laptop back here."

"On it, boss."

"Baby, let your folks know that a prospect is coming for Juni's laptop." I lift her off my lap and set her on the couch, kissing the top of her head.

My mom grabs my wrist as I pass. She looks up at me, giving me a smile to let me know she approves. I kiss her on the head, before following my brother out of the room.

The further I go from Joss, the more my stomach tightens, but I also know that what Mav has to say is bad news.

We enter the room we use for church, and we all take our seats before Maverick starts.

"You aren't going to like this, brother. You heard me saying that Juni has been talking to some teenage chick called Chloe. Well, Chloe isn't a teenage chick, man. 'HE' is a middle-aged man that fucking grooms young girls. I'm using some software to track him down via her phone apps they use, but so far, he is a clever fuck and is blocking his signal. The same with Juni's cell phone, if she still has it. He may have tossed it, but I do think he has her. Their last conversation was talking about meeting up today after school for ice cream."

"Fuck," I growl, my fists clenching on the table.

My heart is raging in my chest. I haven't even met this girl yet and I feel protective of her, all because of her mom. Hell, I would be like this if it were any young girl taken.

My brothers all rage and fume around the table, saying shit, planning how they want to kill the cunt, but not before me.

"He is mine when we find him. Find him, Mav," I grind out.

"He is all yours, brother. You calling it?" Magnum speaks out. My head snaps in his direction.

Am I calling it? Maybe. But fuck me, there are more important things to deal with right now.

CHAPTER SIX

JOSS

Sitting in the main room at the clubhouse, I sip the hot coffee, Risky, got for me. Now Jodie is with us, she arrived not too long ago from work. I love that these women are still working at their ages. Don't get me wrong, they are far from old, but they are a good age and still going strong.

"How are you holding up?" Della asks.

She is a sweet lady. And you can see she adores her husband and her sons, by the way she kept watching them. Like she was waiting for cues on what to do next. If I'm being honest, all the old ladies were doing that.

To me, that shows respect, loyalty, and love.

"My insides feel like if they get any tighter, I won't ever unknot them. I know in my gut that something is wrong. Juni would never just run off. We have had verbal fights before, but she goes to her room or down the bottom of the garden to her little hut to cool off."

Fresh tears build and roll down my cheeks. Della comes to sit next to me, pulling me into her embrace, and I take all her warmth and strength. We rock gently back and forth, while I cry.

"I miss my baby." She coos and soothes me, while I cry. And I feel comforted, even though I have only just met these people.

It wasn't long after the prospect left that he came back with Juni's laptop and took it straight down the hall that Finan and the other men disappeared down.

God, Finan. How could I feel so connected with a man after only knowing and spending so little time with him?

Seeing him here, and remembering what he looked like at the trail, he's younger than me. I thought maybe my mind was making him seem older in my head, but I clearly have a few years on him.

Pulling back from Della, I give her a tight-lipped smile. Then I dry my face using some tissues that are on the table.

"The club will bring her home. That I know," Risky says with so much conviction in her voice, all I can do is nod.

"I hope so."

"Hope is a good thing," Farrah adds. "Hope, faith and belief. That club always get their hunts done, and I know they will find your darling girl. I love her name, by the way."

"Thank you." I grin. "It was a choice her late father picked for her, even though we didn't know we were having a girl." I sigh and think back to what Owen used to say.

My baby girl will carry my attitude and stubbornness forward. She will do me proud.

God he was so happy when I got the message through to him that I was pregnant, he had replied with his own letter expressing his love and happiness. Showing the scan photos to his buddies. We talked vis email, mostly but I would send care packages and letters because he likes seeing my stomach grow.

That makes me smile but breaks my heart at the same time. Is he up there looking down on what is happening, thinking I'm a bad mother?

"I'm sorry. When did he pass?" Jodie asks.

"I was pregnant with Juni. His convoy got hit. He and a few others didn't make it."

Della gasps, Farrah's eyes fill, and Jodie nods in understanding.

"I'm ex-military, so are the older guys in the club. They all served," she explains to me.

"Really? Wow. Thank you for your service," I say.

"Thanks. I got out of active duty when I got pregnant with my first son, Tucker. He plays in the MBA now." She winks at me, and my mouth drops open.

"Who?"

"Tucker Bryant." She beams with pride.

I know who she's talking about because Juni likes to play basketball at school and had talked about a few of her favorite players.

"Oh, wow. Juni plays basketball in school. She's quite good. Thankfully, she took her father's sporty side. Me, I'm happy to sit with my laptop, or read a book, or hike. I like walking, it helps clear my head."

The women smile at me, and I get a weird feeling they know something that I don't. You know when people look at you a certain way, and you get a feeling they want to tell you a secret.

"What?" I ask them.

"You will fit fine with my boy. He's a bit of a health nut," Della speaks.

You can tell he likes to take care of himself by the form of his body. Finan belongs on the cover of some biker magazine, or a gym one. All muscles and tattoos, that perfect light stubble that covers a sexy jawline.

Can jawlines be sexy? Well, anyway, Finan's is sexy, and I just want to nibble on it.

What the hell?

How can I be thinking of this when my baby girl is still missing? My nose burns, and my vision blurs as new tears make a return and flow freely. I cover my face with my hands and sob.

I'm a terrible mom. I never knew what she was planning. I should have checked more, better even. When she told me about Chloe, I had a bad feeling in the pit of my stomach. I should have known.

My whole body shakes at images of the fun times Juni and I have had over the years.. The way she walked into the ocean for the first time as a toddler, the feel of sand between her toes. When she got her first booboo on her knee. She didn't cry; she just wanted me to kiss it better. The day she started preschool, Juni walked right into the room, not bothering to look back at me like some of the other children. Just walked in, put her little pink backpack on her hook, and joined some other children on the mat.

Juni has always carried a sense of independence about her, just like her father. He was never afraid of anything.

My daughter was always up for trying new things, whereas I was always happy to stick with things I knew.

I would try and do things for her, even if it scared or worried me. I would do anything for her.

A hand is placed on my back, slowly running up and down, soothing me. It only makes me cry harder. I want to be the one soothing my daughter, not me being taken care of.

"My chest hurts," I cry. The intense feeling of my chest crushing my lungs and my heart as me struggling to pull in much needed air.

My breathing is choppy with each sob I let out. My body shakes, fear fills my veins, knowing that she is out there, and something is horribly wrong.

"Shh, honey. The guys will find her and bring her home." This comes from Estelle.

She's with Sarge, and that guy scares me, but he looks like he can get shit done and doesn't care who he steps over to get it done.

"I just want my baby," I cry again.

I know that I won't survive if she doesn't come home. I can deal with any physical and mental damage; I will support her no matter what. Having her damaged is better than not having her at all. That will kill me. My life won't be worth living.

Doubling over, my forearms rest on my thighs, my face still buried in my hands, as I try to lock the pain out. To keep the fear at bay. But it's winning. Nothing can take this pain away.

Rocking back and forth, I cry. I cry for Juni, for whatever she is going through. I cry for me, for not being able to do anything to help her.

I know that the club are looking into it, but I feel completely helpless right now. No parents should have to feel like this. The lost feeling, the pain of losing a child. Our children are supposed to outlive us, they are supposed to have a complete, full and joyful life. Not suffer from the horrific things that they do. No child should suffer in any way shape or form.

A child's life should be filled with laughter, ice cream, friends, and a loving family. They are taught to feel love, to feel heartache. That will make them grow as a person. To learn new things, to teach new things.

As a society that is filled with high criticism, we should learn to evolve from that. There is no need to tear each other down. We should want to lift them up.

I want Juni to experience all of that. I want her to fall in love, to have her heart broken by a frog, only to find her prince the next time. We all want what is best for our children, and anyone who does not think that, does not deserve to be a parent.

"Baby," comes Finan's voice.

It's soft, almost in a hesitant way, like he's approaching a wild animal. Bringing my head up, the tears still falling down my cheeks, I take in the ruggedly handsome man kneeling before me. His eyes are soft but full of worry.

He is frowning, and a man this good looking should not be frowning. Without thinking, I bring my hand up, using my thumb to straighten out the small frown lines on his face.

"You shouldn't frown. You are too handsome for that," I whisper, making a small smile appear on his face.

"You still look beautiful even with puffy, red eyes from all the crying. We will find her, baby."

He takes my hands and pulls me to my feet, wrapping his arms around me. I sink into his hold, my arms around his waist. I soak in his warmth, his strength. It's crazy that I barely know this man, but we seem connected in some way.

That scares me.

I lost one man I loved. I am not sure I can do that again. Plus, he is younger than my years. There isn't a realistic reason that a hot guy like Finan would want to be with an older single mom like me.

I know that I should pull away from his embrace, stand on my own, but he is so warm and safe.

The more I'm around him, I can feel this thing between us building. The way he calls me 'baby' makes me shiver, makes my body want him, yet I know now is not the time.

My daughter is missing, and I need both Finan and the club to bring her home to me.

I have to trust in the club that they will find her, and possibly deal with whoever has taken her. Finan moves, his arm sliding around my back, keeping me tucked to his side as we turn to face the room.

"I need to take Joss home. We'll check out Juni's room, see if there is anything else there, and get back to you," he says to Magnum, who nods.

I look at all these men, who look imposing and intimidating, yet feel safe. And these are not all of them. I was told by Risky that some of the club members are out on a hunt but will be recalled to help with finding Juni.

They will lose money because of me, but they will also do what Finan wants because he is one of theirs. They stand loyal to each other, and that shines through with everyone standing in this room, including the women.

This club is built on respect and loyalty.

I feel the warmth spread through my body, knowing they are doing this for me, for a woman they barely know, including Finan. We only talked for a few hours that day.

Yes, it ended in a kiss, and he has been on my mind ever since, but does that warrant all of this action?

Does he this do this for every client?

Am I a client?

Shit, my head hurts so much right now.

"Go. Maverick will keep looking. If he finds anything, you will be called. Same with you. You find anything, you get back to me, got it?" Magnum states, and Finan nods.

Finan goes to lead me away from the group of people, but I stop and turn around to face them.

"Thank you for doing this. I know you don't know me, and you do this for a living, but I can't ever explain how much this means to me that you are helping to bring my baby girl home."

Tears flow down my cheeks, but I don't brush them away. There is no point; they just carry on their path.

The men nod, and the women all give me sad, tight-lipped smiles.

Rookie steps over to us and claps Finan on the shoulder.

"Take a look at her girl's room and see what you find. Take care of your woman, son."

"Will do, Dad. Love you, Mom," Finan calls to Della, and she blows him a kiss.

Swoon, this man loves his mama. That is all kinds of sexy, if you ask me.

He leads me out to where my car is parked, holding his hand out to me.

"Keys, babe." His voice is rough and makes me shiver.

I dig for my keys and hand them to him, then he's helping me into my car, then putting the seatbelt on for me.

I roll my eyes. "I could have done that myself, you know." I lick my lips and pull in a breath when my eyes connect with his intense ones.

We are so close, I can see the bright blue color of his eyes, and the little specks of darker blue that stand out against the light.

"I just want you safe, Joss," he states with conviction, so I nod, because what woman would argue with that?

Finan leans in, brushes his lips softly against mine, before pulling back. He looks me in the eyes for a second longer, then pulls away, closing the door.

I watch as he comes round the driver's side and slides into my seat, pushing it back to accommodate his long legs, making me giggle.

"Laugh it up, baby," is all he says, before he starts the car and drives us to my house.

CHAPTER SEVEN

FINAN

I drive through the streets leading away from the clubhouse, where I have just found out that the cunt who took Juni is a child groomer. He is known to the police and got out of jail eleven months ago, but the prick is back to his old games.

I will hunt this fucker down and rip him into tiny pieces so no fucker will ever find him.

No child will ever fear him again.

He will never hurt anyone once I am done with him.

A sniffle comes from my left. I turn my head to see Joss crying, while she looks out the window. I can't imagine how fucking hard this is to have a child missing. I haven't even met Juni yet and I feel protective of her.

Any fucker touches one of my future kids, and no fucker will find them. We are a very protective MC. I was brought up to keep my own safe, at all costs, and I will do that until I take my last breath.

Reaching over, I grip her hand in mine, making her snap around to look at me. The look on her face is one that shows her true heartache.

"We will find her. Come hell or high water, babe. We will."

"You can't promise that, Finan," she sobs.

"I can and I will, Joss. Me and my brothers will stop at nothing to get your girl home to you. You have my word."

"Okay," she concedes, but I can tell by the tone in her voice that she doesn't believe me.

It isn't long before we are pulling up outside her house. I see an older car and a bike parked in her driveway. The car must belong to her parents. No idea about the bike, but you can be sure I will find out.

I turn and pull out the key, but neither of us move to get out of the car. I twist in my seat to look at her, only to find her watching me. Her eyes are red, swollen, and blood-shot from all the crying, but that is to be expected.

Leaning over, I take both of her hands in mine, tugging a little so she shifts in her seat to face me.

"You wouldn't have come to us if you didn't know what we could do. Push aside that I work for them, because I don't. I part own Rugged Hunters. Me and my brothers do. We are the next generation of Rugged Skulls, and we wanted to bring something to the club, something we knew we could succeed on, and we do. Does it get messy on some hunts? Fuck yes. Hell, my brother got shot a few weeks ago."

She gasps, her hand over her mouth, but I reach up and pull it back down to where our knees are touching. Holding her firm, I carry on.

"This is freaking me the fuck out because I don't usually talk like this with people I don't know, but with you, I feel something different than I have before. Joss, you have to believe that we will do whatever we can to get Juni home to you in one piece. But I do need you to understand that things could happen before we get to her."

"What do you know?" Her question rushes out of her, and I stiffen.

"We found some things on Juni's phone and laptop. That is why Mav wants to see if there is anything in her room, to solidify what we have found out."

"Finan, tell me. Is my baby girl going to get hurt?"

Her eyes are wide with fear, her lips parted a little.

74

Bringing my hand up to cup her cheek, she leans into my touch, which again surprises me. I'm not used to this kind of affection from a woman I want to sleep with.

Joss has me feeling things I haven't experienced yet. She is making me want to explore those and see what they feel like. I don't think like most bikers, I feel and see things differently.

"Is that your parents' car?" I ask, changing the subject, because I don't want to tell her in the car. She turns her head to look out the window and nods.

"Yeah, and my brother, Matt."

I nod and unclip my seatbelt, then do hers. "Stay." I state firmly when she goes to open her door.

"I am not a dog, Finan," she states, and I scoff.

"Did I call you a fucking dog?" She shakes her head. "Exactly, so do not insinuate that I did." My voice coming out in a harsher tone.

I get out of the car, ignoring the look of shock on her face. Fuck, this is why I stay clear of people I don't know. My family is used to my short outbursts. They understand that sometimes I struggle putting out the right emotion.

When I reach the door, I pull it open, and Joss sits there looking unsure. Shaking my head, knowing that I have fucked things up before they have even started, I go to step forward, but Joss jumps from the car and grips my cut, pulling me closer.

Her tits press up against my chest and I bite back a moan, not wanting to show how I am feeling like a fucking horny teenager right now.

Her head hits my chest, and my hands find her trim waist. Dropping my head, I kiss her soft black hair, waiting for what she does next. I am not good at this. I'm used to women dropping to their knees. I don't need to do small talk. They know what they are there for.

The more time passes, the stiffer my body becomes—*all of my body*. My cock is raging in my jeans with her pressed so close, and fuck all can happen.

"Baby, I think we need to go inside. The curtains are twitching, so I bet they are chomping at the bit to find out what's happening."

Pulling her head back, she looks up at me, and I get lost in her brown eyes. Licking her lips, she takes a deep breath.

"I'm sorry for what I said. You were right, you didn't call me a dog. I'm super-tired and sensitive right now, but you are helping me, so I shouldn't be taking my fear and panic out on you. For that, I am sorry, Finan. Forgive me?"

My lips twitch at her words. Not caring that her folks are watching, I lean down and kiss her lips. Using the gasp she lets out, I slip my tongue into her mouth, savoring how good she feels and tastes.

Her fists tighten on my cut, pulling me closer, but I know that if I don't stop, I will take her here and bend over her car. Breaking the kiss, I tuck some of her hair behind her ear, and speak.

"We need to stop and go inside. I want all of you, Joss, you make me feel things that I don't usual feel. You spark something deep in me, but now is not the time. You need to be in the right mind. Juni comes before us."

Her eyes soften, and she graces me with a small smile.

"Thank you," is all she says, then she leads me into her house.

As soon as we step inside, her family is on her, pulling her from me. Her parents hug her, kissing her cheeks, rushing out a bunch of questions.

"Who are you?" comes a gruff voice. I turn my head, taking in Joss's brother, Matt.

He's about my height, his build is smaller, but he has about the same amount of tattoos as I do. With his scruffy jeans, biker boots and an old concert t-shirt, he looks the part of a biker, but Joss never said anything, so I can assume he just likes riding.

"I'm Finan. Me and my club are helping to find Juni."

"So, you know where she is?" This comes from her father.

I look at the four people now looking at me, and I can feel my insides start to tighten, my palms sweat. I wish like fuck that I brought Calder or one of my brothers with me. They can take over and let me sink into the background, but here I am, front and center, the one place I hate being.

Shit.

I flex my neck, trying to ease the tension that is building. Seconds pass—fuck, whole hours could have passed—before I speak. Thankfully, Joss steps to me, taking my hand and leading me over to the dinner table.

"Finan is a member of the Rugged Skulls MC." She points to my cut. "He and the club are looking into what happened to Juni." She sniffs, as fresh tears flow. I need to go to her, but her mom wraps her up in her arms, so I stay seated.

Every fiber of my body it itching to pull her into my arms, to keep her safe against me, but I hold firm.

Her brother cocks an eyebrow at me in question, but I give him nothing.

"Tell us what you found," Joss calls to me.

Taking a deep breath, I push down my personal shit, because I know that Joss and her family are counting on me, us the club, to find Juni.

"Fucking hell, look at him. How the hell can he find my niece when he can't fucking talk to us? He is a pussy, useless," her brother snaps.

His words hit home, but they make me angry rather than make me sink lower into my shit.

My fists clench on the table and I glare at him. Without taking my eyes off him, I hear Joss defend me.

"Jesus, Matt. He just met you guys. He has some news to share. It must be bad since he's finding the best way to tell us, right, Finan?"

I glare at her brother for a few more seconds, letting him know this shit don't slide with me, before turning my head to look at Joss and her parents.

"Yeah, babe." The endearment slips out. Joss smiles at me, so does her mom.

Her dad frowns, but it's her brother who speaks up. "Babe? What the fuck? You fucking him or something? Is that why they are helping? Just to get in your panties." he growls.

"Watch your fucking mouth around her, or I will rip your tongue out," I snarl back. His eyes go wide as his father bitches back at him.

"Enough, Matt. You will never speak to your sister like that again, do you hear me?" His voice leaves no room for argument. Matt sinks into his chair, folding his arms and looking down.

Little shit.

"Finan." Joss calls my name and I look to her. "Tell us." The anguish on her face kills me.

"You know that Maverick looked into Juni's phone and laptop. He looked at the chats between her and this Chloe girl." She nods, and I breathe in deeply. "Chloe is not a fifteen-year-old girl. She is a forty-three-year-old man, who is a known sex offender. He got out of jail almost a year ago, for raping three girls. He is good with technology, so he knows how to hide, but Maverick is better.

"He's looking into where the guy lives and tracking his movement, but so far he has done what he is known for: hiding. It was by chance they caught him the last time. We have other MC's keeping an eye out. We sent a photo of him and Juni, so they know who to look for. I didn't think you would mind me sharing her photo with men I trust."

She shakes her head, her tears slipping down her cheeks. Her skin has gone pale. Her breathing is coming in harsh, fearful pants as she lets the information sink in.

"Do you know where he is?" This comes from her dad.

"We do. I have three brothers out looking at his last known location, where he has been getting visits from his parole officer. I'm waiting to hear from them. Maverick is still looking on the web, plus the dark web."

As soon as I say those words, her brother explodes. He gets to his feet, his chair toppling over. His fists are clenched as he paces back and forth.

"We need to find her before he hurts her—if he hasn't already. Fuck."

That is something we all want, but I know deep down that it will take time. Time we don't have, considering what the sick fuck has done before. He likes to rape his victims multiple times, and he likes to carve his name on their hips, so they remember him. It's fucking crazy and unreal that he only got nine years, but they claimed before it was his first conviction and he can be reformed. They gave him a lower sentence.

Bullshit, if you ask me. One conviction, one victim, is enough for a death penalty, and I and my brother are more than happy to carry the killing out.

"Oh God." I watch as Joss and her family fall part. Well, all except her father, who is looking at me like he's trying to read my mind.

We stare at each other, neither of us saying anything. He looks to his wife and daughter, who are clinging to each other, then in a flash, Joss gets to her feet and rushes to me. She slides into my lap, wrapping her arms around my neck, and sobs.

This time, it's her dad who cocks an eyebrow at me. I give him a slight chin dip, letting him know that I have her, no matter what.

He has nothing to worry about from me.

CHAPTER EIGHT

JOSS

Breathing in Finan's scent is making me dizzy. He smells so good. I want to climb into his body and stay there until his brothers bring Juni home.

I fight back more tears, because I know they won't do me any good, crying all the time. Juni needs me to stay strong for when she comes home. I have to believe that she will come home.

"Baby, look at me." I shake my head against his neck, making him chuckle. "Joss, I need to go and look in Juni's room. There might be something there that can lead us to her and bring her home."

"What kind of thing, son?" my dad asks. Looking over to him, I see the anguish on all their faces.

I can only imagine that reality doesn't set in when a family member is missing until you get bad news. Then it all hits home and you fear the worst.

His arms wrap around me tightly, and I snuggle closer. His warmth is something I need right now. Something to hold me down, so I don't crash and burn. I will be no use to Juni if I crumble.

Finan's voice brings me extra comfort. It's crazy that his voice is like a balm that helps. Some words even have an Irish twang to them; I would imagine from being brought up with an Irish dad and uncle.

"The guy that we think took Juni, we know that he researches them, finds out what they like, so he can have something in common with them. Music, movies, things like that. Even things they collect. Every girl he has taken, he has sent them a glass flower statue. It's a symbol that they are delicate, yet breakable."

I gasp, my hand going to my mouth, as my stomach lurches. I jump off Finan's lap, darting in the direction of the stairs. I can hear him running behind me, his heavy boots hitting my carpeted floor.

I get to Juni's room and step over to where I know the object is. There, next to her bed, is the flower.

Standing there, frozen to the spot, I slowly reach what's in the box, turning to look at the man behind me, with a clear glass flower resting in my palm. The only color is purple that makes up the center of the piece.

"Purple is Juni's favorite color." My world starts to crumble.

My knees give way, that has Finan rushing across the room, catching me. He gently takes the flower, placing it on the bed next to us.

Matt rushes forward with a plastic food bag and tucks the flower inside of it. He nods to Finan, before leaving the room. Finan's arms tighten around me, keeping me from shattering into a million pieces.

Rocking gently, I cry, my body wracking with pain, fear. His large hand soothes over my hair, calming me down, but nothing seems to work.

"Baby, you need to breathe for me. I can't handle you crying like this." I get shifted on his lap as he struggles to get to his feet, clearly not wanting to let me go.

"Here," I hear my dad say. I adjust my head and see my father helping Finan to his feet.

"Her room is just there. Lay her down and hold her. We will let you know when your club is here," Dad says, and Finan nods.

"I appreciate it," he says as we pass him. Finan has a firm grip on me, holding me to him.

"Take care of her. I'm glad she has you here. I know in my bones you will bring Juni home."

I bite my lip from crying out as another wave of pain hits me. My baby is out there, and Lord knows what that sick bastard is doing to her. The belief of her coming home to me in one piece is fading.

Finan walks to my room and lays me on the bed. Thoughts of laying in my bed with Finan are quickly dashed when he kisses me on the forehead and walks out of my room, closing the door behind him without a backward glance.

My heart sinks, and more tears flow. I curl into a ball, making myself small and tight, trying to keep the pain locked away.

I will my breathing to slow down, my heart to calm and fill with hope and faith once again. With my eyes squeezed tight, I drift into a shallow sleep.

The bed dips behind me, and I startle, looking over my shoulder.

"Shh, babe. It's just me." He brushes away a tear. I didn't know I was still crying.

Turning from him to dry my eyes, I feel that the pillow beneath my head has a large wet patch. Was I crying in my sleep? I must have been.

Breathing in deeply, I turn to face him again. He pushes down on my shoulder, so I'm lying on my back. Hovering over me, I take in his utter beauty.

His tanned skin, light blue eyes that look like they could steal your heart and never give it back. His stubble is neatly trimmed, giving it the designer look. His hair is shaved at the sides with length on that he uses product to spike up, but not in that weird ninety's way.

My hand comes up to touch his jaw, and he leans into my touch, with closed eyes. It's like he's savoring the connection between us.

While his eyes are closed, I scan over his face, committing it to my memory, because it can't help but have that flicker of doubt that he won't want this beyond finding Juni. He seriously couldn't want to be with us with the possibility of having the baggage we will have to carry after this kidnapping.

He is as handsome as they come; he could have any woman he wants. Why lump himself with a single mom?

Fuck, these insecurities have never risen before. He is bringing this uncertainty out in me. My eyes focus on the tattoo on his chest. It's then I realize that he's shirtless. Damn, he is fine, with a capital 'F.'

"What are you thinking about, babe?"

I blink and bring my gaze up to meet his. His frown mars his face again, and I don't like seeing it there, but I have noticed that it is there most of the time. It seems that Finan is a thinker, and a worrier.

I lick my lips, feeling how swollen they are from all the biting of them and my crying. Finan's gaze drops to my mouth, and he lets out a low groan.

"Joss, you have to stop doing that. I am trying real fucking hard to not take this further, but I can only take so much. Shit." He groans the last word.

His words are like a bucket of cold water on my heated skin. I know he can see the look on my face because his frown deepens. I can't take looking at him when he's thinking that he knows he can't touch me, or do anything sexually with me

He doesn't see me how I see him. He doesn't want me like I want him. Fuck, I knew this age gap was an issue. Tying to pull away from him, Finan moves into action.

Finan stops me from moving, lifting his body, so he's settled between my thighs, and I am disappointed to feel his jeans against my skin.

"Why the sudden coldness, Joss?"

I shake my head, not wanting to talk to him, but he cups my cheek, making me look at him.

"Tell me. Please." His voice is firm leaving no room for argument, and I cave.

Damn him and his sexiness.

"What you just said. That you didn't want to go any further with me, touching me or anything more, I mean." I divert my gaze, looking over to my large window nook that I love.

Both Juni and I would sit there on rainy days and drink hot chocolate.

Can't wait to do that again. Hell, she can have as much hot chocolate as she wants.

"Look at me, Joss." I finally turn my head to do as he says. "Baby, that is not what I meant."

"What did you mean?" My voice is small, and I hate it.

My gaze connects with his, his eyes penetrating mine. The sight of the affection coming off this man takes my breath away. I can't speak for a few seconds, as I take in the beauty that is Finan Price. But it's not only the outside that looks good with him. I have seen and felt firsthand that he is good inside also.

He is one of the good ones, as my mother would say.

Leaning on his elbow, his other hand cups my cheek, his thumb brushing over my cheekbone. Licking his lips, he dips his head and brushes his mouth against mine before he speaks.

"I want you. That is evident." He thrusts his hips, letting me know how hard he is. "I will have you, but the main focus right now is getting Juni home. I won't want to have you at a time like this, then you regret it and push me away," he explains, and I get what he's saying.

His words resonate in my mind, causing my nose to burn and more tears to appear. God, I am sick of crying. I need to stop and be strong for my baby girl.

Experiencing things with Finan will be new to me. I have only been with Owen, and that was a long time ago. There has been no one since him. Yeah, I have dated, but none went further than a few kisses that didn't make me feel anything.

But this with Finan seems on a deeper level. When I talked to him on the trail that hot day, it seemed like we had known each other for longer than the few hours we had. Something in me clicked, and I never felt like I was betraying Owen, even though I have always known that he would want me to be happy.

"Okay," is all I say, then Finan smiles and leans in to kiss me.

He steals my breath from my lungs, and I would happily give every last breath to him, if he keeps kissing me like he is right now. His tongue dances with mine, he nips at my bottom lip, making me hot and flustered. My body pulses in time with his.

His dick is hard between us, and my pussy is wet and needy, but I understand that now is not the time, but we keep kissing.

He keeps taking and taking.

I keep giving and giving.

"Mine," he says against my lips. He mutters something else, but I can't quite make it out.

My hands are on his hips, but I need to feel more of him, so I move my hands to his back. His skin it hot and smooth. He shivers, and I smile against his lips, making him pull back to look down at me.

His eyes are dark with lust, and the sight turns me on more. My breasts feel heavy with need, my nipples are hard, and my body is pulsing with desire.

"You aren't the only one feeling this, baby. I want you in all ways. For some reason, I feel connected to you, as Hallmark as that sounds. My inner voice seems to quiet when I'm around you."

I frown at his words as my hands find their way to his cheeks, holding his face so he keeps looking at me.

"You can be whoever you want with me, Finan Price. Never let anyone tell you otherwise. We all have our flaws; we all have issues. No one is perfect. The world isn't perfect. God is not perfect. Have you not seen Supernatural?" I wink at him.

He shakes his head at me. "Babe, I don't watch much TV."

"Shame." I yawn, suddenly feeling exhausted again.

"Sleep, baby. We should have news soon."

"You will wake me if you get something?" I say to him.

"Promise."

With that, I nod believing his word. Finan repositions himself at my side, pulling me to him, hooking my leg over his thigh. Once comfortable, he places my hand in the middle of his chest with his hand on top of mine, keeping me in place.

He kisses the top of my head, and I sigh, sinking into his body. Everyone keeps telling me I need to sleep and eat, because I need to stay strong for when Juni comes home, and I know they are right, so I let the sleep take me.

CHAPTER NINE

FINAN

Me and the boys surround the house we're checking. It's the third house we have hit. These sick cunts are sticking together. They are not telling us anything. No fucker will give away where this cunt takes his victims.

When I told Joss that we had a lead, she looked at me with so much hope, and the thought of going back home, with no Juni, or any information, is making my blood boil but my stomach twist with knots.

I know that Joss will be heartbroken, but me and the club are doing everything we can to track her down. Maverick has been on every site he can think of and more. He has his hackers on it too, but this cunt is good.

My blood burns in my veins, like someone doused me in gasoline, as we round the corner. My gun is up in front of me, aiming at any prick that comes at me.

A noise from inside the house gets my attention, and my heartrate kicks up a notch. My fingers flex against the hard metal of the gun. Stepping slowly, I move close to the door, with Royal behind me.

He taps my shoulder, letting me know he has my back, then I reach for the door handle, twisting it slowly, trying to not make much noise. I want to surprise whoever is in here, praying with everything that I am and know that Juni is inside. Fuck, I would give anything to find her here.

The door opens and I move in, Royal hot on my heels. We search the kitchen but see nothing. The noise comes from the front of the house, where I know Calder, Travis and Lennox are.

The older members, including my dad, are positioned all around the house but further back, so if anyone manages to escape, they will be there to catch them.

"Fuck, yeah." I hear someone grunt, and my blood boils over to boiling point. It is so fucking high I would me match for Lucifer himself.

I rush forward, just as I hear a whimper.

With my gun raised, I move into the room.

He is naked, fucking a woman who looks as dirty and strung out as he is.

I kick his thigh, making him fall to the side. The woman rolls to the side, curling into a ball. My stomach twists when I see how young she is. She looks easily around Juni's age.

"What the fuck, man? I paid upfront."

I kick him again, in the stomach this time. He howls in pain, but I move in for more. Tucking my gun in the waistband of my jeans, I grip the piece of shit by his hair, snarling in his face.

"Where is Rolland?"

"Who?" he whimpers. But I can see by the slight widening of his eyes that he knows who Rolland is.

"You know who I'm talking about. Where is Rolland? Tell me, or I swear to fuck, you are going to wish the police had found you fucking that underage girl." I look over my shoulder and see Travis carrying the girl out, covered in a towel.

Knowing the girl is out of the way, I lay into the sick fuck in front of me. Smiling at him, his eyes widen and his mouth parts because he knows what is coming. He is not leaving this room alive. His reign of terror ends today.

"No. Please. I will stop. I won't touch anyone anymore. I swear it," he cries, but I just laugh, looking at my brothers.

"You believe this shit?"

"Hell no. They never stop. Some bullshit about it being in their blood. It's a fucking choice, motherfucker. You can stop any time. It's a choice, not a fucking addiction," Lennox spits out.

He shifts his body, so he's leaning against the front of the sofa, naked as the day he was born, and I am about ready to kill him, but I know I need some information.

Bending at the waist, Calder gets close to the fuck, putting the fear of God in him when he presses the barrel of the gun against his temple. The sick fuck whimpers, looking between the six of us standing in the room.

He knows there is no escape.

I spread my legs in a defensive manner, folding my arms, watching the guy's face as Calder starts to ask questions.

"Do you know where Rolland is?" Calder snarls.

The guy's gaze snaps to my brother's. I watch him like a hawk. This is why my dad and the other members call me a human lie detector. I people watch; I know facial expressions. Years of watching crime shows.

"No. I don't know where he is, I swear." He says all of this while slightly nodding his head, giving his little lie away.

I smirk and shake my head at Calder when he looks over his shoulder at me. He returns my smirk and looks back at fuckface.

"Now, see we know that is a lie. Why don't we try this again, maybe with something simpler? Did you know that girl was underage?"

His eyes widen again, and he fidgets in his seat on the floor. My eyes narrow, watching how he tilts his head, looking between Calder and my brothers. It's like he is trying to figure out what to say, maybe try to lie to get himself out of here alive.

"I was told she was legal," he mutters after a minute or two.

Royal clicks his tongue, stepping forward, closing the gap, and the guy shakes with fright. God, these fuckers have no care what they do to their victims. They have to live with what he does to them. He won't be alive much longer.

"Now, you see, that is bullshit. She looked well below the legal age, guy. My brothers and I don't take kindly to people taking something that doesn't belong to them, or mistreating something that they have," Royal spits out, getting closer.

As soon as he is within striking distance, he swings, clocking the cunt right in the jaw. His head snaps to the side, blood spurting across the floor.

Travis comes back into the room and whines.

"You fuckers started without me." He pouts, making us laugh.

"Where's the girl?" Royal asks him.

"Edge and Opal took her to the local hospital to get checked out," Trav explains. "She is sixteen, brother."

"No, I'm telling you, man, the guy who sold her to me said she was legal, barely but legal. He even gave her the drugs." With each word, his eyes narrow, like he is trying to convince himself of his lies.

He nods a few times, without realizing he is doing it, again giving away that he is saying some bullshit stories.

A person's body will betray them when the heat is on. You may be saying the words but your body will give away little tells saying something different.

I click my fingers, getting the fuck's attention. He looks to me, spitting more blood on the floor.

We are in a stare off, my brother stepping aside, while I step closer.

I don't take my eyes off him, watching as his facial expressions give away so much. I'm like a kid in a candy shop thinking about everything I am about to do to this guy—well, until he gives me what I want.

"I'll tell you what. Give me Rolland and we will forget this ever happened. We take the girl; you go back to fucking women your own age. Deal?"

He shakes his head, his body vibrating with pain and fear, but I can see in his eyes he thinks I'm letting him go.

I get down on my haunches, to get eyelevel with him. He stares at me, as I stare at him, waiting for his decision.

I want the information. I need to find Juni.

With another look at each of my brothers, he knows there is no escaping us, so he sighs. His body sagging against the old, dirty, ripped couch.

"I haven't seen Rolland in over a week. We were due to meet up, but he never showed. I tried calling him on the number I got, but it was disconnected. I am not lying, man. Did you check his apartment?"

"Where is it? We only found a house in his name," I grind out, raging inside that we missed this.

He gives me the address.

I look over my shoulder at Lennox, and he nods, pulling his phone out to call Maverick, to get him to look into this new development.

"Anywhere else he might go?"

He tilts his head again, looking at me. A sick smile covers his face, before he speaks, so I brace for what he is about to say.

"He has taken someone from you." I say nothing. "I bet he is enjoying her right now. Fucking some sweet pussy. You look like a man with taste."

This time I snarl at him, but he keeps laughing, until my fist connects with his jaw. His body slumps to the side, and I keep going at him.

My fist connects over and over with his face. All I see is red. My vision is clouded, his blood is covering his face, my knuckles, and the floor beneath him. My breathing is heavy, my chest constricting with the lack of oxygen with me holding my breath as I beat this cunt to a bloody mess on the floor.

Teeth cut into my knuckles, then hit the floor.

"Alright, brother, that is enough." I hear Calder's voice, but I keep hitting.

All I see is Joss crying. Juni calling out for her mother, begging the guy to stop.

"Stop him," gets bellowed, before I'm tackled to the ground.

We hit the floor with a thud, and I groan, my shoulder hitting the corner of a chair.

Blinking through the rage and pain, I see Calder on top of me, pinning me down. His hair hangs over his forehead, his eyes showing his worry, but he doesn't need to.

"I'm fine. I had it under control," I snap.

"No, you didn't, brother." He gets to his feet, offering me his hand to help me up.

I groan at the pain in my shoulder.

"Finan, you need to calm down, son." My body spins to see my father and the other members, minus, Opal and Edge, as they took the young girl to the hospital.

"I am calm," I growl, then step over to the fuck on the floor.

His face is unrecognizable. I let out a humorless scoff, before pulling my gun out from the back of my jeans and pointing it at the piece of shit.

Without thinking, I pull the trigger, ending his reign of terror on young women.

I walk out of the house, seeing that not one of his neighbors have come out to see what all the commotion is about. Says a lot about this neighborhood, doesn't it.

I get to our SUV, and my brothers surround me as the smell of burning wood fills the air from Travis setting the house on fire, with the dead fuck inside.

Let him burn in Hell. May Lucifer reign Hell down on him in the worst way.

"You okay?" Royal asks, and I nod, not speaking.

Leaning into the back seat, I pull out the leather bag we have that carries an extensive first aid kit and cleaning items.

Using some baby wipes, I clean the blood off my hand and face. Bagging the used ones to burn when I get home, I pack away everything I used. We try not to leave any evidence behind that might lead back to the club.

Blowback would be bad since the club worked fucking hard to build up the legal businesses.

Leaning against the side of the SUV, I flex my neck, clicking the joints to ease the tension that is there.

Today is not over yet. I still have to tell Joss that we can't find Juni. I can only fucking pray that Maverick finds something.

Just thinking of Mav, Royal's phone rings, as my dad, Prez, Sarge and Slide walk over to us. I have no idea where they went.

"You okay, son?" My dad asks, and I nod.

"Fucking hell, Fin, I thought you would beat him to death," Calder groans, and I look to him, snarling. But Sarge gets there first.

"He deserved so much fucking more," the old member growls.

He is the one people still fear after all these years. Hell, he used to scare the piss out of us when we were younger.

"I'm not saying that shit, but come on, brother. This is Finan we are talking about. He is the cool, calm and collected one. He was vicious as fuck in there." Calder looks to me. "You never lose your cool."

"A woman does that to you," Magnum pipes in. My gaze finds his, and he nods, knowing that I will do anything for Joss and Juni, like he would for Risky and his kids.

I don't understand the deep connection I feel for both Joss and her daughter, but it is there. I hope I will have the time to digest and deduce it down to understand it.

Every member would give their life for another person in this club.

My dad closes in next to me and slaps his hand on my shoulder. I twist my head to look at him.

"Maverick found the apartment. He's using his mother's maiden name on the rental agreement. He hacked into the security cameras. Rolland hasn't been home in two weeks. We don't think Juni is there, son." My dad's voice fades, and I picture Joss breaking down again when I break the bad news.

I step away, my stomach knotting to a point of vomiting.

She will hate me, I know it. I promised to bring her baby home to her, but I didn't. We are back to square one on this hunt.

But I know that the Rugged Hunters won't stop until we bring her home. No matter who has to die along the way.

CHAPTER TEN

JOSS

"Any news?" I ask for the millionth time.

My knee is bouncing, and I'm sure I've bitten off my thumbnail with all the anxiety that is coursing through my body at waiting for news from Finan and the club.

They found a lead on the man that took Juni, but they have been gone for over six hours. I was hoping they would find her and bring her back to me.

"Nothing yet, honey. I'm sure they are using all their time finding her."

I nod at Della, then get to my feet, pacing back and forth. I have done this on and off since they left. Maverick has locked himself in his room, or should I say barricaded himself in because I kept bothering him for information.

The girls dragged me away, every time, telling me to let the man do his job and find the scumbag that took my daughter.

"I know but I just want to know. I want her home," I mutter, as I keep pacing.

Everyone is here, to my surprise. All the old ladies are here, all the girls, including Royal's wife, Tree, her sister Kady, and their cousin Lilith.

"My brother is the best out there at finding shit. He will find Juni, and Finan and the club will bring her home," Hazel tells me, and I look at her.

She's older than the other girls here, maybe by only a few years. She is married with a baby of her own, a little boy. Hazel is Sarge and Estelle's daughter, the middle child, as Zeb is older than her, and then Maverick.

"I am trying too hard to not focus on her being hurt. I am really hoping and praying everything that is good that they bring her home to me. It has been too long, and I know that they say the longer they are away, the less chance of them coming home alive."

I cry again. Arms wrap around me, and I sink into their embrace. I can smell a woodsy scent, but a feminine one. Bringing my head up, I see that it is Astrid holding me. Her dirty blond hair just past her shoulders. She kind of reminds me of Kristen Stewart.

"The guys will bring her home. They are a bunch of assholes, who fart too much, drink too much and sleep with way too many women—well, all except Royal, who is married now," she tells me. I go to smile, then it hits me that she included Finan in the group of sleeping with loads of women.

Stepping back out of her hold, I go to speak, but the door swings open, and Magnum steps in followed by every single member of the Rugged Skulls MC. Bar the prospects who were told to stay behind to watch over us.

My heart seizes in my chest as I wait for Finan to walk through to door with Juni tucked in his arms.

All the men have sullen looks on their faces, making my heart sink each time I look at them. None of them look at me. It's like they want Finan to take control here.

Astrid pulls me to her, holding me, tightening incase my knees give out. My jello legs also feel like lead, if that makes sense. My body waits with so much anticipation it doesn't know how to react.

"Breathe, babe," Astrid whispers to me.

My body won't function. It won't come alive until I see my girl.

It's Astrid who tenses when Lennox walks inside. He looks around the room like he's searching for someone.

When he finds the woman next to me, his body loses some of the tension, then tenses and looks away.

I hear Astrid breathe out a defeated sigh, but I pay them no mind besides this interaction, because Finan walks into the room, looking at his boots, and my heart sinks when I see that he doesn't have my daughter.

"NO. NO. Where is she? Where is my baby?" I run to him. His arms dangle at his sides as my tight fists hit his chest.

He takes my cries and my hits, not stopping me, not protecting himself.

"Why? You promised me. You promised to bring her home. You lied to me." I cry and hit him harder.

My body grows weak, my arms heavy, like lead.

It feels like my heart just shattered and Finan set the pieces on fire. A part of me knows that it's not his fault, but my fear is fueling my need to cause him pain, so he can feel what I am feeling.

"ENOUGH," gets bellowed.

My body jolts at the sudden volume of the voice from the man I'm hitting.

Looking up at Finan with wide eyes, my mouth drops open in shock that he just yelled at me. Taking a step back, I wrap my arms around my middle, still looking at him.

I take in the dark circles under his eyes, the little blood splatter on his neck. My hand goes to my mouth, thinking it's hers.

"It is not Juni's blood, sweetheart," Calder says from across the room. He must see what I gasped at and guessed my mind when there.

"I'm sorry, Joss. We hunted him down, followed every lead, but we still got nothing. Magnum even called in other clubs to help search for her. Maverick has run himself into the ground looking for her. Fuck, we all have."

He takes a deep breath, looking at me. The sorrow that shines back at me is frightening, and gut wrenching. He's feeling like he failed, like he let me down, because he didn't bring Juni home.

The anguish mirrors my own, and he hasn't met her yet.

"I failed you. I didn't find her. I—sorry, so fucking sorry. We still have people out looking, but—"

"He needs rest, Joss. He is dead on his feet. Plus, his hand needs to be cleaned up properly," Rookie says as he steps over to us.

I look up at him, then look over my shoulder, seeing that everyone is watching us. Della is crying, being held by a crying Farrah. Risky, Syn and Jodie are all standing like they are ready to pounce at the slightest movement from me.

I bite my lip, holding in a sob that is sure to break free. They took me under their wing, held me together when I was falling apart, and this is how I repay them. I hit Finan, a patched member, their son, brother, and nephew.

I blamed him for not bringing Juni home to me. A piece of my heart breaks off, falling into the pits of Hell. I can see the way they are looking at me, the disappointment.

Shaking my head, I turn back to Finan, seeing the scowl on his face is still there, as he looks down at me. Knowing that I have messed up, I nod and pull in a deep breath, ignoring the ache in my chest, the tingling in my nose.

"I'm sorry," I look him in the eyes and say. "It's not your fault, and I have no right to blame you. You didn't take her; you and the club have done everything to bring her back. If it's okay with you, I'd still like it if you would look for her. I will go to the police so they can start their search too."

With each word, my heart dies a little bit more. Finan's frown deepens as he looks down at me, but he says nothing.

I know when I'm not wanted or needed. In this moment, it is rightfully felt.

I try to smile, but I fail miserably.

Turning my head to look at Rookie, I see he is also frowning at me, but I see confusion on his older face.

"Would you keep me up to date with information, please? That way I can pass it on to the police."

With another deep breath, I turn to face the club, my fists at my side, clenching so hard I have no doubt my nails are leaving imprints on my palms.

"Thank you for everything."

My heart hurt when Owen died, but this... this feels so much worse, and we aren't even in a relationship.

"Goodbye, Finan. Thank you, for what you have done."

With a heavy heart, I force my feet to step away from him. Each step feels harder to take than the last. I wrap my arms around my stomach, holding myself together, also making sure that I don't vomit over the floor and embarrass myself even more.

My first stop will be the police station, to hand over what information I have learned from the club. Hopefully, they can start their search now and issue an Amber Alert. Juni has been gone long enough. I know that I should have gone back the next day, but the club told me they would handle it.

The door swings shut behind me with a thud, and it feels like the final nail in the coffin for something that may or may not have played out.

Just as I reach my car, I hear my name being called.

I look back and see Finan storming toward me. My heart skips a beat as he closes the gap between us. He doesn't waste any time with what he wants. He cups my face, leaning in to kiss me. Then he is speaking.

"You don't get to walk away after what happened inside. We talk this shit out." He bends at the waist, flipping me over his shoulder with a yelp.

I grip the pockets of his jeans, to hold myself up a little, so the blood doesn't rush to my head, as he carries me inside. I hear whistles and cheering but keep my face pointed in the other direction.

One, out of embarrassment, and two, so I don't see any more disappointment on his family's faces.

I know I messed up blaming him, and I will say I am sorry until I am blue in the face. I let my pain guide me and hurt the people who are helping.

I hear a door opening, then I'm being laid down on a soft bed. My gaze connects with Finan's as he kicks the door shut with a resounding thud. His eyes are dark, filled with lust and desire, but I see uncertainty there.

"Finan, I—" He cuts me off.

"Nope, you said your piece, now I get to say mine and we will go from there." All I can do is nod at him.

I watch as he removes his cut, laying it over the chair he has next to the bed, then he kicks off his boots and socks. I watch in complete fascination as he crawls up the bed, forcing me to lay back against the pillows.

I look up into his dark eyes, and my heart stutters from the sheer sight of this man looming over me.

He makes me feel and want things I'm not sure I'm ready for. We need to look at the age difference between us. That alone scares me. He could get tired of me, so easily. He could want different things because we are at different stages of our lives.

Does he want kids? Do I want more kids? I already know the answer to my own question. Yes, I would love to give Juni a sibling.

"I hate that I failed to bring Juni home to you. We have looked and hunted down every lead we have found, but come up empty, and I fucking hate that, Joss. More than you know. It isn't in me to fail. I struggle to understand when I can't do something, which is why I research, and I watch. I teach myself. So not finding her is killing me. Knowing and seeing what this sick fuck has done, it pains me that I couldn't get to her."

"And I put all that shit onto you out there. I don't blame you or the club for hating me. I should just go, Finan. It is causing too much upset me being here. Like I said out there, I'd like if you kept looking for her. The more the merrier as they say."

My voice is low, with a hint of longing to be in a better place with him, but I know I have blown that, and rightfully so. I was in the wrong to do what I did.

"You aren't going anywhere. You are right where you belong. Yes, some of my family are pissed, but they understand your fear is ruling you right now. Anyone of them out there would be feeling all kinds of emotion if something had happened to us when we were younger."

My hands find his cheeks, his eyes close at the contact, and I feel something shift between us. His hips rock a little, and I can't stop the gasp that escapes, making his eyes snap open. My panties become damp, as she twitches to feel him.

He looks down at me, seeing the aroused look on my face. One side of his lips tilt up as he rocks against me again. He shifts his body, so he's leaning on one elbow, while the other hand finds my stomach, then he is pushing the material of my t-shirt up my body, baring skin to him.

Dropping his head, his mouth connects with mine, while his hand explores my ribs, then I feel his thumb skim over the underside of my bra, while his tongue plays with mine.

The material of my bra is tugged down, exposing me to him. Finan breaks the kiss, dropping his head to suck my nipple into his mouth.

I arch and moan his name, causing him to stop.

"You okay?" I nod, unable to speak. He smirks at me and goes back to sucking, biting my nipple.

He moves to free the other breast and pays that attention too. I'm a withering mess next to him. I can feel how hard his cock is, pressed against me.

My body wants to melt into the bedding. He makes me feel so sexy and alive. Something that I haven't been feeling since Juni was taken three days ago.

"I bet I could make you come by just playing with these." His voice breaks my inner thoughts, and I look down at him.

He is grinning up at me, flashing me his perfect smile and his pearly whites.

"Maybe," I say, my voice low, deeper than normal, showing how turned on I am.

"I want you to feel something other than what you have been feeling. I want to make you feel so fucking good. We need you, alive and full of want to survive what we bring home to you," he says, and I nod, gripping his face and smashing my lips to his. He tweaks my nipples, making me cry out a breathy moan.

"Make me feel something. Anything, baby," I mutter against his lips.

His hand moves down between us, then he is sliding his hand down my leggings, dipping his fingers into my panties and over the small section of hair I leave when I shave. My heart beats against my chest, and my pussy grows wetter with every second his skin touches mine.

His fingers slide between my pussy lips, gliding over my clit, and I moan, loud, my hips coming off the bed at the contact.

His fingers move further down, until they come to my wetness.

"Oh, fuck, you are so fucking wet, baby. Damn, you are tight," he growls as he dips a finger inside of me. He moves in and out of me, adding a second finger, before looking at me.

"Baby, if you didn't have Juni, I would say you were a virgin with how tight you are." He kisses me again as he finger fucks me, slowly, deeply.

Without saying anything, I move my hands to the waist-band, pushing my leggings down along with my panties. Finan helps until they are a heap on the floor.

"I might as well be. It's been a while," I mutter, before taking his mouth again.

My cheeks heat up. I keep my eyes closed so I don't have to look at him, but he reacts.

"How long?" he asks, pulling back from my mouth.

I lick my lips, almost groaning loudly because I can taste him on me.

"Fourteen years," I say, then bury my face in the crook of his neck and breathe him in.

Damn, he even smells good. Woodsy, oil and sweat.

Finan moves away, making me look up at him. He's smiling, then he kisses me without saying anything. His hands start to move again, and I spread my legs wider for him.

It feels strange being naked, baring all to a man again. It has been way too long, but Juni was always my priority. She used to tell me to start dating but it never felt right, until one day I met a man on a mountain, that makes my body react in a way it has never done before.

"Oh, God." Just the touch of him sends my body into a frenzy.

The touch of a man is long overdue. Making myself come did the job, but I could come just from the simple touch of this man.

His fingers move inside of me, bringing me closer and closer to climax. His thumb presses down on my clit, with the slightest of circular motions. I gasp for air and push my head into the pillow, as Finan looks down at me.

"Is this okay?" he asks me, and I frown.

"It's perfect, handsome. I'm so close. Press harder," I pant out, and the man listens.

"Oh, fuck. I can feel you tightening around my fingers. Can't fucking wait to feel you strangle my cock, baby," he growls, and my body likes the sound.

"I'm coming," I cry, as my body goes into delicious spasms.

My eyes are squeezed tightly, as the flourish of my climax courses through my body, making my body tighten in the most delicious way. My breathing is coming in harsh pants, my heart beating wildly in my chest.

Finan says nothing, but neither do I. I can feel his eyes on me, even though I can't see him. He makes me feel things that I haven't in a long time, but I can't help but wonder if this feeling with him will pass.

Finan kisses my lips, before he snuggles next to me, pulling my body tight against his, as the sleep takes over. I fall into the darkness, something I have been struggling with since Juni was taken.

My nightmares start, but Finan is there for every one of them.

CHAPTER ELEVEN

FINAN

I rub my eyes, getting the grit out from not sleeping. It has been five days since Juni was taken and Joss hasn't left the clubhouse. She has stayed in my bed, every night. Letting me hold her while she sleeps. Joss told me that she sleeps better with me wrapped around her, keeping her safe.

Prez has been in contact with the sheriff, and they have run out of leads too. Knocking on doors of Rolland's known crew, no fucker has seen him. The fucker that I killed, his death was ruled an accident, saying he fell asleep with a cigarette in his hand, while drunk and high. No blowback for the club.

Maverick is next to me, with Astrid on the other side of the table, doing her thing. She has brought back some huge knowledge of the dark web. Click and her old man,

Override, of the Unforgiven Riders MC in the UK, have done good by her, taught her so fucking much. She is a different woman since she came home.

My gaze flicks to the door, as Lennox comes in with a tray of coffees, fueling us, but he is also keeping close to Astrid. Not that she is giving him the time of day. She is polite, but that's it. He hates it, that she is pretty much treating him like a stranger.

"Thanks, brother," I say when a mug is placed next to the laptop I'm working on.

I am not Maverick, or Astrid, but I know some shit. With years of watching and learning, you pick some things up. These two are the best hackers I know. They can find anything and anyone, which is why this is so fucking frustrating that we can't find Rolland.

"Thanks," comes Astrid's voice.

"You need to rest your eyes. You have been at it for hours, babe," Lennox says to her, leaning one hand on the table next to her laptop, the other on the back of her chair, caging her in.

I don't mind the slight tense of her shoulders at the closeness, and if Lennox saw it, he doesn't acknowledge it. She doesn't look up at him, just keeps tapping away on the keys.

Watching these two is like watching some TV show that is filled with angst and drama. Lennox knows he fucked up by doing what he did. As they say, like father, like son.

Astrid may be Slide and Farrah's daughter, and very laid back like her parents, but damn, she can be stubborn and hold a grudge like no other.

"I'm good," is all she says to him.

He stays in place for a second longer, before sighing and walking out of the room. I keep my eyes on her, and I see her gaze flick to the door he just exited. Smirking as I look at her, she looks at me, poking her tongue out when I cock an eyebrow at her.

"Leave it, Fin."

I hold my hands up in a surrender pose. "I didn't say anything."

"But you were thinking it. Always watching, plotting and shit. It is fucking freaky," she whines, and I chuckle.

"If I didn't watch, I wouldn't have been able to save your ass a time or two, missy. The same with the brothers. This is me," I tell her.

She nods and bites her lip. "I know, and we love you for it, Fin."

Astrid sinks back into her seat, her shoulders slumping. I agree with Lennox; she looks tired. Fuck, we all are. The three of us haven't stopped in days. Sleeping for an hour here and there.

I watch as she rubs her eyes, yawning, and I feel like shit for not pushing her to sleep more, but like I said, stubborn.

These guys are my family through and through, and we will do anything for each other.

Seeing Lennox and Astrid go through the awkwardness of their friendship, then Astrid wanting more, seeing it crash and burn, all because Lennox wanted to respect her father and the club.

In all honesty, I think Slide would have respected him more if he went to him directly and told him he wanted her, but he chose the wrong path, as did his father years ago, but we all know how that worked out.

"Go have a nap," I tell her, but she shakes her head.

"No, I'm close. I got accepted into a chat, where the men like young girls. They have a preference. The sick fuckers. It turns my stomach reading what they talk about. It pisses me off that more is not being done to shut these fuckers down, but I also know from my time in the UK, that when one gets shut down, five reopen. It's an impossible job.

"We need to do more in the prevention side of things. Make people aware, make the kids more aware of how dark and unsafe the internet can be. The things I saw over there, the people we helped shut down, should be dragged out into the water and dropped deep, so the sharks can rip them apart, painfully."

"Damn, remind me not to piss you off," Maverick says, as he stretches his arms over his head.

Something clicks in his body, and he sags in relief.

"You will do good to remember that, cousin," Astrid pipes up.

"So does Lennox deserve to be dropped with the sharks?" he asks her.

Fuck me, this man has a death wish. We all know to avoid bringing up what happened years ago. We was surprised that she stayed away so long, but we were also told that the UK did her good. Her family went over to see her, some other members went too, including my family, because we stopped over in Ireland to visit my father and uncles' family.

"Fuck you, Mav." She flips him off.

Mav laughs, wiggling his eyebrows at her, making her fume even more, but she goes back to working.

We sit and troll through hours and hours' worth of websites, things getting worse and worse the more we dig. My stomach rolls from what I read, but also because I haven't eaten in fuck knows how long.

As if she knew, Joss comes walking into the room with a tray of food, with Lennox hot on her heels. She gives me a small smile, but with a knowing hint what Lennox is doing. He is trying to make amends, but Astrid is having none of it. I truly think he has burnt his bridge, but one thing about Lennox is that he is like his mom, stubborn as fuck, so this should be interesting.

"Thought you guys should eat something. I should have brought it in earlier," Joss explains.

She places the tray on the table, Lennox following suit, keeping his eyes on Astrid.

Wrapping my arm around Joss, I scoot my chair back and pull her into my lap, kissing her bare shoulder, as she is wearing a cami. One of her arms goes round my neck, her hand resting on my collarbone, playing with the hem of my tank.

I shiver from the little contact from her fingers, my cock twitching in my jeans, but now is not the time for this shit. We have work to do.

"How are things going? I'm sorry to ask all the time, but I'm getting more and more fearful that we won't find her." Joss's voice cracks, and it fucking kills me to hear it.

She tucks her head in the crook of my neck, crying gently. My hand rubs up and down her back, soothing her. There is fuck all I can do right now, and it messes with my head. This is why I have limited contact with people outside of the club. It gets under my skin when I can't control things that people do, but I can't hurt every fucker either.

My gaze slips to Astrid. Tears run down her cheeks, as she bites her lip. We are all feeling a fraction of what Joss is feeling, but we feel it. Lennox steps to her, his arm around her shoulder, pulling her head to his stomach, holding her while she silently cries.

Astrid pulls in a deep breath and quickly pulls away from my brother like the contact burned her. Lennox sighs, moving to lean against the wall behind her, staying close in case she needs him again. They may be at odds right now, but he will die for her, and she knows it.

"You can ask as many times as you want, honey. I just fucking hate that this fuck is good," Maverick states, but then Astrid cuts in.

"But not as good as me," Astrid cries triumphantly. "I think I got him."

"Show me," Mavericks states firmly.

Astrid turns the laptop around to face us, and all we see is a bunch of chats going fast up the screen, like there are so many people all talking at once. The screen is back, the text is yellow as it scrolls fast and faster.

Joss sits up in my lap, looking at the screen, frowning.

"What does it say? Shit, they are talking way too fast," she cries.

I soothe her again, as Maverick watches the lines move up the screen. We sit and wait for him to work out what is being said, Astrid looking over his shoulder. Lennox rushes from the room, no doubt going to get the rest of the club.

We don't move unless Prez says so, and I know that Sarge will want to check into things before we make a move.

"Okay, I think I know where he is. Or at least where Juni might be. From the looks of what people are saying, he has two girls with him. One with dirty blond hair, which is Juni, and the other is a redhead, both under sixteen. Fuck." Mav curses, closing his eyes.

He looks to me, and I see it in his eyes. This is not good. His gaze moves to to Joss and gives her a pitiful look before bringing his eyes back to me.

"What? What is it? What does it say? Maverick, please tell me," Joss cries, leaning across the table, trying to see more of the laptop.

I go to speak, but Magnum, Opal, my father, and the other brothers pile into the room. My dad comes to stand by Joss and me, while Slide and Edge go to their kids.

My brother, Royal, Jack and Travis come in behind them. We called everyone back until we have more solid information, plus Prez didn't want a trail of dead bodies leading back to us.

I won't apologize for trying to get information.

"Talk," Prez pipes in.

"Do you think that Joss should be in here for this?" Sarge asks, and Joss makes a panicked sound, so I pull her tight.

"She needs to hear this," I state, looking at my president. Magnum looks at me for a few seconds, like he's reading me, then he nods.

"Go," he says to Mav.

"We think Astrid found Rolland. He is keeping the girls locked in an old storage unit, on some land. But we don't know where the land is yet. We need to dig deeper into his past again, try cross-referencing old family members, people he served time with," he explains.

"It looks like he is planning on selling the girls," Astrid adds.

Joss lets out a strangled cry, and I hold her tighter. She sobs against me, my heart aching for her. I look over to my father, and he nods, telling me that I have his full support.

My gaze connects with each of my brothers, each giving me a nod.

I kiss the top of Joss's head, and my arms tighten around her. Before I speak, I look towards Sarge.

"I trust you, old man, but I think us youngsters need to be on the hunt for this one." Before I'm even finished, all the older brothers are shaking their heads.

My father's hand is on my shoulder, his other one, smoothing down Joss's head, offering her his comfort too. Seeing my dad treat her like she is one of us already makes me damned fucking proud to be a Rugged Skull.

"Not happening, kid. Not on my watch. While I'm still able to breathe, while I am still able to fuck my wife, I will always be Sergeant at Arms of this club."

I see a flicker between Magnum and Opal, and it piques my interest, but I stay quiet.

"Jesus, Dad. Fuck, I think my dick just shriveled up and went back up into my body." Maverick gags.

Joss bursts out laughing, shocking the fuck out of us all. She sits up, staying in my lap, and dries her face with her hands.

We all sit in amazement, watching this woman cackle like a crazy chick, but I think she needed to feel a different emotion. If someone suffers the same emotion, they let it take over, laughter helps. Fuck any other kind of emotion, it can help lift your spirits.

Joss takes a deep breath and looks around the room, before her gaze settles on me. Her eyes are bloodshot and a little swollen from the crying; her lips are red, puffy, and damned lickable.

"Sorry. I know I shouldn't be laughing knowing what my baby could be going through. I needed that. I needed something to break the darkness that was creeping in. Like Risky told me, I need to stay strong for Juni. I will be useless to her if I'm an emotional wreck when she comes home."

She sniffs and looks around the room again. I follow her gaze, which stops on Magnum.

"Thank you, for allowing the club to help find my daughter." Magnum shakes his head at her.

"No thanks needed, darlin.' Family takes care of their own."

"Plus, these old bastards are not a part of Rugged Hunters. It's just us sexy fuckers," Calder pipes in.

She giggles, snuggling back into my body, and damned if she doesn't feel good. She fits me perfectly. Can you feel deeply for someone after only knowing them for a short time?

Fuck, I think I'm losing it. The way my brain works, is that I need to comprehend most things, if there is something that I don't know I make it a mission to find out everything there is to know.

This thing with Joss is something different, so at times I think that I have a gage on what is happening but at times, similar to this one, I feel like I am feeling and doing the wrong things.

Can someone feel deeply for someone that barely know?

"Watch yourself, boy," my father growls from behind me in his deep Irish accent.

Calder winks at him, sitting next to me.

"Next move?" Opal asks, looking between Maverick, me, and Sarge.

"We track down the land. Shouldn't take Astrid and I long. We will split the load and go from there. Be ready for when I find the info. From all the chatter, it looks like they are doing the sale in the next few days."

I watch as Maverick looks to Joss, then me.

"He had talked about sampling the goods already." He sighs, his shoulders slumping. "I hate talking about this in front of you, Joss. It's like kill the messenger scenario, right now," he moans.

"No. I need to hear it," she says softly. "I want to be prepared for what she will be like when you bring her home."

"Okay, we wait for the info then we plan to go hunting," Prez growls, and everyone agrees.

I eat my food with Joss on my lap, watching Maverick and Astrid do their thing. Lennox keeps a close eye on her, but she stays focused on her task at hand.

Joss eventually falls asleep on my lap, so I take her to my room, where she sleeps until we get the call.

Now we hunt.

CHAPTER TWELVE

JOSS

I take a sip of my coffee and groan in delight at the sweet java hitting my taste buds. Today has been a day for coffee or alcohol, but I need to keep a clear head. Finan and the men left early hours of this morning to go and find the land that we are praying to everything God ever known to man, that they find Juni and the other girl.

I am currently watching Risky, Luna and Astrid making lunch for everyone. The kitchen smells amazing, something that reminds me of when my mom is on a cooking frenzy for family time.

My phone lights up with a notification, so I franticly look down, expecting it to be from Finan, but it's just an email from a client. I sent out a mass email explaining the situation, stating that all work will be put on hold for the time being. So far, everyone has been respectful and offered their positive vibes for Juni to come home.

Her case has hit the local news, and the club thinks it will spread as it is an Amber Alert.

I listen to the women talk, reminiscing about when the kids were young, when they were younger and meeting their old men. It's nice to hear. I fall in love with their love stories. I am an old romantic, my bestie, Joy, always says.

She always pokes fun of me because of all the old, cheesy love movies I watch over and over again. Plus, the amount of romance books that are on my e-reader.

I smile, thinking of her. She has been there for all my life. Her mom and my mom are also best friends. They met in college. Joy was there through all of my big moments in life, and me hers.

Joy was my rock when I lost Owen, and when Juni was born.

"You doing okay over there?" The sweet voice pulls me from my thoughts.

I look over and see Della smiling at me. She looks good today, not so tired. Finan told me that she is due to go in for surgery next week, to remove a cancerous lump in her breast.

She will be fine; she has to be. So many people will hurt if anything happens to her.

"I'm okay. Just trying to keep focus, not let my mind wander to the horrid things that keep trying to creep in. It's hard." I offer her a sad, small smile, and she returns it.

Stepping over to me, she pulls me in for a hug, kissing the top of my head. It is crazy how much I feel connected to this woman. She's like a second mom, but I have only known her for a short time. Finan said that his mom has that effect on people.

"If there is one thing I do know, it's that my boy doesn't like to fail. He learns from something he can't do and makes sure that he succeeds. That has always been Finan's way. Just remember this: he will stop at nothing to bring your daughter home. In that, I believe."

"You'd better believe his ass will, or he will face the wrath of Juni's favorite aunty," comes a voice from behind us. I spin around and see Joy standing there, in all her glory. Tight jeans that look painted on, a tight camisole that shows her oversized breasts that are fake, because Joy was flat-chested right up until she was nineteen, then she had the surgery done because she hated being called a boy. Her confidence soared after that.

"Oh, my God. When did you get in?" I ask, running to her.

We hug, holding each other tight. I hear her sniff and pull back to look.

"Are you crying? The great and powerful Joy Gamble." She scoffs, waving her hand in a dismissive way.

"No. When the hell have you known me to cry?" She plays with my hair, moving some strands off my face, then she brushes some invisible lint off my shoulders to distract me.

"Well I know a few, Joy." I quirk my eyebrow.

She fakes being hurt and disgusted, because she knows the moments about which I am talking.

"We said we would never speak of that again. You—you fucking bitch," she replies with a smile on her face.

I giggle, then turn to the room. Some of the women are smiling. We are also getting some confused looks. Taking Joy's hand, I pull her further into the room.

"Ladies, I would like you to meet my best friend, my sister from another mister, my non-blood sister. Joy Gamble."

The ladies come over, and introductions are made. I also don't miss the way that Luna's gaze lingers on my friend longer than the others.

She is Joy's type, all-natural beauty, not ashamed of her sexuality. The last relationship Joy had, the chick wasn't even out to her family and made it out like her and Joy were just friends. Joy ended the relationship because the woman refused to tell her family that she was gay.

Since then, she doesn't date anyone who is still in the closet.

I do catch Joy looking over to Luna a few times before we walk outside and sit around the fire pit to have a talk.

I need to fill her in on everything that is happening, as there were some things that I kept from her.

With a drink in hand, we take a wooden chair each. I tuck my feet under my butt, sipping on the soda I brought with me.

"So hit me with everything. Do not leave a detail out, sister," she scolds, and I do.

I fill her in on the hike, meeting Finan that day and him always being on my mind. The fight with Juni that morning about Chloe. My mother-in-law, who has been a fucking nightmare over Juni being missing, telling people that I am an unfit mother.

She doesn't care that Juni is missing, just the attention she can get from her preppy, golf club friends and the press. The club has kept the press away, putting me on lockdown here at the clubhouse, until Juni is home.

I tell her about the man who has taken Juni and possibly another young girl. She holds my hand while I tell her this, rubbing her thumb over the back of my hand, like she used to when I lost my husband.

Joy scoots her chair closer to me, slinging her arm around my shoulders, and we awkwardly hug, but it's so nice to have her here. My parents pop in every day, but having Joy here is something I didn't know I needed.

With each word that I speak, I see her rage turn feral; she is almost foaming at the mouth. She loves Juni as much as me, because that is the type of person Joy is. She loves hard and forever. And two, Joy can't have children of her own—well, not the traditional way. When she was younger, she fell down a mountain we were hiking, and a tree branch went through her abdomen and pretty much destroyed her womb.

By the time I have finished telling her everything, we hear a commotion behind us. We both look over our shoulders to see a group of young women walking toward us.

Luna is followed by Astrid, Posey, Royal's wife Tree, and her sister Kady.

"Damn, she is sexy." Joy mutters, and I slap her with the back of my hand. "What? She is." She winks at me.

"Ladies, we thought we would come and keep you company." Tree speaks first with a friendly smile. I can see why Royal loves her; she is stunning and sweet.

"Yeah, so it had nothing to do with the fact that our resident lesbian wanted to eye-fuck the new chick," Astrid throws out, and we all laugh.

Luna winks at Joy, who smirks back.

"Eye-fuck away, baby." Joy bounces her eyebrows, and I groan, covering my face.

I hear the girls laugh, and I join in.

"So, what's up with you and Finan?" Kady asks. "I mean, that man is hot as fuck, broody, quiet, and they say they are the ones to watch out for." She wiggles her eyebrows with a huge smile on her face.

"I'm not sure. I like him. He makes me feel things I haven't felt before, even with my late husband. That may make me sound like a bitch, or whatever, but I can't help the way I feel," I explain.

"I feel a 'but' coming," Posey speaks up.

I look to her, and see the look she is giving me, like she is genuinely wanting to know what I am thinking.

Is now the place to discuss this? Are these the right people to talk to about what I'm feeling and thinking? I mean, they have grown up with Finan. They are a family.

I sigh, sinking into the seat beneath me, then look to Joy, who is giving me a tight-lipped smile, with soft eyes. She knows how hard it was for me to move on after Owen, that I hated dating, because it felt like I was betraying him.

Then one night she told me that he is gone, and he is never coming back, and that he would want me to find a man I loved, that Juni loved, and get the same love back.

"I'm older than he is, by seven years. I'm a single mom who works from home. My entire world revolves around my daughter. Should a man his age be wanting to be lumped with that? He can have anyone he wants. He is hot, ruggedly handsome, with a good soul and heart." I sigh after I explain my issue.

"Joss, let me ask you this. How would you feel seeing Finan with another woman?" Tree asks me.

My stomach knots and I feel like I'm going to be sick, but I push that feeling down. I look down at the rip in my jeans, pulling at a thread there, before looking up and seeing everyone looking at me.

"I don't know," I whisper.

"Oh, bullshit. You would hate it. Admit that much," Posey snaps.

I look at her, taken aback by her sudden outburst. We all stare at her. Her eyes are closed, while she takes deep breaths, before opening her eyes and looking at us.

"Fucking shit. I'm sorry, Joss. I'm dealing with some stuff, and I took it out on you."

"It's okay. We are allowed to blow from time to time. It's unhealthy to keep things locked away."

"Oh, we all like to blow from time to time." Kady winks, and I laugh with everyone.

"Damn, girl. I like you," Joy speaks up, holding her hand up so Kady can high-five her.

"I'm just scared that he will look around one day and realize that he doesn't want us anymore. He will see a hot babe one day and feel trapped being with me and Juni. I can't allow her to fall in love with him and then him disappear."

"Just her?" Luna pushes. I shake my head, looking down.

I know that it will crush me if he leaves. I can feel myself falling right now, so spending more time with him will only be worse and ruin me in the future. I am torn as to what to do.

"But think of all the hot sex a younger man will give you. That man is built, from what I have seen, sister. I have no doubt he could fuck you into the mattress." Joy bounces her eyebrows, and I smile.

"Can we not talk about sex please; it has been months for me." This comes from Astrid, making us giggle.

"I can beat that, babe," I say.

This piques their interest, as Joy laughs uncontrollably.

"Now you have to tell us. How long has your dry spell been?" Posey asks.

"Fuck off, Miss-Tittie." I push Joy away, laughing. "Not everyone is like you, who likes to eat any pussy that is offered," I say between laughs.

"There is nothing wrong with eating sweet, pussy." Luna throws her two cents in, making us laugh even harder.

I needed this. I needed to pull myself out of the hole I was slipping into. These girls have lifted my spirits, so I'm strong for when Juni comes home. Finan told me that he won't come home without her.

"Damn straight." Joy winks at Luna again.

Fuck me, shit is going to go down with these two. But they are both adults; they make their own decisions and face the consequences.

"Okay. Okay, no more sex talk. I need to get laid, and preferably by someone who knows what he is doing, or doesn't hate me," Astrid says, then she covers her mouth with her hand.

"Oh, do tell." Kady rests her elbow on her knees, her hand tucked under her elbow, looking intrigued.

"Not happening. Sorry." She doesn't look sorry. I see Tree shake her head at her sister, who thankfully takes the hint to not push further.

"Joss, tell us about Juni. What is your favorite memory?" Tree asks.

I brighten up. I love talking about Juni. She is the light in my world.

Taking a sip of my soda, I explain one of my many favorite memories.

"When Juni was almost one years old, we took her to see her father's grave. My parents and I. She was walking, barely, but doing so well. When suddenly, she sped up, walking straight to her father stone. Calling 'Dada.' It shocked us all, but at the same time it made my heart melt. The last time she was there, she was four months old. So how did she know where to go?"

"She knew. Her daddy lead her to him," Luna says, smiling at me, and I nod.

"Yeah. She sat on his grave, talking—well, babbling away to him like he was right there with her. Not once did she show an ounce of fear. That day has always stuck with me."

All the girls are smiling, loving the story. Tree wipes a tear away.

"When she was a baby, I would often catch her talking to a corner of the room, like someone was in there with her. In the end, we heard her say 'Dada' and 'Daddy,' so we knew his spirit was with her. She sees it all. "

"I bet Opal will have a blast meeting her," Posey chimes in, and I look at her, frowning.

"Have you not noticed that when he touches you, you feel calmer?"

I think it over, and my eyes go wide, making her smile when she sees that I remember.

"Oh, my God. I remember that when he touched my thigh, I felt a calm wash over me, but I was too distracted by the fear and Finan touching me and growling," I explain, sitting forward.

The club kids nod in understanding.

"We can't explain it. He just does it. Never once told us how," Astrid says.

We spend the rest of the time talking about Juni and her childhood. They talk about their lives growing up in the club, and the feeling of being home settles over me, also knowing that Juni will love it here.

I just need to get my head around the age gap between Finan and me.

CHAPTER THIRTEEN

FINAN

When people say their blood is boiling, it is not a figure of speech. When they say they can't hear anything besides the blood whooshing through their ears because their heart is beating so fast, they are not lying.

I have my earbuds in while we scope out a derelict building with a half barn, but all I hear is the beating of my heart. The blood bumping through my veins. Each of us have spread out. Even my father and the older members are here. Hell, even Preacher is with us, leaving the job he was on to help out.

It was all hands-on deck when Maverick and Astrid found where Rolland was keeping Juni and the other girl.

After the days of looking, it turned out that Juni was being kept less that forty minutes away at some old farm that was owned by one of Rolland's old cellmates.

It took some time, but we found her. Now we go in, kill that sick fuck, and bring Juni home. What happens after that is up in the air. I'm not sure what will happen between Joss and me after this is over.

Sweat beads on my brow, trickling down my back, soaking my t-shirt. With my gun raised, I step closer. My dad and me are going in the front. All I have to do is wait for the word from Sarge, and I'm going in ready to kill this cunt.

Seconds, minutes tick by. The guys are getting into position.

Down the gravel drive, we have Risky and Jodie waiting in a van. They will help take care of the girls, because they might be shit scared to see all of us men. Men they don't know. Also, we don't know what condition they will be in.

My stomach tightens as I think of Juni and the other girl being hurt. How can anyone hurt another human being for fun? It is fucking crazy how these men think they deserve these young girls. They genuinely believe they love them. But I know some are just sick as fuck and like fucking and hurting young, innocent girls.

Well, no more. That ends today for Rolland. I will make it my mission to take down every fucking pedophile and make them suffer.

"Going in," Sarge says.

"Three."

I tighten my grip on the gun.

"Two."

I snarl, my lip curling.

"One."

I take a deep breath, closing my eyes for a split second, controlling my body. I need to be clear-headed on this.

"GO."

The sick fucks talked about the girls being held in some shipping container, but we found none on the property from the drone that we sent up, so I can only assume it's stashed in the barn.

With a deep breath, I twist the handle on the red door, pulling it open, with my gun up in front of me. I am not taking any chances with this cunt. The smell of hay and shit hits my senses, and I hold back the gag.

With my gun still raised, we stalk forward, careful of each step. My father's hand is on my shoulder, confirming that he is at my back, watching my six.

I see Royal, and Magnum come in from the other side, while Sarge, Travis, Opal and Edge stalk in through the main bar doors, slipping between the large wooden doors.

Slide, Calder, Maverick, and Jack check out the house that is on the property. No movement has been seen in over five hours. That's why we took the decision to strike now. We will deal with that fuck if we catch him.

My main priority right now is the two girls.

Scanning the area, each of us take slow steps closer to the red container. I see the doors have no lock, so I assume the girls are restrained inside, or he is that cocky that he has scared them enough so they won't run?

We step closer, Prez, Sarge, and Royal right at our sides. I go to step forward, to pull the door open, but my father stops me.

"Sarge," he mouths, and I nod. Now is not the time to argue with them.

The rest of us form a semi-circle around the large steel doors, watching Sarge step forward, gun up in front of his face, covering himself.

My gaze flicks around these men who will do anything for the men at their sides, as they would do for any of the innocent, especially children.

We protect those who are unable to protect themselves.

He nods to Magnum, then he pulls the pin up, twisting it so he can pull the door open.

As soon as the door starts to move, the petrified squeals come from inside, makes my blood turn to molten lava.

Stepping forward, Sarge, Opal and Prez move closer, guns still up, ready to fire if needed. They step into the room, then I hear the soft voice of Opal, letting me believe the room is clear of Rolland and just the girls are in there.

"Shhhh, honey. We are here to take you home. I promise we won't hurt you," Opal soothes them. They cry, and it kills me.

Not wanting to wait any longer, I rush in. They both let out a sudden cry, and Prez glares at me.

"You was told to wait," he hisses at me.

"That's my woman's daughter. No fucking way was I waiting," I snap back.

That's the first time I have called Joss my woman.

When I step to the girls, I kneel down like Opal is, looking between them. Both have a black eye, which are also red and bloodshot from all the crying.

They both have their wrists tied with rope, which Sarge quickly cuts off.

As soon as they are both free, the other girl throws herself at Opal, while Juni looks at me.

"Hi, Juni, my name is Finan, and we have been looking for you, sweetheart. Your mom sent me."

Juni shakes her head at me, crying more. Shuffling closer, I take her hands in mine. I hate seeing the red, angry looking marks that have marred her smooth skin. She fought, she pulled and tugged. That is why they look so bad.

"I promise, baby, your mom sent me. Would you like to talk to her?" Her head nods vigorously, as I pull my phone out with a smile on my face.

I need to keep her calm, make her trust me enough so I can get her out of here and home to her mother.

Pulling up Joss's contact, I hit the call button.

"Finan?" Her voice comes through the speaker, and Juni's eyes go wide with shock, and I nod.

"Hey, baby. There's someone here who wants to speak to you."

I can hear her crying on the other end as I hold the phone out for Juni to take. She's nervous and hesitant at first, before she takes the phone.

"Juni? Juni, baby, are you there? Oh, God, baby, talk to me please," Joss cries, and my heart cracks at the emotion in her voice; fear mixed with elation that we found her baby girl.

"Mom? Is that really you?" Juni sobs.

Movement catches my eyes, so I turn my head, seeing Opal stand and carry the other girl out of the barn.

"Yes, baby girl, it's me. Oh my God, he found you. Baby, Finan is with me, okay? He and his club, they will keep you safe. Please let him bring you home to me. I need to hold you, to make sure you're okay."

They cry for a little more, talk a while, before she hands the phone back to me.

"Joss?"

"Please, bring my baby home to me." Her voice is firm, but I can hear the tremble in it.

"On our way, baby. Be there soon."

Pocketing my cell phone, I look back to Juni, who is staring at me with wonder in her eyes. My heart soars a little at seeing less fear coming from her aimed at me.

Holding out my hand for her to take, she looks down to it, then back to my face, before she places her tiny hand in mine. We get to our feet, and I bend at the waist to pick her up bridal style, not wanting her to walk out of here.

Both girls look tired, their skin a grayish color. Just the thought of what this fucker has done to them has my blood boiling.

My dad is right there with me, watching me with Juni, who is resting her head on my chest, tucking both her hands under her cheek.

We step out into the sunlight, and Juni winces at the sudden change, tucking her face into the crook of my neck. The feeling that she trusts me makes me feel like I am on top of the motherfucking world right now.

This is something I haven't felt before.

"Son, take her to the van. The girls will look over her," my dad says, and I nod.

Juni's head snaps up, looking between my father and me.

"You're his dad?" she asks Rookie.

"I am, darlin.' He's one of my two boys. My other son is over there. His name is Calder."

Juni follows to where he is pointing, and we see my brother coming toward the group. His face is like thunder, lips curling, nostrils flaring, and his brow is down. Fuck me, this looks bad.

The second he clocks the three of us, his face softens, like he doesn't want to scare Juni any more than she already is.

"Hi, Juni." His voice is soft, charming. He knows that most girls, even the teenage girls, like the way he softens his voice. There is something similar to what Opal does with his touch. Fucking freaky as shit.

"Hi," she squeaks.

"Brother, put Juni in the van with the old ladies. We have shit to deal with." I don't miss the slight nod toward the house.

"Language," I snap.

They chuckle around me, including Juni, and I smile down at her.

"Dude, she's fourteen. She probably swears as much as us," Calder chimes, winking at Juni.

The smile that graces her face makes me fucking thankful for my brother.

"I do, but don't tell Mom." She looks up at me, begging me not to snitch on her.

I smile shaking my head, turning to look toward the van, seeing Risky waiting for us.

"Juni, this is Risky. She is Magnum's old lady. Magnum is the club's president, so that means he's in charge. Risky and Jodie will take care of you, and the young girl with you," I explain.

"Okay." Her voice is sounding a little stronger.

I go to set her in the van's back seat, but Juni grips my cut in her fist, holding me tightly, afraid to let go. I shift so that her butt hits the seat, but her grip is still firm.

Covering her hand with mine, I pry her fingers loose, setting them in her lap. I cup her cheek, making her look at me so she knows that I mean what I am about to say.

"I won't be far, I promise. I need to go and see what Calder wants to show me. I swear, Juni, you are safe here." I look over my shoulder at Rookie, and he nods. "How about I leave my dad here to guard you. Would that make you feel better?" She nods to me, and I lean in and kiss her forehead.

"Juni, this is my dad, Rookie. Dad, this is Juni, Joss's daughter." I make the introductions, hoping it will help soothe some of Juni's fear.

"Okay," she whispers.

I nod to my dad and follow Calder, seeing Prez, Opal, and the rest of the brothers follow.

The closer we get to the house, the tighter my stomach knots. My heart races with pure anger.

"Brother, you need to brace yourself," Calder says from my side.

I look at him, his face showing a grim expression that is tinted with rage.

"That bad?" He nods.

I push open the front door, gagging at the smell that welcomes me.

Jack is standing in the kitchen, leaning against the counter. Clearly what I am about to walk in on has affected him deeply.

"You okay, man?" Royal asks his twin, stepping toward him.

"Fuck, man, it's bad. She's only a few years older than Dom. Fuck." I see tears in his eyes, and that alone tells me how bad it is.

Tearing my gaze away from the twins, I step into the bedroom off to the side of the kitchen, my gaze landing on what is causing my brothers' upset and rage.

There, on a mattress that is set on some wooden pallets, is a body of a young girl. Clearly she is dead. She has been for a few days from looking at her body. Rigor mortis has set in. She's laying on her back, spread eagled, tided to the corners of the bed.

The sick cunt did a number on her before leaving.

Why? I can't fathom why people have the need to do this.

I cover my mouth with my hand, as the contents of my stomach try to make an appearance.

"Where is he?" I snap, stepping out of the room.

"Slide has him in the living room. He was hiding in the basement watching porn on a laptop."

Rage fills my veins; my body heats up with the bursts of rage that course through my body.

When I step into the room, Rolland is on his knees, blood dripping from his nose and mouth. No doubt having a tuning from my brothers.

My fists clench at my sides, and my gun burns against my back, wanting to be used to end this sick motherfucker.

Images of how I want to make this man suffer rush through my head, but my heart is telling me to not waste any energy on him. He is not worth the time or breath. But I need to know why. Why Juni?

Stepping over to him, I swing, punching him in the jaw. I hear the crack as his screams fill the room.

He grins at me as blood and saliva dribbles out of his mouth, onto the already dirty white wifebeater he's wearing.

"I guess one of those were yours. Did I step on your toes, *brother?*" he asks, spitting more blood onto the floor.

I swing again, this time catching him in the temple. My knuckles scream in pain, but I push past it. I need to end this fuck, but not before he answers my questions.

"I am not your brother, you sick fuck. Juni belongs to me and her mom. Not dirty scum fuckers like you. Not someone who takes pleasure in hurting innocent young girls. Well let me tell you this, all of that ends today. Because where you're going, no fucker likes a man who likes to hurt children."

His eyes widen in fear. He shakes his head, pleading with me over and over again to not hand him over to the police. This makes me smile. Hearing his fear, seeing it.

"Why Juni?" I snarl.

"What?" he stammers.

"I said: why Juni?" I get up in his face, gripping his shirt, before hitting him again.

He cries out, before looking up at me from the floor as I stand to my full height of six-foot-three.

"WHY?" I bellow, making him jump.

"Her hair. She has nice hair, alright," he whimpers.

"Holy fuck," I hear someone mutter from behind me.

He took Juni simply because he liked her hair. Fuck me.

Shaking my head, I pull my gun out from the waistband of my jeans, cocking it, before aiming at the cunt on the floor. I pull the trigger, happy to see the fear in his eyes when his gaze lands on the barrel of my gun.

Dropping my hand to my side, I turn and walk out.

"I need to get my girl home to her mom," is all I say, as I make my way back to Juni.

Her face lights up when she sees me, and fuck me, that does shit to my heart. Let's hope her mom still wants me around now that the job is done.

CHAPTER FOURTEEN

JOSS

I bite my thumbnail, watching my drive, waiting for the van to pull in that is carrying my baby girl. Finan sent me a text saying they are on their way, so Joy and myself came home to wait for them. I wanted to be at our house when she got home.

I was informed that Jodie and Risky would be looking her over, making sure if she needs to go to the hospital or not. Thankfully, she is unhurt besides a black eye and some cuts on her wrists.

I will take that.

"Where are they?" I mutter to myself, but I know Joy heard me.

"They will be here soon. Give them a chance, okay? She is safe, honey. Finan got her."

I nod and look back to the window.

My heart leaps out of my chest when I see the big black van pull into my drive. I rush for the door, swinging it open, not bothering to close it behind me.

"Juni," I call her name as I close the distance.

The back door swings open, and I see a booted foot step out. I halt as Finan's body emerges from the back. He looks at me with a smile on his face, his eyes looking tired but happy.

He leans into the van, before pulling back, with Juni clutching his cut tightly. He whispers something in her ear, and her head snaps in my direction.

"MOM," she cries, and darts to me as soon as her feet hit the ground.

I hear murmurs around us, but I hold my baby tightly to me. My heart aches with the love I have for this girl. I feel complete with her in my arms, like the whole world has been filled.

Holding her tightly to me, I look over her shoulder at Finan, who is a little blurry from the tears I'm crying, but he still looks as handsome as ever.

"I can't thank you enough, Finan. You and the club," I sob.

"There is nothing to thank us for. We're just happy she's home, safe and sound. Risky and Jodie cleaned up her wrists, no stitches needed. It just needs to be kept clean and dry for a few days, so the skin can heal. Why don't we go inside and talk some more, yeah?" he says, before looking around at my neighbors.

I nod and get to my feet, dragging Juni up with me. Leading her into the house, I hear men talking behind me.

"Church tomorrow, brother," Magnum states.

"My juicy Juni," Joy cries when Juni runs to her.

Knowing my daughter is safe, I turn to look at Finan, who is just closing my front door. He stops short, looking at me. His gaze gives away his uncertainty. I tilt my head to the side, watching a ray of emotions mar his handsome face.

Juni lets out a loud laugh, breaking the connection between us. Finan's spine straightens, and he moves forward.

"If your mom will leave you out of her sight for a short time, why don't you go and shower, sweetheart," he says to Juni, who smiles at him.

"No. I want her with me. I'll help her clean up. I can't let her out of my sight." I fight him on his suggestion.

Shaking my head at him, he steps forward, cupping my cheeks.

"She's okay. Believe me. I know you're scared but happy to have her home, but we need to talk," he says.

Turning my head, I look to my daughter, and my heart stutters in my chest, seeing the way she is looking at him. After everything that has happened, I see trust in her eyes, and adoration.

"I'm fine, Mommy. I'll come right back down to you."

Fucking hell, when did my baby grow up? She's acting like she wasn't kidnapped four days ago. It's me who is struggling with this and not her, but I suppose she could be masking what she is really feeling.

"That is a good idea," Joy pipes in. "I will go with her." Joy gives me a look and a nod, letting me know that I need to speak to Finan. I nod at her and watch as she leads Juni up the stairs.

Suddenly, my daughter stops and runs back toward Finan. Her arms wraps around his waist as she holds on tight, her face smooched against his stomach. He holds her just as tight, kissing the top of her head.

I cover my mouth to hold in the sob that is trying to show me up. Watching the way she reacts to him melts my heart. A hand wraps around my shoulder, pulling me tight to her.

"She trusts him. Says a lot, babe." All I can do is nod because she is right.

"Thank you. For saving me, I mean," Juni says to Finan. He smiles down at her, tapping her nose.

"Anytime. Go, I need to speak to your mom." Not once does he look uncertain when he speaks to her. It is a far cry from what he has told me, or I have seen with him.

Juni and Joy head upstairs.

"Come sit." He takes my hand, leading me into the living room and over to the sofa. He sits, pulling me next to him, never once letting go of my hand.

We sit facing each other, our knees touching.

"Let me get everything out before you speak." I nod.

He takes a deep breath and starts explaining what he found.

"We found Juni and another young girl locked in a storage container. Both relatively unharmed. Besides both having black eyes and the cuts on their wrists, they are okay. Juni told me that neither Rolland nor anyone else ever once touched them."

"That's good, I guess." I try to smile but fail. "But I don't understand why he took her, or the other girl. Why them?"

"I will get to that in a second." He takes a deep breath again and continues, "Baby, they weren't the only girls there. We found another girl in the house. She didn't make it. Raped and beaten. Maverick found out she was just eleven years old and has been missing for ten days. Astrid found out that Rolland didn't touch Juni because she was to be sold to a guy in New York.

"We already have information on him and have a club close by that will take the fucker out and anyone associated with him. None of them will hurt another girl again."

I nod, letting the information sink in, looking across the room where there is a photo of Juni and me at the beach from last summer. We had such a great time that day. Finan's hand grips mine tighter, gaining my attention.

"Baby, the reason he took Juni was because of her hair. He simply liked her hair."

"What?" I gasp.

"Fuck knows how these cunts think. There is no rhyme nor reason why they do what they do. They are just fucked up."

"Oh, my God," I cry.

Finan pulls me into his lap, holding me tight, soothing me with sweet words and kisses to the top of my head.

How can these men, and women, do these horrific things to these innocent kids? Sickos, all of them, and they should be punished for what they do. More needs to be done about them, not giving them a short sentence and some counselling. Maybe they should suffer what they put their victims through.

"She can't ever know that is the reason, Fin. Juni loves her hair, and I know she will want to change it. Can we keep this between us?" I beg, his eyes soften as he nods at me.

"The club are linking up with other clubs in locations that we found people that were connected with Rolland and his crew. We are all teaming up to take them down. Some won't make it, some will end up behind bars again," he explains, and all I do is nod against his chest.

Knowing that some of these sick men will die at the hands of club members, is a torn feeling but right now my anger is controlling how I feel.

I have no idea how long he holds me, but before long, Juni and Joy come back downstairs.

Juni snuggles with me, while Joy sits in the love seat. Finan stays, watching Supernatural with us. He even comments that Dean's car 'Baby' is *fucking sexy*, making Juni laugh. I know one day she will crumble; everything will pile on top of her. But I also know that she has people around her to love and support her through it. For right now, she is back being a teenager again, crushing after overaged actors.

By nine, Juni is sleeping on my lap, my fingers brushing through her hair. I can smell her bubblegum scent that she loves so much, and it makes my heart happy to have her here, home and safe.

"Let me carry her to her room," Finan says, reaching for her.

"She's heavy, Finan. She can walk."

He shakes his head. "She is out cold. Let her sleep." I nod, and he lifts her bridal style and carries her to her bedroom.

I smile after them, loving seeing how close they seem after just a few hours. I suppose it might have something to do with Finan saving her.

I look over to Joy, who is smiling at me.

"What?"

"You like him," she replies to me, smirking.

"You know I do, but I am still struggling with the age gap thing." I shake my head, trying to force the thought out of my head of Finan with a younger woman, someone his own age.

Joy sighs, getting to her feet and coming over to me, cupping my face.

"Go with it. Deal with the fall out tomorrow. Juni is home and safe. Give him a proper thank you." She wiggles her eyebrows at me and walks up the stairs to the spare room.

Shit, can I sleep with Finan? Is now the right time? I just got Juni home. I know she is safe and well, but shouldn't I be focused on her right now?

Shit. I scoot to the edge of the sofa, resting my elbows on my knees and my face in my hands, breathing in deeply, trying to focus my mind. So many different things are swirling around my mind right now. I can't seem to think straight.

"She's down. You okay?"

I twist my body around to see him walk back into the room, and nod.

"Yeah, just letting things sink in. Thank you again for bringing her home to me." I force the tears to stay away, swallowing past the lump in my throat.

"Nothing to thank me for. I'm glad you came to the club. Plus, I got to see you again." He smiles at me, and my heart melts, my nipples tingle, and my pussy wakes up.

"Yeah. I was wondering how I would see you again after that day." I smile shyly, looking away.

He sits next to me, using his forefinger to tilt my chin his way, so he can see my face.

"I would have found you eventually." He leans in and kisses me.

It's soft, gentle at first, maybe a little hesitant. He seems concerned whether this is the right time, but damn, I want more.

I lean in, pressing my lips to him harder, letting him know exactly what I want.

Finan picks me up, then gets to his feet. My legs go around his waist as he carried me up the stairs and into my room. All the while I'm lapping at his neck, making his skin pebble and his chest rumble with every growl.

He lays me on the bed, looking down at me. When I reach for his cut, he sits up, removing the leather and dropping it onto the storage stool I have next to the bed.

"You need to tell me now if this is too fast or you are not ready for it, because once I taste you, once I get inside of you, Joss, there is no going back. You are mine," he growls, and my pussy spasms from the tone of his voice and the declaration.

I have to take Joy's words and go with it. I have to live for me too, have something that I want, and Finan is what I want. Even if it is for a short time.

"Fuck me, Finan. I need to feel you inside of me," I say, not adding that I will belong to him.

So much can change in the blink of an eye. So I will take what I can.

It takes him a split second to get off the bed and strip down. I gawk at him, taking in every muscle, every tattoo, every dip of his defined body.

His skin looks golden brown, a natural sunny tone. It is also flawless, besides the scar on his right hip.

I sit up, running my finger over it, making him shiver. He's looking down at me like a predator waiting for his meal to submit to him.

And fuck me, I will submit to anything for this man in this moment.

He shivers when I run the tip of my finger over the scar, leaning in to kiss it, then looking up at him for an explanation.

"Stab wound," is all he gives me. I nod, before running my tongue over the scar.

That earns me a growl. I smile against his body, moving my lips closer to where I want my mouth.

"Baby, you don't have to." His voice is deep, thick with desire.

With my hands on his hips, I look up at him, licking my bottom, tasting him there.

"I want to. A thank you of sorts." I grin.

He frowns down at me, and it hits me that I said the wrong thing. Fuck, we didn't talk about payment for me hiring them.

"I didn't look for Juni so I could get in your panties, Joss. It was the right thing to do. We would help anyone who needs it," he yells at me.

Biting my lip, I look away, not liking the frown on his handsome face, but Finan doesn't let me get away with it.

Cupping my jaw, he makes me look up.

"You can suck my cock whenever you want, beautiful. But this is never a payment. I will never make you do something as payment. This is all fucking pleasure, baby, and believe me, I'm getting a taste too."

My skin heats at the promise in his voice of him eating me, licking me to climax.

Dipping my head forward, I kiss the tip of his cock. The smooth, shiny purple head is begging to be sucked and licked, so I do just that.

Opening my mouth, I slide down his length, making sure my tongue makes contact on the underside. Finan hisses, his hands gripping the side of my head gently. Pulling back, I see how wet his shaft is, and move back down again, sucking harder.

That gets me another growl, his body tightening with tension. Letting go of his hip, I cup his balls, making his hips thrust forward. His cock sinks into my mouth further, hitting the back of my throat.

I don't gag because I don't have a gag reflex.

"Holy shit, woman." I like how deep his tone is, filled with arousal.

My pussy pulses, my panties becoming damp with need for him, but I don't care, because I know he will take care of me when I'm done tasting him.

I move my hand up and down his cock, twisting the skin when I pull back to the tip, sucking and nipping at the head.

His balls tighten in my hand, and I can't wait to have them in my mouth, but tonight is fast paced, and I want to take my time with him.

"Fuck, baby, I'm close." That makes me double my efforts and make him come down my throat. "Fuck, yes. I'm going to coat your tongue with my cum. You are going to taste me for days, baby. Fuck yes."

He howls out the last word as he comes.

I smile to myself, before licking his cock free and moving back on the bed. Reaching for my panties, the most horrific blood curdling scream stops my movement. Finan, in a flash, is dressed and out the door. I quickly throw on my shorts and run after him.

Juni is on the bed, rocking back and forth in Finan's arms. I move over to them, Finan moving back slightly so I can get to my daughter. I hold her, cry with her, while Finan holds us.

I am thankful for him being here, but I can't help but think that what we just did was a mistake. Bad timing. I am a terrible mother for doing what I just did after what my daughter has been through.

Fuck, I need to rethink my life.

CHAPTER FIFTEEN

FINAN

On my back, I groan at the pain and pressure as I lift the weights above my head. Jack is spotting me. Luna joined us this morning. She is over on the treadmill, wanting to run her tension out, she said.

"You okay, brother?" Jack asks.

Straining, holding my breath, I replace the weights bar on the hook, before looking at him. I sigh and sit up as Jack comes around the front of the bench.

My arms scream, but I need this kind of pain today. I have heard fuck all from Joss since I left her place the day before yesterday. Believe me, I have fucking tried. I called and text, not wanting to just turn up at her place, but got nothing back.

To say I am pissed is an understatement.

"Just pissed that Joss is ignoring my calls and texts."

I use my towel to dry my face, before downing the rest of my water. Moving over to the fridge, I take out another bottle, finishing off that one at once. Damn, I wish I had fucking whiskey right now. That might help me forget the look on Joss's face the last time I saw her.

She looked heartbroken when Juni woke up screaming from a nightmare. I held them both close until they fell asleep in Juni's bed. Then I went to sleep on the couch, leaving the next morning before they woke up.

I thought giving them some space to have mother, daughter time would be good. Give Juni some time to recover from what she went through, so I text instead of going to the house but got nothing back.

"Maybe she is giving all her time to Juni. She has been through a shit time, brother."

"Yeah, I know." I sigh. "But fuck, man, I thought she knew I would be there for her. For both of them."

I think over everything what was said between us, and I never got the vibe that she would fucking ghost me, especially after she sucked my cock in her bedroom. The way she looked at me when I said that I wanted to taste her also, she fucking wanted it.

Clearly I read her wrong.

Even if she fucking told me that she wanted some alone time with Juni, I would understand. I'm not that much of a dick to demand all of her time, but shit, just to ignore me. That is messed up.

"When she was at the clubhouse, she was worried about the age between you guys. Maybe that's her reason to not text you back. It's a shitty reason but it is one. Joy told me that she hasn't dated anyone seriously since her husband died. She's tried but she felt it was wrong, but with you, Joss seemed to want to try, but the age gap was a huge issue for her," Luna adds as she joins us.

I stare at her, looking at her like she is crazy. There is no way that is the reason, right?

"Add in that she is a single parent of a teenager. That can add some extra baggage," Jack throws out there.

"Juni is not extra baggage, fucker," I snap at him, making him smile.

"I know that, so do you. Look at you, Fin, you are a young guy in an MC. You have women throwing themselves at you, and before you jump down my throat, I know you don't feast on them, but she doesn't know that."

Fuck my life with a fucking punching bag.

Why the hell didn't she just talk to me about it? We could have worked this shit out. Fuck, I have no idea the last time I fucked someone. It was months before I met Joss that I got my dick sucked.

"I need to talk to her again." I need to go to her house and make her face me.

I want to hear it from her if she wants nothing to do with me. She can tell it to my face, give me her shitty reasons, so I can try and squash them all and tell her that I want her and only her.

"Speaking of talking, what's up with you and her friend, Joy?" Jack asks Luna, wiggling his eyebrows.

It is uncanny how him and Royal are identical in every way, but so different in the personality department.

"Nothing to speak of." Luna shrugs, looking around the gym.

I look at Jack, and he winks at me, making me grin. Oh, it is grill time.

"Yeah, doesn't sound like nothing," I state, folding my arms across my chest.

She scoffs and moves over to the bench to start her leg lifts, but we follow her. I go to speak again, but my phone rings.

"This is not over, young lady," I joke, earning myself to be flipped off by her.

"Hey, Dad," I greet my father.

I hear both Luna and Jack talking, so I step away to hear my father better.

"I need you for a job. Come to the studio. One of the girls needs to go to the clinic, but she lost her fucking license again. Her husband is filming so he can't take her. Everyone seems to be fucking busy today," my father grumbles into the phone, and I smile while walking back to the locker room.

"No problem. Let me shower and I will be right there."

"Nice one, son. Later." He hangs up, and I hit the showers.

Stripping down, I tuck my clothes into my locker, before wrapping a towel around my waist and stepping into the cubical.

Images of Joss all wet in front of me on her knees like she did that night, flash through my head. My cock likes the flash movie, and he hardens. Sighing, I wrap my hand around my cock, using some soap as lube. I jerk my dick up and down, leaning one hand on the wall in front of me, remembering the feeling of Joss's lips wrapped around me, sucking, licking, and tugging on my balls. She knew what I liked.

It doesn't take long before I'm coming, groaning her name as my orgasm hits, my balls emptying into the water at my feet.

My muscles seem less tense. I shake it out, washing up, then drying off and heading to Rugged Online Entertainment studio.

———————

Pulling up outside the studio on my bike, I see my truck already pulled out to take Whitney to the clinic.

She comes out as I unlock my truck, in all her flashy glory. A skirt that looks like if she bends over an inch, she will flash the world. Her tits look like they were forced into a top that is five sizes too small, and her heels are so huge, they must hurt. Why do women wear such high heels?

"Aww, Finan, thank you for doing this, baby. I need my month's tests done, and I got pulled again for speeding, apparently, so they took my damned license." She smiles while trotting over to me.

"It's okay. I have no plans." I open the door for her to slide in.

Once she is in, I closed the door and walk around to my side and get in, then fire the truck up.

I pull away from the studio, waving to some of the old ladies as we pass through the clubhouse compound, Whitney doing the same.

"Damn, that woman gets sexier every time I see her," Whitney states, looking at Synclare.

I laugh, shaking my head.

Whitney is not one to shy away from her sexuality. I mean, she is a porn star after all. So is her husband, who also works for us. They are only allowed to fuck other people in the studio. Outside of it, they class it as cheating. Each to their own, I guess.

Me, I will never share my woman.

Thinking of Joss with another man makes me clench the steering wheel a little tight, so tight my knuckles turn white from the pressure.

"What has you so wound up, honey?"

"Nothing," I reply, keeping my eyes on the road in front.

"Finan Price, why don't you try that again."

People may only see Whitney as a porn star, but she is a great lady. Always respectful, always happy to help people out when she can. Hell, she is even friends with my mom, after all the years they have worked together.

Both her and her husband know their time in front of the camera is coming to an end, but they plan to stay on with us, on the production side of things.

"This chick I like, she ghosted me. No big deal." I try to shrug it off, but I know she won't let it slide.

I am not in the mood to talk about Joss and me, but I know that Whitney is one to push and get what she can.

She stays quiet for a few minutes. I look over to her, and find her looking at me, like she is trying to get a read on my situation. Well, that won't happen. It's me who reads people, not the other way around.

Focusing back on the road ahead, we make it to the clinic, and I sit in the car while she goes inside.

I feel like I can finally breathe, thanking the fucking gods that she didn't push any further, but I also have to drive her back to the studio, and she will pounce then.

Lifting my hips, I pull out my phone from my jeans pocket and click on Joss's name, hoping she will answer this time. It rings, and rings. I hit the end button in frustration.

Why am I even bothering?

Because you like her, dickface, the voice spits out in my head. Fuck.

I scroll through my social media, seeing some old school friends that have kids and are married already. I sigh and shut it down.

Using my app for local news, I see that Joss's in-laws are still kicking up a stink on Juni's abduction. Prez has a prospect outside of Joss's house to keep watch, as some local news journalists are wanting to speak to them.

I know the club's lawyer is handling some shit for Joss, because her mother-in-law is claiming that she is an unfit mother who allowed her daughter to be kidnapped. Thankfully, the sheriff and the deputy jumped on that and said that Juni was taken from school. There was nothing that Joss could have done to prevent it.

But still those fucking rich cunts won't leave her alone. Juni is going over to her grandparents for a visit this weekend. How do I know this? Maverick. He has been keeping tabs on them both for me since she won't get in touch.

I plan to make my move then.

I sink down in my seat, resting my head back, closing my eyes to catch a nap before Whitney comes back out. My head has been pounding with a headache since I got up this morning. I thought the gym would help, but nope.

I see an extra-long nap in my future when I get back to the clubhouse, maybe some whiskey that will knock me the hell out. I don't drink much, but when I do, I go all out.

The door opening startles me from my nap, and Whitney looks apologetic.

"I'm sorry, sweetie." I sit up in my seat and smile at her.

"No worries. Ready to head back?"

"Yep. All done until next month. I hate doing these. I mean, we are all clean, but I understand it's the club's policy," she explains.

She is right, the Rugged Skulls MC take care of all of their employees.

We drive back, stopping on the way for a coffee, because Whit says she has a full day ahead of her.

The girl at the window hands me the coffee, and I drive off. I double take as I pull away. Fuck. Was that Joss and Juni walking into the mall?

I pull back around to see if it is them, and to my fucking surprise, it is. They are laughing and smiling, and something hits me right in the chest. I reach up and rub the heel of my hand over my sternum.

She is okay without me.

She doesn't need me.

As if she senses me or she sees my truck, Joss looks my way, and the smile drops from her face. I see her gaze flick over to Whitney, and it may be bad for me to be thankful that she sees me with another woman, but fuck me, this is a kick to the nuts.

I shake my head and keep driving, but I can't stop myself from looking in the rearview mirror. Joss stands there looking at my taillights. I can't make out her face, but I can imagine she is hurt, and pissed, but guess what. So the fuck am I.

I cut the engine to my truck when we reach the studio, but Whitney doesn't get out. She shifts her body to look at me, so I face her.

"What?"

"Who was that? She was pretty."

"It was no one. Leave it." I get out of the car, and so does Whit. She meets me around the front of my truck, her hands on her hips.

"You are as stubborn as your father, Finan. If that hot chick is someone you want, then go get her. Move that cute little tush of yours and get her. If my marriage can survive us fucking other people for a living, then you can sort through whatever shit you two are dealing with. Now," she fluffs up her hair, giving me a megawatt smile. "If you will excuse me, I have a very hot chick to fuck. Toodles."

With that, she walks away, and I watch her.

Fuck me, she is hot for her age, but my cock doesn't like what he sees. On no, he only likes one short woman with golden skin, with soulful eyes and dark, short hair.

Fucking cunt on a stick.

CHAPTER SIXTEEN

JOSS

Juni seems brighter today. I kept her home from school the last few days, making sure she is doing okay both mentally and physically. So far, she hasn't shown any signs, but I did a quick online search and they said that trauma victims can take a while to show signs of PTSD, or even a trigger can set things off, so I have been keeping a close eye on her.

Her school were super supportive with me keeping her home, even sending schoolwork home for her to do, but like every teenager out there, she whined about having to do it, but I refuse to let her fall behind.

"Oh, this is cute." Her voice comes from the other side of the rail filled with clothes.

We are at some new and hip shop, according to my daughter. I step over to her and see she is holding up a matching black and white, plaid skirt and blazer. Smiling, I take it from her to check the price tag, and I am shocked how cheap it is, yet it is made well.

"You want this?" I ask, making her smile wide.

"Really?" I nod to her question.

She lets out a squeal of delight, gaining the attention of some people around us, then she is rifling through the rack for her size.

I smile at seeing her happy. I just hope and pray that it stays there. Her happiness is what I live for. To see her happy in life, to succeed in what she wants.

We each deserve to get what we want.

Speaking of wanting things, Finan's handsome face pops into my head. I have been dodging his calls and texts since he left the morning after Juni was brought home. I needed time to wrap my head around things; Juni being home and safe. Him being younger than me, and the possibility that he could dump me at any time.

It's not only me who will be hurt, but it will also be Juni. She talks about him, wanting to know how much I like him, how hot he is. Damn teenage hormones.

I blow off her questions about him not spending time with us, getting to know her, by saying that he is working. I can't bring myself to talk to my teenage daughter about my issues with the age gap.

She is older than her age, I know, but maybe it's time to talk to her about how things are. I mean, she needs to understand that not everything is a fairytale when it comes to relationships.

She likes watching all those tween movies that are filled with sweet love, mixed with a little teen drama and angst.

Maybe I need to approach this subject rather than dodging it.

We shop a little more, then pay for the outfit with some accessories to go with it. Next up is shoes, then we are booked in for a mani-pedi. Mother-daughter time.

"What do you say we grab something to eat before we go to the salon?" I nudge Juni with my shoulder.

"Okay. I could eat."

While we are walking to the food court, I breathe in deep and ask her the question that has been burning on my tongue.

"Juni, you know you can talk to me about anything." She nods but doesn't look at me. "Are you sure you are okay? Nothing bothering you? Nothing you say will make me love you any less."

She stops in her tracks, looking at me with a slight frown. Okay maybe asking that while walking through the mall isn't the best time.

"Mom, I love you, but you need to stop freaking out, okay? Cool ya beans. If and when I need you, I promise to come to you."

My nose burns with emotion, and I pull her in for a hug while I blink back the tears. Nothing says crazy emotional chick quite like crying in the middle of the shopping mall.

We hug for a few seconds, before I plaster a big smile on my face, holding her cheeks.

"When did you get so old and wise?" I joke. Her smile widens, before she steps to my side, linking her arm with mine, and we start walking.

"Since the day I was born. I am a mix of you and Daddy, right? That's what Aunt Olivia says."

"Your aunt Olivia is a wise woman herself. She wants to come and see you. I told her that you would call and arrange something. But as for your grandparents, everything must go through me, okay?" She nods, taking on a serious look.

"I don't want to see them. They made out that you put me in danger when I was taken. It was my fault, not yours." This time, I see tears in her eyes.

Looking around, I see the nearest pathway that leads through two stores and out to the parking lot for a little privacy.

We sit on a short wall, and I take her hands in mine.

"You listen to me. None of what happened was your fault. You hear me? None of it, Juni." I speak firmly, letting her know that I am dead serious on what I am saying.

"It was that disgusting monster's fault and people like him. They prey on young girls like you. But you, or any other victim, male or female, are not to blame for what their kidnappers do. Do you think victims want to be hurt, taken from their loved ones? Of course they don't. Neither did you. They hunt, and are manipulative, cunning, and sick in the head. There is no excuse for it. But at the end of the day, it is *their* fault. *They* are the ones to blame."

I punch home just to make sure that she understands. Tears run down her pretty young face, so I swipe them away.

"We are a blotchy mess now. Come on, let's go and get some pampering done. I think we both deserve it."

"We do. I love you, Momma." She hugs me, and I kiss the top of her head, holding her tight.

"I love you too, baby girl."

We link arms again and head down the parking lot side to the nail salon, where our appointment is.

The hairs on the back of my neck stand on end and fear washes over me. Thinking it is someone who wants to try and take Juni again, I cling to her tighter, because they will have to kill me to get her.

I look around, keeping the smile on my face so not to scare her, until I see him.

There, in his big truck, is Finan. He looks so handsome, making my heart pinch with guilt at the thought of pushing him away after everything he and the club did for me. But that feeling quickly stops when I see that he is in his truck with another woman.

The closer he gets, the more I see of them. The woman with him his stunning. Dark blond hair, perfect make-up. Typical biker type.

Maybe I did dodge a bullet after all.

I see Finan shake his head, before he speeds up and drives past us without so much as a second look.

My stomach knots, almost to the point of me throwing up.

"Mom?" Juni's voice pulls me from watching the truck pull out onto the road.

I blink and look at her, plastering on a fake smile and tugging her along.

"Come on, it's nail time. We have to nail it," I joke.

Juni groans, making me giggle.

I keep my forced smile in place while we sit and get our nails and toes done. Juni goes for something bright. She has each finger a bright shade, with the tips a different color. They look amazing, and she loves them.

I went a little darker, with having dark maroon on each finger, except for the two ring fingers. They are full glitter. They look pretty, if I do say so myself.

The entire time we're in the salon, I push back the images of Finan and that woman. I focus on Juni. But now we are driving to my parents' house to drop Juni off for the weekend, the images come flooding back.

Who is she? Has he been seeing her while killing and doing things with me? Oh, my God, is she is girlfriend, and he cheated on her with me? Even as I think that thought, I know it's not true. Finan is not that kind of man.

Then why was he with her?

I stop my thoughts when we arrive at my mom and dad's house. They live very comfortably in their huge house that they worked very hard for, that and my dad knows how to invest.

Me and my brother didn't want for anything growing up, but we had to learn to work hard.

'You can't expect to get everything for nothing' is what we were always told by my father. I have passed that down to Juni.

If you want something, work for it. Do your hardest to get to where you want to be. Will it be smooth sailing? Hell no, but totally worth it when you reach your goal.

As soon as the car comes to a stop, Juni is out and running to my parents, who are standing on their front porch.

My parents hug her, even though they have seen her every day since Finan brought her home.

My stomach does that twisty thing again when I think of him, so I push it down again. There is nothing I can do about it. Clearly me ghosting him pushed him into the arms of another woman.

Maybe this is for the best.

I climb out of my car and meet Juni and my parents in the kitchen. This is Juni's favorite place in their house—well, except her bedroom, which she designed herself for her tenth birthday.

The entire back wall is made up of bi-folding glass doors that open out onto a fabulous deck, with a patio area, and pool.

"You hungry, honey?" my mom asks me, and I shake my head.

"No, we ate before having our nails done," I explain, and she nods with a smile.

I sit on one of the high stools, tucking my feet on the bar, leaning my elbows on the counter, watching Juni add topping to her bread.

"Child, you just ate five tacos at the mall." I nod to the huge sandwich in front of her.

She shrugs. "I'm a growing girl, Mom."

"Oh, leave the kid alone. She can eat anything she wants. It's our time, so we get to spoil her." My dad winks at me.

"You always spoil her," I add, tilting my head with my own grin.

"What can I say, she is my favorite granddaughter."

"I am your only granddaughter, Gramps," Juni says to him, and he winks at her.

"That you are. That is your uncle Matt's fault. He needs to shift his butt in gear. We want more grandbabies to spoil," my mom joins in.

We all laugh, and it is nice to see Juni smiling, so carefree. I still worry about her, but I know she is in safe hands with my parents. There aren't many people I trust with her.

My parents, brother, and sister-in-law Olivia. Hell, I trust Finan more than my ex-in-laws.

Shit, Finan. That man is invading my every thought unless I am solely concentrating on Juni.

"How is Finan and the club, honey?" My mom's question brings me back to the room.

I sit up straight, holding my breath, my gaze flicking over to Juni, watching her reaction at the mention of Finan and the club. She has asked about him, but she never brings up the club. The last time she saw any of them was the day they rescued her.

I bite my lip, looking at each of the people in front of me that are all staring at me expectantly. Then a smirk crosses my daughter's face.

"She's avoiding him. He calls and texts, but she doesn't do anything about it."

"JUNI," I gasp. I thought I had kept it from her. Clearly not good enough.

"Aw, honey, why would you do that? Finan and the club helped in ways no one else could. They brought our baby home to us." My mom sounds so disappointed in me. I swallow past the lump in my throat.

"He has his own life, Mom. He doesn't need to be tied down to a single mom with a teenage daughter." I shrug, then trace the marble pattern on the counter to keep from looking at them.

"Joss, they did so much for you and this family." I nod at my dad's words.

"I saw the way he looked at you, Joss. That look was not the look of someone who wouldn't want to be tied down, as you put it, with a single mom," my mother adds.

Emotion bubbles up, and tears fill my eyes. Arms wrap around me, holding me tight.

I cry for a several minutes with my father holding me. My mom holds Juni while they both cry.

"Plus, I think the sounds that came from his room didn't exactly say that he didn't want to be lumped with a single mom," my mother then adds in.

I gasp, but Juni blushes and bursts out laughing.

My father walks over to her, kissing the side of her head, smiling down at the woman who owns his heart.

"Damn, woman, I am so fucking happy that you didn't lose that dirty mind of yours."

We all laugh—well, I groan a little, then join in with the laughter.

I know what I have to do when I get home. This thing between us needs to be sorted, so I intend to do just that.

CHAPTER SEVENTEEN

FINAN

Once Whitney walks inside the studio, I drive off, then park my truck in my usual space, before shutting it down and walking over to my bike. I pull out my aviators, placing them on my face, then sling my leg over my baby and fire her up.

She purrs between my thighs, making my dick twitch from the vibrations. Fuck, I would love to make a woman come on my bike, my cock buried deep inside of her, while I pull the throttle, adding to the sensation.

My dick thickens in my jeans, making the material become tight, so I push down, hoping he will calm down enough for me to ride.

"Where you going?" comes my brother's voice.

Looking over at him, he walks toward me, coffee mug in one hand, while running his fingers through his hair, brushing it back off his face. His hair is wet, so I know he just had a shower, no doubt after he fucked someone last night and this morning.

"Got some shit to talk out with Joss," is all I tell him.

He cocks an eyebrow at me, sipping his coffee, like he is expecting me to say more. Dick. We stay like that, neither one of us saying shit, until a smile appears.

Shaking my head, I give in.

"She hasn't answered my calls or texts in fucking days. Which pisses me off. You know I don't do well with being ignored. It sets shit off in my head. Makes me think things that aren't actually fucking there." He nods in understanding. "Dad asked me to take Whitney to the clinic, so I did. Then she wanted coffee, so we stopped by the one at the mall. To my fucking surprise, and it being perfect fucking timing, I saw Joss and Juni there."

"And let me guess. Joss saw you in the car with a hot chick." I nod.

"She looked angry, but also upset. What fucking right does she get to feel like that? She fucking ignored me; it's not like I ghosted her. So she shouldn't care if I have turned to another woman," I snap.

Calder's eyebrows shoot up into his hairline, and I know I've gone too far. I sigh, my body sagging. I lean forward, resting my forearms on the tank in front of me, turning my head to look at my brother.

"Fuck, sorry. This shit with Joss is fucking with my head. I'm going over there to talk this shit out with her now. I can't keep sitting around and waiting."

"Then you know what you got to do, brother. Just putting this out there, she doesn't have the right to be pissed off. She is the one pushing you away." With that, he gives me a chin dip and walks away.

I let his words sink in before kicking the stand up and pulling away from my place in the line of bikes. The prospect is there ready to open the gate for me. Nodding to him as I pass, I open up my bike, leaving the clubhouse behind me while I head in the direction of Joss's house.

I can only hope that Juni is already at her grandparents when I get there because shit is about to go down with her mother and me.

Good or bad, the unknowing ends today.

I arrive at her house and see that her car is not here. Maybe she is still at her parents' house dropping Juni off.

I park my bike and swing my leg over, dismounting. Tucking my keys in my pocket, I walk over to the steps that lead to her front porch and take a seat, leaning against the rail.

Pulling out my phone, I scroll through the apps that I have, which aren't many. When I'm done with my social media check, I close the apps down and open up a game that I have actually enjoyed.

I get lost in the game but think over everything that has happened since I met Joss.

I've noticed that she is making me feel things I don't usually feel, and I'm not sure how to handle that yet. When it comes to family, I know that I love them unconditionally, and will do anything for them, but I have never felt like this toward an outsider, someone that I met who's not family.

Like I've said, I am not one to work to get a chick into bed —not that there have been many. Yeah, I'm a biker, I'm surrounded by bikers who like sex. I've been told often enough that I'm a good looking guy. Believe it or not, I usually get my dick sucked and that is enough for me, but Joss makes me feel like I could get lost in her body for the rest of my days.

That may sound cheesy as fuck, but I know me, and I have to listen to what I know.

When I called and text her and she didn't answer, my mind started stirring. Did she use me? Was she lying when she came to the club to ask for help, using my connection with her to get it done for free?

This is what I'm talking about. Shit is running through my head, even though I know she isn't that type of person.

Settling in for the wait, I look around the neighborhood. The houses are pretty similar in size and structure, but some have different colors on the framework and shutters.

Every lawn is kept to a high standard, and the cars all look expensive. I know that Joss has a good job, even has employees that she takes good care of. Maverick looked into her, even though I asked him not to. But when the club takes on a client, they have a full background check. Well, unless they are an MC.

Is this why she doesn't want a biker at her place—fear of what the neighbors will think?

Fuck.

I watch as an older couple walk past the house, walking their dog, decked out in full exercise gear. I raise my hand in greeting, and to my fucking surprise, they return it with smiles.

"Afternoon," the guy says. I nod back, as I watch them walk off.

Okay, so maybe not all stuffy neighbors.

The sound of a car approaching gets my attention, and I look just as Joss pulls into her driveway.

Her gaze connects with mine, and I hold my breath, wondering if she will bolt or get out.

I fucking hate that I feel like a chick in one of those romance movies, waiting for the guy to come to them and confess their love. Damn my mom for loving those cheesy movies and guilt tripping me into watching them with her.

Calder soaks that shit up, saying he can use the techniques on new chicks when he wants to try a woman from a different background, rather than easy pussy, as he says.

The seconds tick by before Joss finally gets out of the car, still holding my gaze.

She steps to me, biting her lips before she opens her mouth.

"Hey." Her voice is soft, but I hear the slight nervous tremor to it.

"Hello," I return, and get to my feet.

CHAPTER EIGHTEEN

JOSS

On my way home from my parents, all I can think about is Finan. Knowing that Juni is safe, I can finally let my mind wander to the man who has been occupying my mind when my work or daughter isn't.

Finan is a man you want to keep. To brag that he is yours. But, am I what he wants to keep and show off? I know the club helped me; his family was so amazing with me. But would they be happy if he shacks up with a thirty-one-year-old single mother?

So many things run through my head as I drive with the windows down, the wind whipping my hair all over the place, but I don't care. I need to feel free. To blow the cobwebs away and enjoy my 'me time' after I have called Finan to talk.

I pull into my drive, my heart stopping when I see him waiting for me.

Sitting on my steps, is Finan in all his biker glory.

Leaning against the wooden rail, one leg is outstretched resting on the same step his butt is. The other foot is resting two steps down, showing just how tall he is. His jeans cling to his thighs, the black t-shirt sits under his cut, the body a little baggy but the arms tight around his biceps.

His tribal tattoos stand out against the dark material.

He looks relaxed, which is a far cry from what I am feeling right now.

He gets to his feet, keeping his aviators on, hiding his eyes from me. Taking a deep breath, I get out of my car, hitting the lock button as I step over to him.

"Hey," I greet, my hands hanging heavy at my sides.

"Hello."

"What brings you here?" Lame, I know, but hell, I have no idea what to say right now.

Shaking his head, he takes slow steps until he is almost toe to toe with me. I have to crane my neck up to look at him.

His scent hits me, and I have to fight to keep a sigh in but fail epically. Finan chuckles a little, then he removes his sunglasses. His gaze penetrates mine, his hands lightly touching my hips.

"I see what I do to you, Joss. You do the same to me, baby. But what I want to know is." He pauses for dramatic effect. "What are you going to do about it?"

I lick my lips, watching has his eyes track my tongue. Now it's his turn to make a sound, but his growl does stupid things to my lady parts.

Even though I want him to take me to bed and ravage me, bring me to orgasm over and over again, I know we have things to talk about.

"Talk."

His lips twitch at the corner of his mouth, drawing my attention there. God, even his lips looks sexy. How is this possible?

Everything about this man is beyond sexy. The funny thing is, he isn't even trying. Being showy and trying too hard is not something Finan does. It's not his style.

He keeps looking at me for a few more seconds, before he steps back and to the side, moving his arm in a royal wave, signaling for me to go first so I can open my front door.

I step forward, walking up the steps and toward my door. With every step, I can feel his eyes burning into my ass. I may even add a slight sway to my hips.

I may be older than him, and a single mom, but I am not dead. I like to feel wanted and sexy, but that is where my thoughts halt.

My head is messed up over my thoughts for this man. One second I want him to strip me naked, and then the next I think he will bolt the second a younger woman comes along.

Sighing, I open my door, dropping my keys in the bowl next to it. Keeping up my stride, I head to the kitchen, dropping my purse on the island. I look down at the worktop, keeping my gaze off Finan, but I know he is there. I can feel him, smell his amazing scent that should be bottled. It reminds me of sandalwood, and oil.

Nothing is said for a short time. Pulling my gaze away from my hands, I look up to see Finan leaning on the wall, arms crossed across his massive chest, making his biceps bulge. I so, *so* much want to run my tongue across them.

To trace every intricate detail of his tattoos.

"The way you are looking at me, we won't get to talk, Joss, because I will be taking you to your room and fucking you so hard, you will feel me for days. Even though I want that to happen, and very fucking soon," he reaches down to adjust his erection, letting me know that my looking is turning him on, "you wanted to talk."

"We do need to talk." He nods and steps closer to me, and my breathing picks up.

I bite the corner of my lip, unable to stop my eyes fluttering closed when he leans in, brushing his nose in the crook of my neck and breathing in deep.

That simple touch sends a wave of arousal through my body. My pussy throbs, and my panties become damp. My quiet moan makes Finan growl. His hands find my hips again, tugging me toward him.

All thoughts of talking fly out the window when Finan sucks on the skin of my neck. My knees almost buckle, and I'm grateful that he is steadying me. He pushes me against the wall more, holding me in place with his hips, while his hands wander.

His lips move from my neck, over my jaw, making me shiver. My eyes close, letting the heated sensation cover my body, prepping me to take this man because I know what is coming.

He's distracting me from our talk, and it's working. All I can feel is him.

His lips find the corner of my mouth, his hot breath coating my skin.

"Do you still want to talk, or do you want to fuck?" The need in his voice makes my body throb for him.

Damn this beautiful man.

"Shit," I moan as he sucks on my bottom lip.

A growl emanates from his chest, vibrating against my body.

In a flash, I'm picked up, his hands under my butt, and he is moving. Carrying me up the stairs, down the hall to my bedroom.

He lays me down on the bed, covering me with his large body. His biceps bulge as he keeps his full weight off me, but I want him to smother me.

Hooking my hands around his neck, I pull him down; I want to feel him everywhere all at once.

He kisses me like a man possessed. It's not soft and sweet; it is hard, hungry. It feels like he is devouring me, and I like it. Sex with Owen was always hot, but it was never like this, and we are still fully clothed.

"You are wearing too many clothes, baby," he mutters, then he is pulling my t-shirt up over my body, kissing the path the material just used.

I'm lying under him in my bra and shorts, with him looking down on me with hunger in his eyes. Because of carrying a baby, my already large breasts got bigger and never lost the size after I gave birth.

I have talked about getting them reduced, but the way that Finan is looking at them right now, might change my mind.

His fingers nimbly unclasp the front, and my bra pops open, my breasts becoming free. My nipples turn painfully hard as the chilled air hits them, making Finan growl again.

"You are all kinds of growly there, handsome," I comment.

A wicked smile crosses his face, and his eyes sparkle with mischief.

Without saying anything, he drops his head, taking one of my nipples in his mouth, sucking, tugging it with his teeth.

My back arches off the bed.

My hands find his head, my fingertips digging in the short hair at the back of his skull. Both of his hands massage each breast as he plays with my nipples, almost bringing me close to falling over the edge.

"I want to feel your skin against mine, Fin," I pant.

He pulls back, letting go of my nipple with a pop.

"Anything you want, babe." He climbs off the bed and strips. Each item of clothing seems to take a million hours to be removed, even though I know it takes him mere minutes to disrobe.

"Holy cow." I lick my lips, eye fucking him where he stands.

His cock is thick, long, and almost has an upward curve to it. Oh, that is going to hit in all the right places.

With my eyes devouring his body, I blindly remove my shorts and panties. Throwing them on the floor.

Finan growls again, and it makes me smile, before I bite my lip, opening my arms to him. Inviting him to come to me so we can get on the road to feeling good.

He doesn't waste any time as he places one knee on the bed, gripping my ankles, pulling me to the edge of the mattress. I let out a yelp, making him give me a sexy smile.

I go up onto my elbows, watching as Finan drops to his knees, diving in and licking me from bottom to top. Waves of arousal rush through my body like a tsunami, making me cry out his name.

His tongue does some wicked things to me, playing with my clit, but not adding enough pressure to make me come.

"Finan, please?" I beg, not caring that I'm loud.

"Please, what, baby? Tell me what you want." His voice is deep, his breath blowing against my wet pussy.

Before I can answer, he goes back to torturing me with his tongue. My hands grip the back of his head, holding him to me.

He growls against my clit, before sucking it into his mouth as he slides two fingers into me.

"Shit." I gasp at the sudden feel of him penetrating me with his digits.

Over and over again, he sucks in time with his fingers pumping away. I pant, moan his name as my body heats up, getting closer and closer to climax.

"Now," Finan suddenly grinds out, hooking his fingers, catching my G-spot, and I explode against his mouth.

His fingers slow as he licks me over and over again, lapping up my climax.

With my eyes closed tightly, I pull in deep breaths, while feeling Finan moving up my body. He kisses my thighs, my hips, over my stomach, and makes his way up to my breasts, where he once again sucks my nipples into his mouth.

I arch again, my nipples feeling sensitive. He says my name, making me look at him. He holds my gaze as he slides between my legs.

"Going to fuck you now, Joss. You don't want that, tell me now. I walk away. But once I get balls deep in you, there is no going back. You are mine, baby. No backing out."

I let his words sink in, letting the way they make me feel settle in my mind.

Can I push away the issue with his age? Is this thing with him worth the risk?

The thought of him with other women makes my stomach churn with jealousy.

Cupping his jaw, I pull his lips to mine, kissing him deeply.

"Take me."

The smile he gives me makes every fiber of my body quiver. He reaches between us, lining up his dick, before pushing into me.

The feeling of fullness makes my body react in the most delicious way. My neck arches back, giving him access and the invitation to kiss my neck, to suck on the skin there.

Finan buries his face in my neck, kissing me, while his hips push forward, burying him deep inside of me. There's a slight twinge of pain as he bottoms out, making me gasp.

"Sorry, baby. I'm big, but you took me perfectly."

His voice is strained, but he doesn't sound apologetic.

With my hands on his hips, I dig my fingertips in, making him hiss. I lift my head, biting the skin where his neck meets his shoulder.

"Fuck, do that again," he asks.

I do as I'm told and bite, before licking the same area. Finan's hips pull back before snapping back in. I gasp, and he moans. He does this over and over again, rolling his hips on occasion.

"Shit, that feels fucking good," he pants.

His upper body lifts off mine, and he braces himself on his palms, as he moves again. His hips rock into me, his pubic bone catching my clit with each second of contact. I gasp and moan his name.

My breasts feel heavy, and my nipples tingle, as do the muscles in my lower body. I know I'm close. Wetness coats my inner thighs, so I know he has some on his skin. This has never happened to me before, but Finan is making my body experience new things.

The idea of him carrying my scent makes me gush more and tighten around him.

"Oh, fuck, baby. Yes, do that again." I clench, and he growls.

I fucking love growly Finan. It is sexy as sin.

His pace picks up, and my orgasm hits so fast and hard, I can't speak to warn him.

I cry out his name. "FINAN." My body goes so tight I know I will be sore later.

He keeps pumping into me, pulling every ounce of climax out of me, before he lets out the loudest growl I have heard from him, and he stills. His body falls onto mine.

I can feel his cock twitching inside of me as his climax subsides. To feel him throb makes my pussy pulse, sending mini jolts of lightning through my core, making me let out little puffs of air in shock.

I wrap my arms around him, enjoying the feel of his weight on mine. We both breathe easy, enjoying the moment.

Burying my head in his neck, I breathe in his heady scent and sigh. Fuck me, he smells so good after sex. Hell, he smells good all the time, but after sex, he is off the charts.

"We are so fucking doing that again." He hisses as he pulls out of me, making me let out a soft whimper. He kisses my stomach before he climbs off the bed, and I see the condom on his flaccid dick.

"Shit," I mutter, making him look at me with a frown.

"What is it?"

I point to his dick. "I didn't even ask about a condom. Shit. I was so wrapped up in you, I forgot."

The smile he gives when I explain would make any woman swoon.

"I like that I made you lose your mind. I will always protect you, Joss. Even from me if needed. We'll use a rubber until you tell me to stop, and believe me, I can't fucking wait to feel you raw."

He winks and walks into my bathroom to dispose of the condom. I look up at the white ceiling and smile to myself.

Holy shit, I just had sex with Finan. A biker. A sexy, hot biker. Holy cow. Joy will throw a freaking party when I tell her.

That woman will do anything for a celebration.

It has been way too long since the last time I had sex, but hell, it was worth it, and I bet that Finan could play my body to the highest level, and I would sing right along with him.

My stomach growls as soon as he steps back into my room, breaking the sexual high I was just in. He chuckles at me, then reaches for his jeans.

"Come on, let's feed you." I nod and throw on his t-shirt before he leads me downstairs.

I need food, then we need to talk.

CHAPTER NINETEEN

FINAN

Every Saturday morning, I go for a ride if I have no plans, and today is no different—except for the woman smashing her tits to my back, her thighs cradling my hips. Joss's hands are settled on my stomach, under my t-shirt. Her fingers are stroking over my skin, making my balls tighten and my cock press against the zipper of my jeans.

I have one hand on the handlebar, directing the bike along the highway, and my other is resting on her thigh, which is encased in a pair of jeans that I swear to fuck were made for her.

Never in my life, besides family, have I had a woman on the back of my bike. That seat is held for my old lady, so this is fucking monumental.

When my dad talked about having my mom on the back of his bike, I used to think he was making shit up. No person can make you feel like you can conquer the world by just sitting on the back of your bike, but fuck me, he was right all along.

Having her here feels right. It feels like home.

Something settles in my chest, something that includes Joss and Juni.

I squeeze her leg, and she replies with a gentle squeeze of her thighs against me. My cock screams to be let out to play.

When I finished feeding Joss yesterday, after I fucked her for the first time, we sat on her sofa, talking about why she ghosted me.

"So, are you going to tell me why you avoided talking to me?" I edge, placing her plate in front of her. I've made her pancakes with bacon and fruit. She devours it, like it is her last meal, or she is avoiding answering the question.

"Joss, speak."

She sighs and drinks some of the orange juice I poured for her, before she gives me her eyes.

"I was dealing with everything that happened with Juni. It was a lot to take in."

"Okay," is all I say.

"Finan, you are younger than me, by a good few years, and I am a single mom of a teenager. I am sure there is some girl out there the same age as you that you want. It got me thinking that it would be easier for Juni and me if I kept my distance from you, then you would see that I wasn't worth the effort. Then I saw you with that other girl yesterday and it made me realize that I was right."

Her eyes go wide, and she covers her mouth like she just remembered Whitney.

"Oh, my God! I slept with you, and you have a girlfriend. Oh, fuck. Oh, Finan, why would you do that? I never thought you would do that. I'm a whore," she cries, covering her face with her hands.

Stepping over to her, I pull her hands away, bending my knees so I'm eye level with her. I smile, leaning in to kiss her, but she jerks her head back.

"Baby, I am not with Whitney. I was doing the club a favor because she lost her driving license again. My father asked me to take her to the sex clinic because she was due her checkup. Her husband was working, so I took her."

"Husband?" she enquires, and I smile wider at her, hopefully easing her distress.

"Yes, husband. He's a cool guy. They both work for the club," I explain.

"Work for the club? He's a member?"

I chuckle, kissing her nose, before pulling back to look her in the eyes.

"Baby, Whitney and her husband both work at Rugged Online Entertainment."

"Am I supposed to know what that is?" She cocks her head to the side, frowning at me.

"R.O.E is the club's porn company. The studio is behind the clubhouse."

Her eyes bug out of her skull, making me laugh. I leave her with that piece of information and go back to my stool and eat my breakfast, because today she is coming for a ride with me.

I pull the bike off the ramp and head down to the beach, where I know they have the best seafood platters around. Joss loves seafood. I am fucking lucky that my woman likes food and is not allergic to anything.

When I ride into the parking lot, Joss begins to bounce in her seat gently, showing her excitement.

Once I park, I shut off the engine, as Joss jumps off, removing her helmet and shaking out her short hair.

My gaze roams over her body, taking in her black ankle boots, blue jeans with some rips and scuff marks, and the black thin-strapped camisole she is wearing under a black and white patterned waist-length kimono.

Thank fuck for all the women at the club, otherwise I wouldn't have a clue what ladies clothing is called. Apparently, all us men needed a crash course in women's clothing and other shit, so we could woo a woman if we needed to.

Have you met the men of the Rugged Skulls MC? We don't need help with anything. We flash a smile, some muscle, and tattoos, talk about our bikes and the club, and boom. Easy pussy.

Well, it is for my brothers. Me, not so much. Getting my dick sucked was easy enough, but anything else and I felt out of whack, except for when I'm with Joss. When I'm with her, I feel like a fucking world renown porn star.

"I love seafood. I can't believe you remembered." The smile she gives me makes me fucking thankful that I do remember so much shit.

"I know. Come on, let's eat, so we can get back to your place, so I can fuck you some more. Then eat your pussy. Then fuck you again. The sound of you screaming my name makes my cock harder than ever before." I crowd her, wrapping my arms around her waist. My lips close in on her ear.

"I could fuck you all day, every day, baby, and it would never be enough. Your pussy is like pure silk to me." She shivers in my arms, and I nip at her neck.

I have never been this open with a woman in public before, but I can't seem to keep my hands off her.

Taking her hand, I lead her inside and smile when I see who is at the hostess table.

"Well, if it isn't Finan Price. How are you, honey?" Lila smiles wide as we close the gap. With my free arm, I hug her.

"I'm good. Can we have a table for two please?" I say, then look down at Joss, who is frowning, looking unsure as she takes in Lila. She is a stunning woman, all legs, blond hair, and tits for days.

"Of course, and who is this beauty? You never bring women here, Fin." Her brow pops up in question, and I shrug with a smile.

"Lila, this is Joss, my woman. Joss, this is Lila. The club helped her last year. Her ex took off with her savings and sold her car and other shit from her apartment," I explain.

We follow Lila through the room to our table. I offer Joss to slide into the booth, and I slide in and sit across from her. Lila leaves us with the menus and to fetch our drinks.

"You okay?" I ask Joss as she watches Lila across the room.

"Have you been with her?" Her question doesn't surprise me, what with the way she was looking at the other woman, and I know that Joss is a territorial lady.

I chuckle. "No, baby. She does nothing for me. Now, if you asked me about another certain woman with short, dark hair, beautiful eyes, and a body that was made for sinful things, then I would tell you that my cock gets hard thinking about what I want to do to her."

Her cheeks flush red, and she looks down at the menu.

I lick my lips, seeing her chest rise and fall with each breath, knowing that my words got her thinking of all the dirty things I want to do to her.

Lila comes over and we order our food. I order a lemon pea and prawn risotto. Joss orders creamy garlic shrimp pasta. We sit and talk. She tells me about events that have happened in her life. Her husband, Juni being born, how shitty her ex-in-laws are, except her sister-in-law.

Before I know it, we are back on my bike, heading toward her house, and my dick is begging to be pulled out and be played with.

Getting my cock played with isn't something new, but that was all I did. Very rarely did I fuck random women. My dick getting into someone's mouth was enough for me, until Joss.

It seems like a switch has been flicked in my head. All I can think about is kissing and fucking Joss. Kissing was never my thing, but hell, her lips are fucking heaven.

I take the quick route home. Pulling into her drive, I shut the bike off. Again, Joss is off the bike before I can release the handlebars. She steps up to my side, so I swing my legs over, pulling her between my thighs. She hangs her helmet on the handlebar, before licking her lips, moving in to kiss me.

My arms go around her waist, pulling her closer while I devour her mouth.

Her tongue dances with mine, and I moan at the contact, pulling her even closer, my dick pressing against her stomach. Her hands grip my shoulders, as she nips at my bottom lip.

I pull back, grinning at her.

"It's going to be like that, huh?" She nods, rushing to her door, unlocking it, and running inside.

I shake my head, giving her a head start, before I'm off. I run after her, hearing her squeal my name as she makes it up the stairs. Pulling my cut off, I drop it on the chair, before stripping myself of my clothes, watching Joss do the same.

I walk around the bed, so I'm on the window side, before reaching for her.

I take her hand, pulling her off the bed.

Spinning her around, I press her to the window that faces the water. There are no houses behind hers, just sandbank and the ocean.

I bend my knees, making sure my cock slides between her ass cheeks, and her breath hitches.

"I can fucking smell you, baby. I know you want this. You want me to fuck you where someone could see you? See how fucking hot you look?" I say in her ear.

Her body is shaking with excitement. She is turned on so fucking much, her breathing is coming fast and hard. Well, it's about to get harsher.

Reaching down, I grip her hips with my hands, pulling her back a step, then place one hand on the middle of her back, pushing her to bend slightly. Her tits press up against the glass, and her ass is poking out in an inviting posture.

"Fuck, this ass is sexy as hell. I am going to fuck it one day, babe."

"Yes," she pants. "God, I love it when you talk dirty."

I grin, looking down at her. She isn't wrong. She fucking loves it when I talk dirty, and color me surprised, I like it too. I have never needed to do it before, but I can't seem to shut the fuck up with her. The need to talk dirty seems to be our thing.

Seeing her back arched, her head tilted to the side, looking at me over her shoulder... The look she gives me makes my cock dribble with lust for her.

"Fuck. You are one hot woman, and you are all fucking mine, Joss. You ready?" I ask, slapping her ass.

Her breath hitches, then she moans, pushing back against me. I guess she is.

Reaching for the condom I dropped on the bed, I slide the latex over my thick, hard shaft one-handed, while my other hand explores how juicy my woman is.

"Damn, baby, you are wet for my cock. I'm going to slide right in that tight little hole, stretching it with my cock." She moans at my words, presenting her ass for me more.

I pull at her ass cheek, while I guide my cock into her. My eyes roll into the back of my head as her heat engulfs me. Fuck me, she feels like sin, all warm, wet, and tight.

"Fuck," I hiss, as I push in further.

She pants my name, her eyes squeezed tight as I pull out and slam back in. Her tits push against the glass, almost to the point of flattening.

Joss spreads her legs more, giving me better access, but I need to go deeper. Moving my hand to her thigh, I pull it up, hooking it over my elbow. I suck in a harsh breath when I slide in more, bottoming out.

"Fin… fuck, you fill me up so good," she cries out.

Her voice has dropped an octave or two, giving me that sexy, husky tone that makes my balls draw up.

I plow into her over and over again.

Sweat covers both of us as we breathe in fast, short pants.

I can feel my spine tingle, and I know I'm close.

"You need to get there, baby. I'm going to come. You feel too damn good," I growl.

"Yes," she pants.

I bend my knees, hitching my hips at a different angle, and Joss goes crazy. She starts bucking against me, seeking out her climax. Her hand slaps against the glass, and she tightens around me, strangling my cock to the point of pain.

"Fuck." I drag the word out as I follow her, my orgasm hitting me like a freight train.

Every inch of my body buzzes for this woman. I have never come so hard in my fucking life, and I think that's because it's with Joss.

My legs are like jello, so we stumble back onto the bed. Joss lets out a giggle as I move us into a better position.

I pull her to me, both of us still dazed from the intense orgasm. We both breathe at the same rate, trying to calm the speed down, until she falls asleep with her hand on my chest. I shut my mind off, letting myself fall asleep, right where I want to be.

CHAPTER TWENTY

JOSS

I sip at my coffee, loving how the dark, hot liquid makes my taste buds come alive. After the last two days with Finan, my body needs a break, and lots of coffee. I'm going to need a vacation to recover from my mini vacay.

When I dropped Juni off at my parents, I swore that I would catch up on my work, but after finding Finan on my steps, all that went out the window.

Am I happy he was there? Kind of. I knew we needed to talk, but I thought we would do it over the phone, knowing how much of a distraction he can be.

Do I regret the weekend? Yes and no. We still didn't talk much about our relationship. We just had sex multiple times, all over my house.

My body hums with the memories of how he can play my body like he has been for years rather than it being our first time together, fully.

I clench my thighs together, thinking about his head between them, making me cry out his name in the shower just a few hours ago. Finan is currently sleeping in my bed, while I'm in my kitchen, waiting for Juni to arrive home. She should be here any minute now. She's coming home early because my mom has come down with some sort of stomach sickness and they didn't want Juni to catch it.

I hear the car pull into my driveway, so I walk out to meet them. My eyes go straight to Finan's bike that is parked just in front of my car.

My father spies it, but says nothing right away, as he comes to a stop on my porch.

"Hey, baby," I greet Juni, pulling her in for a hug. I smell her hair and my heart settles.

"I missed you, Mom. Grama is so ill. Grampa's had to have the lady next door sit with her to bring me home." I can see the concern on Juni's face for her grandmother.

"Is it just a stomach bug, Dad? Should she go to the hospital to get checked out?" I ask, but my dad is shaking his head.

"Nah, she will be fine. She thinks it's food poisoning. We ordered from that new restaurant on 8th and Blyth. Juni and I had the same thing, Mom didn't. I will keep an eye on her. Speaking of keeping an eye out, I spied that bike in the drive." He cocks an eyebrow in question.

"Yeah, he's here. We spent the weekend together."

"Finan is here?" Juni pipes up with a huge grin on her face.

I brush her hair back, smiling at her. "He is. He's still sleeping," I explain.

"Right, well I had better get back to your mother. Give me a hug, sweetheart," he calls to Juni, who steps into his arms for a goodbye hug. She moves to the side, and I step in for my hugs too.

My dad gives the best hugs ever. My dad has always reminded me of Bill Murray. One of the things I used to love to do when I was younger was watch Ghostbusters with him, and he would act out some scenes with Peter Venkman. He has done it a few times with Juni too.

We wave him off before stepping back inside, and walk into the kitchen. I am thankful that Finan is still sleeping because it gives me some time to talk with Juni about what happens in the future.

She hops up onto a stool at the island, watching me as I watch her.

"Did you have a good time at Grama's and Grampa's?" I pick up my coffee mug and take a sip, immediately spitting it out as the cold liquid hits my mouth.

"Eww. Cold," I tell my daughter, who is giggling.

My heart swells at seeing her smile.

Topping up a fresh, hot coffee, I turn to my girl and start talking.

"You doing okay? No nightmares? Anything we need to talk about?"

Shaking her head, she smiles at me. "No, Mom. Honestly, I'm okay. I feel safe with family. And I feel even more safe knowing that Finan will be around. He will be around, right?"

Her questions settles something in my chest, but I know I need to make things clear to her, and if I'm being honest, to myself too.

"I want that, Juni, but I'm worried that some time down the line, when I'm no longer the shiny new toy, that he will leave for some younger woman. I have to think of you as well as myself. We are a package deal, baby."

I sigh, folding my arms across my body. Sipping more of my coffee, I lean against the counter behind me.

"Mom, Finan is wicked cool. He saved me and that other girl. He took care of me. He had his brothers look after the other girl, but I got his dad when he went into that house. Plus, you have to admit, Mom, he is hot." She winks at me, and I grin.

God, to have more of her would be amazing. To have another child, so happy and carefree as Juni, would be such a huge blessing.

The smile falls from my face when I think that Finan might not be in the place in his life to want kids, if at all. He is a biker, after all.

"Mom?" Juni comes round to the island and stands in front of me.

"I just don't know, baby. I get that he is sweet, loyal, safe."

"And hot," she adds.

"Yes, he is hot." I give her a weak smile. "But with the age gap, I'm not sure he's ready to settle down. He can have anyone he wants, so why me? I'm just worried that he'll slip into our lives, we'll make a place for him here, and then he'll leave. Drop us like we are nothing. I'm not sure I can handle that, J." I put it all out there.

Is it bad that I'm talking about this with my fourteen-year-old daughter? Maybe, but this involves her life too, and I want her to be a part of the decision.

"Mom, I don't think Finan will do that. He doesn't seem the type."

"I'm just struggling with it all, Juni. He makes me feel things that I wasn't sure I was ready to feel. My love for your father was epic. Dating seemed like I was betraying him in some way."

"Mom, you can't think that. Dad is dead. He isn't coming back. Finan is right here." She points to the stairs.

Her voice has hitched a little. I can hear she is getting upset, but also frustration is lacing her voice.

Leaning forward on the island, I rest on my elbows, covering my face with my hands.

"I know." The sound is muffled.

"I know you said that the age gap was an issue for you. Is there anything else?"

"Child, when did you grow up? You are sounding like a wise old woman right now; Aunt Joy would be so happy to hear you speak like this," I try to joke, but my daughter gives me a look that says she knows I'm procrastinating with my answer.

"Just did, I guess. Being taken woke me up a lot, Mom. Seeing things like that... no girl my age or any age should see or go through that. It made me see that life is not all pop music and social media. I love you even more for protecting me."

My nose burns, and tears fill my eyes as thick emotion takes over. My baby girl is so grown up, but I'm glad that she sees things differently now. Will it keep her safe indefinitely? Hell no. There are no guarantees in life.

"I will always protect you, Juni. I would lay my life down for you, you know that. So would so many other people."

"Including Finan and the club," she adds, smirking at me.

"Yeah," I whisper.

There are so many things running around my head like little energizer bunnies, nothing staying still so I can focus on one thing. I close my eyes and rub my temples. I have a headache building.

"You have to admit, Finan is hot, Mom. He is like really good-looking." Juni's voice has my eyes popping open, while she grins at me.

The smile is wide, sweet, and innocent, but I know she knows what she is talking about. Girls her age are a ball of hormones, and they are discovering boys.

I scoff and go to rinse my mug out, before turning back to her.

"I do not want you dating until you are twenty-five, young lady," I joke with her, making her fake upset.

Her hand is on her chest, mouth and eyes wide open in shock.

"How dare you insinuate that I like boys, mother of mine."

Now it's my eyes and mouth that are wide open. She shrugs, and I run over to her and pull her into my arms.

Did my daughter just come out as gay to me?

Holy shit.

"I will love you always. Who you love does not define you."

"Thanks, Mom. But what about your love life?" she asks me.

Pulling back, I shrug.

"I don't know. I loved your father; I'm not sure I can love another man that way again. Being with Finan is nice, but is he really the marrying type? I mean, he is a biker after all. It's not like they stick to one woman."

"Nice to see you hold me at such a low regard." I freeze on the spot, as the deep, gravelly voice filled with sleep steps into the room.

I can't bring myself to turn around and face him. Cowardly, I know.

Squeezing my eyes shut tight, I breathe deeply, trying to control my heart and stomach that are both trying to break free of my body and run away, like the Road Runner cartoon character.

My fists are clenched on my thighs, my back steel rod straight. My muscles start to hurt with how taut they are.

Opening my eyes, I look at Juni, who is looking at me with wide, shocked eyes.

Fuck.

I close my eyes once more and step down off my stool to face him. I open my mouth to speak, but my daughter gets there first.

"Morning, Finan." Juni tries to break the ice that has filled the room.

Can the ground open up and swallow me whole, so I don't have to face him and deal with what I just said? But no, that isn't going to happen. I look at him.

His brow is creased, showing his dislike for what I just said. I watch as he slides his cut on over his t-shirt, then moves over to the door, where his boots sit from last night.

I watch in fascination as he slips into them. Once his boots are on, he comes over to Juni and kisses the top of her head.

"Morning, sweetheart. I'll see myself out," he says to her, not giving me a second of his time.

Obviously, he heard everything I said and didn't like it. He has been nothing but good to me, so why am I letting my worries come between us? Over the weekend, he made me see things, feel things, and I just threw that all away.

My stomach knots, a cold wave of anguish washes over my body. I run my hands up and down my arms to warm them up, but it's no good. It's like Finan took all my warmth with him.

"Mom?"

I ignore her, staring at the door he just walked out of without so much as a backward glance. Tears fill my eyes before running over and down my cheeks.

I clench my eyes shut tightly, wanting to shut the world out right now, but I also know that I can't. I have a daughter who needs me more than ever.

With me running my mouth, I doubt we will see Finan again, and I know that once again, Juni and I will be at odds over this. She has made it clear what she thinks of Finan, and I just blew any kind of friendship they could have built.

Sniffling, I move around the island and use a paper towel to dry my face. While doing that, I calm my breathing. I need to do it so I can speak, because it feels like he took all my oxygen with him.

How can he make me feel like this after such a short time we have spent together?

Finan Price means something to me. That much is clear now at the thought of potentially losing him.

"Shit," I mutter, resting my palms on the counter and bowing my head. Closing my eyes, I think about how much I messed up.

I am a grown woman, for crying out loud, and this is how I act when a man treats me too good. It makes me question things with him, yet he gave me no reason what-so-ever to question him.

Arms snake around my waist, and I feel Juni plaster her body to my back, holding me tightly, offering her love and support. I keep one hand on the counter and rest my other one over her hands that rest on my stomach.

I soak up her love, letting the moment sink in, letting it hit home what I have just done.

Damnit.

Pulling in a deep breath, I straighten my spine, pull back my shoulders, and stand strong. I messed up and I need to deal with that.

It is my mess to clean up, whether it's I fix things with Finan or move on.

Fix it.

A voice enters my mind, and I gasp, looking around, but see Juni with a mouthful of banana.

He is good for you both. The words enter my head again.

A sudden rush of calm and a content feeling settles over my body, in my head, and mind.

"How about we go do something fun today?" I burst out, making Juni stop mid-chew.

"What about Finan?" She eyes me cautiously.

I blow out a breath, giving her a smile that I hope she believes, even though I am overthinking inside. I know I need to fix things, if I can, but right now he needs to cool off, and I need to get things straight in my head.

"I will deal with him soon enough, but how about going to the beach? We can swim, eat junk food. What do you say?"

"Okay. Sounds fun. Let me go and change." She runs off, then stops at the bottom of the stairs. "Will you wear that red bikini you bought when we were in LA last summer?"

"Okay," I answer adding a smile.

I clean up the kitchen while thinking about how to fix things with Finan. Will he want to talk to me after what I said? God, I bet he will tell everyone in the club, and they will hate me. I'll never be able to show my face there again if he never forgives me.

Moving over to the pantry, I pull out the cute picnic cool box I got while also on vacation in LA. I add some drinks, some savory foods, and some sweet junk foods that we both love.

Once that is all sorted, I head up to my room to change into the red bikini Juni asked me to wear. I slip into the two pieces, then throw a simple white sundress over it. Stepping over to my vanity, I pull some of my hair up, tying it with a small hair tie, before making my way to Juni's room.

She slips out of her room as I get closer. Smiling up at me, Juni puts her bag over her shoulder, leaning in to kiss my cheek.

"You look beautiful, Mom. I love you."

"I love you too," I reply and follow her down the stairs.

Juni is wearing her favorite two piece suit. It's a mustard color top that isn't too short, and the bottoms are almost like boy shorts, with blue, yellow, and white patterned flowers. She has pulled her hair up into a messy bun, making her look older than her fourteen years.

I know that kids have to grow up, they have to develop and evolve, but damn, can they stay babies a little longer? No parents want their babies to grow up too quick so they can get hurt, heartbroken.

Juni is growing up too fast right before my eyes, and I'm not sure I'm ready for it.

CHAPTER TWENTY-ONE

FINAN

My mood hasn't shifted in four fucking days. When I left Joss's house that morning, I thought she would call, but I've heard nothing. Though I haven't reached out either. I thought that after the weekend we had, that it settled all of her fears about being with me.

The age gap, the club... Fuck me, if it wasn't for the club, she might not have got Juni back. I'm not saying that she isn't grateful to have her home, but she made it out like I'm a dirty biker that likes to fuck my way through life, which I fucking don't.

I am who I am, and I won't change for her, or for any woman.

And to top it off, she can't love another man except her dead husband.

Well, her dead husband can't fuck her and make her come all over his cock.

"Fuck." I slam my hands down on the steering wheel.

Calder looks at me, turning his body to face my direction with a questioning brow.

"What has your panties in a twist? I assume you're wearing panties. You did spend the weekend with your woman, right?"

"Not my woman," I snap back.

"What?" he asks, with a tone that says he don't understand my reply.

I shrug. "Not my woman. She made it clear I am not the guy for her. Whatever. Her loss," I snap back, and I see the look my brother is giving me.

He doesn't believe what I'm saying.

I really don't give a fuck. I have been a raging bull since I left her house. My dad slapped me across the back of the head because I snapped at Luna yesterday. Then Slide threw a bagel at me for bitching at his daughter, but Luna just winked and flipped me off.

So many fucking times I have opened my phone to call her but locked it again, not wanting to be the one to go crawling back.

I have no fucking clue if I should be the one to make the next step, or should I want for her to come to me?

This is why I have stayed away from having a relationship with women. I knew that it would get fucked up, either by her or me. Not many people outside of the club can handle the way I think and act. Some say I am rude as fuck; some say I'm ignorant or a retard.

Fuck, I hate that word.

"What the hell happened, man?" My brother's voice pulls me from my thoughts.

"She doesn't want to be with a biker. Can't let go of her dead husband." I lift a shoulder and look out the window, watching the pool hall that we are scouting.

"Bullshit. I saw how she looked at you, brother. I mean, I don't know why she was looking at you with gooey eyes. I am clearly the better-looking brother." He wiggles his eyebrows at me when I turn my head to look at him.

"You're an ass."

"A sexy one, but you love me for beating you in that department too." He blows me a kiss.

"Prick," I mutter back.

"I am serious though, Finan. She likes you, maybe even loves you. I saw the look in her eyes at the clubhouse. It was like how Mom looks at Dad."

I look at him and he tilts his head at me with a small smile in place.

"Maybe," I sigh.

I lean on the center console, pulling at my bottom lip with my thumb and forefinger, thinking over what he just told me.

Can I get over her not wanting to be with a biker? Fuck knows. She needs to explain all her shit to me, but I can't see that happening. She has left it days again to get in touch.

"Come on, Fin. You know you want something more with her. Fuck knows why. A variety of pussy is the best days of living, my brother. Why tie yourself down with just the one? Unless her pussy is tight as fuck."

"Fuck off. Do not talk about Joss like that." I punch him in the shoulder, making the prick laugh.

"Now tell me you don't care if fuck all happens between you two."

"It's not my choice, Cald. She doesn't want to be involved with a biker, a man younger than her. I can't change her mind, can I? You never heard her talking with Juni. I could hear the unease in her voice. She is torn, and I can't be with someone who isn't all in. You know how I think. It's not worth the anxiety, or overthinking. Unless she comes to me, saying she is all in, I am out."

"Oh, man, do Mom and Dad know you're out of the closet?" the little shit jokes.

I roll my eyes, flipping him off. "Not like that, fuckface."

"Well, you never know these days. Everyone is bi, or trans, or some other fucking gender-something. Each to their own and all, but fuck me, it is confusing to keep up with all the new titles."

I nod because it is confusing if you are not well educated in it. To me, you have to want to learn to evolve. Some are stuck in their ways, while others are happy to learn and move forward.

We all have our own way of thinking, and I am a firm believer that we are all in our right to think that way.

"So how did Juni take the conversation? Did she mention that she could have a potentially hot uncle in the near future?" He grins.

"No, she didn't mention you. She did say I was hot, and that Joss should go for it." I shrug and look out the window again.

It was nice knowing that Juni was on my side, but it's not her I have to please as much. It's her mom.

"There he is," Calder grinds out, then calls on the radio that the mark has arrived.

This one I am looking forward to catching. Fuck, most of them I look forward to, but this cunt beat an eighty-three-year-old lady and stole her money, car, and other shit to sell for drugs.

The police found her car dumped in some parking lot, but nothing else, including her wedding ring. So her son hired us to get everything back and do with as we please to the fuck that hurt his mother.

We get out of the car, following the fucker into the dark building. Calder is with me, while Jack and Lennox take the fire exit at the back. We always cover all entries in and out of the buildings we are watching.

I pull the door open, narrowing my eyes at the sudden dimming of the light. My eyes adjust as we walk over to the bar that looks like it has seen better days.

I spy the fucker over in the back corner, doing some freaky handshake and patting the other guy on the back.

I take my position at the bar, keeping my eyes on the guy, while Calder ambles over to the wall that leads to the restrooms, but this gives him a good vantage point to watch also.

"I don't want any trouble," the older guy says from behind the bar.

With my elbow on the wooden top, I look over my shoulder at him, then back to the back table.

"No trouble."

His eyes tell me that he doesn't believe me, but I don't give a fuck. The mood I'm in right now, I am ready to bust some heads open, and that is not me. Joss has me twisted up inside. And I don't see a way around it.

I scan the bar, taking in the people that are scattered around. There is a couple in one booth. Clearly he is finger fucking her under the table, what with the way her head is thrown back and his hand is tucked under her skirt as he kisses her neck.

Moving my gaze to the table close to them, there is a guy in older clothes, reading a newspaper from what I can see, not paying any mind to the room.

There are a small group of guys talking loudly, joking around, but they don't give off a bad vibe, so I move on.

Catching the gaze of my brother, he nods, letting me know he is okay, and watching.

Loud voices fill the room as the conversation between our guy and the one he is talking to starts to get heated, but I don't make a move yet. If we can get out of here with no scene, that would be fucking great.

They both jump to their feet, and Calder steps forward, ready to strike if he runs, but the cunt clocks my brother and scans the room. He must think I'm the weaker one because he bolts for me.

I step away from the bar and brace for impact. I grin at him, but that seems to make him angrier.

Even with my gun in the waistband of my jeans, I am in the mood for a fist fight.

"Come at me, fucker," I snarl as he plows into me.

We fall to the floor. He lands a punch to my ribs, and I wince. Then go on the attack, wrapping my arm around his head, holding him in place while I hit him in the ribs, shoulder, side of the head over and over again. We are both breathing heavily, grunting in pain as we each get hits in.

I plant my foot flat on the floor to flip us over, so I can get the upper hand, but the cunt kicks out, catching me in the gut. He sends me sailing back against a table, scattering the chairs across the floor.

I can hear shouting but can't make out what people are saying.

"Fight me, bitch," the cunt screams.

"You're calling me a bitch? You are the one who beat up a defenseless old lady, motherfucker." I lunge for him.

I slam my shoulder into his stomach, and we tumble to the floor again with me on top this time. I punch him in the side of the head, once, then again. He brings his knees up, knocking me off balance, but I regain then go in for more hits.

The shouting gets louder, then I'm being pulled off him. I kick out at him before I'm slammed on the floor, stomach down, my hands being cuffed behind my back.

"Calm the fuck down," gets snarled in my ear.

Fucking cunt on a stick. My mom will freak the fuck out when she finds out I have been arrested.

I'm pulled to my feet, and I quickly look around the room, searching for my brother. Calder is marched toward me, cuffed as well, with a smirk on his face. The female officer scowls at him, only making his grin wider.

"Baby, I like it kinky too." He winks at me as he passes, and I shake my head.

"Shut up," she snaps at him.

I get jerked and lead out to a police car that Calder is sitting in.

"We are fucked, man. Not only will Prez kick our asses, but so will Mom," my brother says to me, and I nod.

"I know, and she doesn't need this shit right now. Maybe dad won't say shit to her." We can only hope and fucking pray.

Looking out the window, I see the mark being cuffed and put in the back of another squad car. I smirk at him, and he goes fucking bat shit crazy in the back.

Not giving him any more attention, I face forward, calling to the cop in the car with me.

"Hey, that guy I was fighting with. There is a warrant out for his arrest. Check it." I give him the fucker's name, but the cop does nothing.

Fucking typical.

"Fuck. I do not look good in orange, brother. Will you protect me, being the oldest?" Calder jokes next to me.

"Shut it," I snarl and look out the window.

"Why do you fucking bikers think your shit don't stink, huh?" comes the cop's voice from the front of the car. My head snaps in his direction, before I look to my brother, then the other person in the car.

The female officer looks behind at us, then frowns at her partner.

"Hey, mine doesn't, thank you very much. That title belongs to Lennox," Calder calls out, then he winks at the woman again.

"Shut the fuck up, biker."

"Oh, how fucking original," my brother jests back, and I roll my eyes.

Here we fucking go again. He will end up being tripped and getting a black eye to match the split lip he already has.

Thank fuck that when the fucker hit me, it was all below the shoulders, so no bruises will be visible. That way, I can hide it from my mom—if Prez and Rookie don't tell her. But I know that the club will fucking love seeing Calder and me squirm when it comes to being scolded by Della Price and the other old ladies.

I wonder if Joss will fucking care if I'm hurt.

She has probably forgotten about me by now. This is what she wanted. Space from me. Me not in their lives.

Shit, I fucking miss her. Just the thought of her showering with me, helping to ease tension in my body after that fight, and then making love to her to settle us into a sleep in the same bed... Shit, I shouldn't be acting like a fucking chick.

"Fuck."

"What?" Calder whispers.

"I need to get in contact with Joss," is all I say.

"About fucking time, brother. That's two down." His voice takes on a weird tone, as he looks out the window with a faraway look on his face.

What is that all about? Is he seeing someone? Fuck no, he would tell me. We tell each other everything.

We arrive at the police station, and both of us are pulled from the car and processed. The club's lawyer turns up hours later, after Calder made the call to Prez to explain what was happening. He already knew what kicked off because Jack and Lennox called, but that is the only good news.

The lawyer told us that we have to sit and wait until Monday to be released. Prez's orders, the fucker.

He wanted to teach us a lesson to not lose our heads on the job or get caught.

So I'm stuck in a cell with my blood brother for three fucking days. Could be worse, I suppose.

CHAPTER TWENTY-TWO

JOSS

I run my finger over my bottom lip, smudging my lip-gloss. I stand up straight, staring at myself in the mirror.

Not hearing from Finan for five-plus days pisses me off. I text him to see if he wanted to meet up for a chat, but it went unanswered.

Smoothing my hands down my sides, I brush them over the blue floral skirt that I paired with a cream lace camisole that I have tucked in and added a thick brown belt, and wedges.

"You look beautiful, Mom. Hot." Juni leans against the doorjamb, watching me get ready.

"You think? You don't think this outfit is too young for me?"

She scoffs and gives me a look that tells me I am being silly.

"Mom, no. You need to let go of this age issue that you have going on. You are thirty-one, not ninety. You can rock any outfit you wear, and Finan is going to flip his shit." She grins at me.

"Language," I call to her, making her giggle.

"Yes, sir, captain." She salutes me.

"Go and get your things for school. We leave in ten," I tell her, and she runs off to her room.

We talked again last night with Joy, and they both made me realize that I have been on edge and grumpy without Finan, and that can only mean that I like him. They made me see that if I didn't have such deep feelings for him, then I wouldn't feel this way.

I take one more look at myself and leave my bedroom, calling for Juni. We head out to the car and drive to the school.

"I want an update on what happens, okay?" she says from her seat.

"I'm not sure how this will go, baby. But I will do my best."

"Mom, just tell him how you feel. I promise he feels the same way. Just don't let him go into his shell. Take charge.

Love you." She leans over and kisses my cheek before jumping out.

She waves as she rushes around the front, meeting her friends at the side.

I sigh and drive off.

I'm going to the clubhouse to talk to Finan. I can only pray and hope that he is willing to talk to me. Some time has passed, and he might have moved on.

Thinking of Finan with another woman doesn't sit well with me, and that is just another sign that he is meant to be mine. I have had a lot to think about regarding our relationship, and I have let what people have told me settle in. And they are right. Owen is gone. He is never coming back. And he would want me to find love again.

I arrive at the clubhouse and the prospect opens the gate for me with a nod. I give him a grateful smile, before parking my car.

I get out, drying my sweaty palms on my skirt. Hooking the strap of my purse over my shoulder, I walk inside, pulling in a deep breath.

People are sitting around the room. They sit up straight when I enter but then relax when they see it's me. It's like they are waiting for someone.

"What is happening?" I ask Della, who is sitting on the chair closest to the door.

She frowns at me, tilting her head. "You don't know?"

"Know what?" I ask her.

I grip the strap of my purse tighter, dreading what she is about to tell me, but the door swings open before she can speak. I spin around to see Magnum, Opal and Rookie walk into the room.

Finan and Calder walk in behind them, looking ragged and tired.

What the hell happened?

I go to speak, to ask, but Finan looks up, his gaze landing on mine when he looks round the room.

"Why are you here, Joss?" His voice is deep, gravelly, showing his exhaustion.

My stomach knots at the feel of coldness from him. I bite the corner of my lip, before swallowing the lump in my throat.

"I came to talk to you. You didn't return my texts." His tired eyes widen a fraction, like he is shocked that I reached out, then they turn cold again.

"Got nothing to say. The non-reply should have been enough for you to understand. I am not in the mood for more bullshit reasons why you can't be with me. You don't owe Rugged Hunters for finding Juni. Just leave."

I gasp in shock at his harsh tone and coldness.

"He's bullshitting you. He has been in jail since Friday night. That is why he didn't reply to your text," Calder calls out.

Jail? What the hell happened? Was it linked to what he and the club did for Juni?

I go to ask him but the look on his face has me frozen to the spot.

Finan snarls at his brother, before looking back to me. "Go home, Joss."

He turns to walk away, and my fear of rejection doubles. I glance around the room, my fingers knotting together out of nervousness.

Della gives me a small smile, nodding. Looking at his father, Rookie offers the same type of nod. Are they giving me their blessing to be with their son?

"Finan Price, you stop right the fuck now," I yell at him.

I hear some chuckles, but I don't look their way.

"Oh, she used the 'mom' tone on him," someone mutters.

"Fuck yeah, hot MILF alert," someone else says. Maverick, I think.

Again, I ignore them. I wait on bated breath as Finan turns to look at me.

I breathe in deep and march toward him.

"You do not get to throw me away, Finan. I am a person, not a thing. If you don't want me anymore, have the fucking decency to tell me to my face. I came here to talk to you, and you will listen," I spit out and wait for what he does next. Time ticks by, then he gives me the barest of nods I have ever seen, but it's my opening.

"Losing my husband was like my heart being pulled out of my chest. I went from being a happily married woman with a baby on the way, to a pregnant widow in the blink of an eye."

I hear gasps, and some quiet crying.

"I grieved, I begged for God to bring him back to me, I felt like my heart was literally breaking, then this beautiful baby came into the world, and I felt somewhat whole again. Juni is my entire fucking world, and I would do anything for her. She was my glue. She helped me keep things together. I had to live for her, and in turn live for myself also. We have a great relationship, and that was what you walked in on, me and Juni having a mom and daughter moment.

"She was telling me how much she liked you, and that I should give you a chance. I expressed all my fears with her, because, Finan, this all involves her too. It's not just me and you in this. My fourteen-year-old daughter will be mixed up in whatever we have. If you decide to leave, it's not only me that you break. It's her too, and I wasn't sure I was prepared for that."

I'm breathing heavily by the time I've finished. We stare at each other, neither of us saying anything. My fists are clenched at my sides, waiting for him to say something, but he doesn't.

I sigh. "I can't tell you to give me another chance. It has to be your decision. Just know that I want this, want us. It scares the hell out of me, but I am sick of being stuck in my safe ways. I need to take a risk for once."

I hear people snigger, and I know it's because Finan's aunt is named 'Risky.'

"Is that all you wanted to say?" My stomach falls through the floor at his words. With nothing else to say, I nod and look to the floor.

Humiliation and heartbreak lashes through my body. I messed up beyond repair.

I turn on my heels and walk toward the door. My stomach is at the point where it will never unknot again. My heart shatters all over again, but I know deep down that Juni will keep me together. I just hope she can forgive me for not being able to fix this.

Clearly my love for him isn't enough.

What? Where did that come from? I stop in my tracks. My hand goes to my chest as I take in deep, fortifying breaths.

Holy shit, I love Finan.

Pulling my shoulders back, I turn on my heel to face the room that is still as quiet as Sunday morning in church.

My gaze connects with Finan's, his scowl still on his face.

"I thought you were leaving?" His voice still cold.

"I was, then I had an epiphany."

"And what's that? That bikers are still dirty, sex-crazed men?" he growls.

I hear someone gasp, but my gaze never leaves his.

"Did I ever call you dirty?" I question him. "If you are going to put words in my mouth, can you make sure they are true facts, please?"

I cross my arms, popping a hip, showing a defiant stance against him.

"Oh, I like her," one of the women says.

"You didn't have to, Joss. The context was there."

"Right. So no matter what I say will change your mind?" He just stares at me, not giving me any indication of what he is thinking.

"Okay, so I will say this and then I will leave. The ball will be in your court then, Finan. It will be the proof that I needed all along."

"What's that?" he mutters.

"That you are not the man I thought you was." I take a deep breath and speak. "I love you, you idiot."

I hear a faint sob to my left, but I push the desire to turn and look down. Finan stares at me, moments tick by, and with each passing second, my stomach sinks.

He doesn't love me back, rattles around my head.

With a nod at the realization, I bite back the tears. My lips tremble as I lick them and rush from the room.

I fumble with my purse, pulling my keys out and unlocking my car. The need to get far away from here is overwhelming.

My car beeps, and the lights flash as it unlocks. My hand goes to the handle, but a rough-looking one slams against the window, stopping me from pulling the door open.

I don't need to look behind me to know who is there. I can feel him, smell his musky scent.

"Did you mean it?" His voice is deep, close.

I nod as goose bumps cover my body from the hot breath on the back of my neck.

His hands move to my waist, pulling me flush against his body. I draw in a breath, as I feel the heat coming from his body.

I twitch when I feel his warm lips on my shoulder. Then his lips move across my skin, making their way to my ear.

He tugs on my earlobe with his teeth. I can feel how hard he is, with his dick nestling against my butt.

"It's been too long since I've been inside of you," he growls as he flexes his hips.

"Who's fault is that?" I ask, pushing back on him.

"I will take fifty-fifty in this, baby. But we can fight about percentages later."

I nod as I get lost in the feeling of his lips on my skin. My panties start to feel uncomfortable as they become damp. This man can make my panties evaporate from the simplest of touches.

"Juni at school?" he asks, and I nod again. My voice seems to have vanished.

In a flash, I'm twisted around and flung over his shoulder. I let out a yelp, causing Finan to slap my bare ass. I get a feeling of dread as he walks into the clubhouse.

Oh no.

"Finan, no, they can see my butt. Put me down, right now," I cry out, trying to reach around to pull the material of my skirt to cover my ass cheeks, but it earns me another ass slap.

"Damn, he is one lucky fuck having her use her stern mom voice on him." When I hear that, I cover my face with my hands, giving up covering my butt because we are already in the main room.

Finan doesn't stop though. He keeps marching through. Then he turns, heading down the hall to his room he keeps here at the club.

I hear some catcalls and whistles, and that adds to my embarrassment.

We get to his room, I hear the door being unlocked, then he steps in, the door being closed and locked behind me.

Finan lets me down slowly, making sure to rub my body all down the front of his as I go.

He looks down at me, the scowl gone. Back in place is the handsome man I fell in love with.

"Say it again," he demands.

I smile up at him, reaching for his jaw with my hands.

Going up on my tiptoes, I brush my lips across his, before pulling back.

"I love you, Finan Price."

His eyes flash with lust, before he slams his mouth onto mine.

I sink into the kiss, his tongue dominating mine. My hands find his waist, slipping under his cut and the material of his t-shirt, making him hiss at the contact. His skin feels hot beneath my fingers.

"I love this outfit, baby, but it needs to come off," he grinds out against my mouth.

I smirk up at him, taking a step back. Undoing my brown leather belt, I drop it to the floor. Reaching behind me, I unzip the skirt, letting it pool at my feet. Kicking it to one side, then I reach up, pulling the front zipper down on my top.

Finan's eyes don't leave my hands, watching as my body is exposed to him.

The material meets my skirt on the floor, leaving me in a cream strapless bra and panties set.

I can feel the heat coming off his body. The desire in his eyes makes my body vibrate with need for him. Like he said, it has been too freaking long.

"Damn, you are fucking hot. Unbelievably sexy." He steps to me, snaking an arm around my waist, dipping his head and sucking the skin on my neck, making me cry out. "And all fucking mine."

"Yes," is all I say.

Finan breaks the contact, stepping back enough so he can undress. Now this is what I am talking about.

Finan is like a slice of heaven, all rolled into a tight ball of sin.

I clench my thighs together, reminding me that I'm still in my underthings. So I remedy that, removing my bra and panties. I stand before Finan naked, while his eyes flare with lust as he kicks off his boots, removes his jeans and socks, and joins me on the bed.

"Commando?" I ask as he sinks between my thighs.

He shrugs. "We stopped at a motel to shower and change before coming home. I didn't want to smell like jail when I hugged my mom."

I nod, touching his face.

"You will tell me everything." With a nod, he kisses me, stealing my breath while he devours me.

There is no other place I would rather be than in this bed with him right now. We have making up to do, then we talk.

CHAPTER TWENTY-THREE

FINAN

Never in my life did I think today would pan out the way it did, but fuck, here we are.

I am laying between my woman's thighs.

When I stepped into the clubhouse, I never expected her to be there. Then she told me she had text, and I was pissed that I missed it. Her words hit me right in the heart, but I couldn't get over the hurt she caused when she said what she did that day. Stubborn as fuck, I know.

It was only when she walked out after telling me that she loved me that I took a breath. Calder slapped me across the back of the head and told me to get her back, because it would eat me alive if I didn't take that chance with her.

So here we are.

I'm about to be buried deep in my woman again, and today is a new start for us. She is the only pussy I will fuck and eat out from now on. Not that I ate pussy before her. Fuck, I hadn't even kissed someone in years until Joss.

I lean down to kiss her, with her hand still on my face, but it quickly moves over my shoulders and down my back, her nails digging into me.

"Need to be in you." My voice has dropped to a deeper tone, making her shiver.

From our time together, I know that my woman loves dirty talk, but right now I want to make love to her, sweet and soft, then fuck her later, hard and fast.

Reaching between us, I grip my cock, using the head to rub over her clit, causing her to moan. I relish the heat coming from her, as well as how fucking wet she is for me.

Keeping my gaze locked on her, I push into her, and my eyes roll into the back of my head. Fuck me, she feels good. Like warm silk, and only made for me.

Her eyes dilate, her lips part on a sweet gasp. Moving inside of her, I watch as her eyes close for a brief second, before I command that she open them.

"Eyes open, baby. I want you to see that it's me making love to you right now." Keeping my upper body off of hers, I move in and out at a slow pace.

I moan when she clenches her inner muscles, sucking my cock back in.

The pace is set slow, agonizing, drawing out the pleasure between us. My balls scream for me to move, to speed up, but I want to prolong this for as long as I can.

"I've missed you," she tells me.

Leaning down to take her lips in a kiss, I mutter, "I missed you too," against her mouth.

Seeing the pleasure on her face isn't helping me drag this out. Her moans, the breathy sounds she makes, is hitting my balls right on target. Pulling out, I kiss her again.

"On your stomach," I growl.

She gives me a coy look, biting her lips as she seductively rolls over, showing her ass to me, looking over her shoulder.

"Like this?" Fuck me.

Her brown eyes pull me in, and I don't ever want to be let go.

"Perfect, baby." I settle behind her and fill her up with my cock again.

She groans deep in her throat, and that sound is like a nut punch. Sexy as hell.

Leaning over her, I place my hands on the bed by her hips. I kiss between her shoulder blades, dragging my tongue over her salty skin. I nip at her skin, making her hiss and push back against me.

"That's it, baby," I growl against her back.

Kneeling to full height, I watch as she fucks me back, slowly, deeply. Looking down, I watch as my cock slides inside of her, the skin around her pussy stretching to take me and fuck me. That makes my balls ready to explode.

She falls flat on the bed, and I lean forward, bracing my hands on the bed again, laying my legs out behind me as I move deeply into her, over and over again.

Her fists grip handfuls of the bedding, crunching it up as I make love to her.

Joss pants my name, moaning, growling in frustration because I'm taking my time. I chuckle, kissing her spine again.

Clearly Joss has other ideas. She squirms beneath me, pushing against my groin, then goes back up onto her knees. I still, knowing what she wants. With her upper body off the bed, I reach around and play with one of her tits, pulling at the nipple, just the way she likes it.

"Yes, baby," she whines. "I need to come. More."

Placing my hand between her shoulder blades, I force her to lay flat on her stomach. I pull out and close her thighs, before parting her ass cheeks and sliding back in.

I hiss, while she cries out at the sudden tightness.

My shoulders bunch as I lean over her, slapping my pelvis into her lush ass, my cock driving into her, making her cry out. So much for making love. Shit, I will do that later. Right now, I need to make her come. My balls are going to burst.

Covering my body over hers, my front flush against her back, I shake my hand between her body and the bed, finding her swollen clit. I tug on it, making her jerk back, and fuck me, my eyes roll back.

How the fuck does she feel this good?

"You need to come, baby. Now," I growl against her ear, before biting her neck, making her cries of pleasure echo around the room.

I have no fucking doubt the whole club heard her, then her body goes tight. Going still beneath me, she moans deep in her throat as her pussy clamps down on my cock, strangling him, keeping him locked to her.

"Finan." My name on her lips in that sexy, breathy tone makes my balls ache then explode.

I fill her up, my hips flexing, drawing out the intense orgasm. I slow my thrusts, pumping the last few drops of my cum into her. Her body goes lax beneath me, and I smile, knowing it was me who made her feel that way.

This right here is one of the reasons a man's ego grows so fucking big. Seeing a woman, especially our woman, completely sated... Best fucking feeling ever.

"Shit, that was intense," comes her muffled voice, as her face is still buried in the bedding.

"Hell yeah it was. Needed too," I add.

I pull out and lie next to her, trailing my fingers up and down her back. She turns her head to face me. Joss moves her arms up so she can rest her head on them while she looks at me.

Brushing some hair off her face, she gives me a sleepy smile.

"Talk to me."

"I'm going to sound like a chick right now, but fuck it. What you told Juni hurt, like a sucker punch, babe. Being the typical man, it hurt my ego, so I left. I just didn't think anything else needed to be said."

"I'm sorry I said all of that. I let my motherly feelings and insecurities get the better of me. I know the club and I know the man that you are, Fin. Everything that has happened with Juni hit me hard. I felt like I failed her, and I just know that I couldn't deal with failing a relationship with you."

Tears fill her eyes, and I move in to kiss her lips.

"No crying. It fucking guts me," I tell her.

She sniffs, drying her eyes on the pillow close to her. I let her have a second to get her bearings before I carry on talking.

"I got arrested because we were on a hunt. Things turned to shit pretty fast, then the next thing, we were fighting. Then a brawl broke out and Calder and I got cuffed. That was Friday. We had to wait until today to face the Judge, Prez called in a favor, and here we are."

I shift closer so my chest touches her shoulder, hooking my leg over her thigh. My dick likes the new position because he perks up.

"Again?" Joss asks. I bounce my eyebrows in reply.

"He has been without you for days, baby. He wants to make up for lost time."

The smile she gives me makes my heart skip a beat.

"I missed him too, and the body he's attached to." She goes quiet for a second, looking at my chest, before bringing her gaze back to mine. "Will we be okay?"

Her voice is soft and unsure. A tremor shows her unease at the question.

Smirking, I roll her over onto her back, placing my body over hers, laying between her thighs that are spread wide for me. With my forearms braced on either side of her head, I dip forward, taking her mouth in a sweet kiss. Slanting my head, I deepen it further, making sure she knows exactly how I feel about her.

My tongue dominates hers. She moans into my mouth, and I swallow every sound she makes. Her pussy feels warm against my dick, her puffy lips cradling my shaft.

Breaking the kiss, I smile down at her, my gaze sliding over her face, taking in her features. Cupping the side of her head, I give her another gentle kiss.

"We'll be okay. We need to learn to talk things out rather than burying what needs to be said, okay? I know I'm not the easiest person to get to know, but I am here, and I want you to get to know me more. Like I've said before, I grew up in the club. Everything was handed to me, but I never took anything that was handed. I was the kid that stood back, watching my brothers fail at shit, then I would work out where they went wrong and try myself, only to nail it right the first time," I explain with a grin.

"Overachiever," she jests, and I kiss her.

"Anyone in the club will tell you that even from a young age, I was a people watcher. Always watching and learning, then I started on the crime shows, learning how to read people. Seeing their reactions, seeing how they gave their lies and truths away."

"So remind me to never lie to you then."

"No lies are allowed around us, baby. I want brute honesty."

"No lies. We talk it out."

"We talk it out, always." I kiss her again, getting lost in the feel of her with me.

Her hands skim over my body, and my dick twitches. He likes her touching me. I lick inside of her mouth, then she is nipping at my bottom lip, pulling the flesh between her teeth.

I hiss at the slight pain, making her giggle.

"Oh, it's like that, huh?" I flip us, setting her on my cock, rocking her back and forth as my dick slides between her pussy lips, coating him with her arousal.

"I want to ride you," she rasps.

"Then ride away, baby," I say with my hands on her hips.

I watch as she moves up onto her knees. Reaching between us to grip my cock in her tiny hand, she guides him to her dripping pussy. She slowly sinks down, and I watch as I disappear into her, one inch at a time.

I keep my head up, watching as she takes me inside of her. My abdominal muscles clench, and my balls draw up at the feel of her wrapped around me. This won't take long; she feels too good for it to last.

"Go, baby. Ride me."

Joss leans forward, resting her hands on my pecs. She uses that as leverage to slide up my cock, then sink back down. She does this at an excruciating pace, her gaze locked on mine.

We get lost in the stare, the feeling of fucking.

This feels more intense than any other time we have fucked.

Her eyes get darker, her breathing harsher as she moves, slowly. Licking her lips, Joss sits up, sinking as far down as she can, making us both moan.

Her hands run down my body, over her thighs, her hips, her stomach, up her ribcage to her tits. She plays with her lush globes, pushing them together, tugging on her nipples, all while rocking back and forth on my cock.

"Fucking hell, that is sexy. I'm going to fuck those one day, Joss."

She nods but says nothing. Her eyes are closed as she rides me. My woman looks like a sex goddess right now.

We are both panting, covered in sweat, as she rides me to our orgasms.

"Yes, Finan. I need more," she pants.

Keeping one hand gripping her hip, I slide the other one across her body, using my thumb to add pressure to her swollen clit. That's all it takes, and she goes off like a fucking rocket.

Leaning back, her hands land on my thighs as she rides her orgasm on my cock. I'm not far behind her. I come with a bellow, drowning out her cry of pleasure.

"Holy fuck." I pant, my gaze locked on my woman, just as she flops forward, resting her head on my shoulder.

Her body heaves with each harsh breath, mirroring mine. I wrap my arms around her, holding her to me. My cock still buried inside of her as little aftershocks ripple through her pussy, drawing more cum out of me.

"Mine," I whisper into her ear.

I feel her lips on my neck before she speaks in a quiet voice, but in a tone that leaves no room for argument.

"Mine."

Damn straight I'm hers, and she is mine.

I know what I need to do.

CHAPTER TWENTY-FOUR

JOSS

Sipping my coffee while sitting in Coffee Cove waiting for my client to arrive, I take in the people enjoying their morning. I love coming here. It's part-owned by the club, because Farrah, Slide's old lady, and her grandfather, Kenny, own it. But Kenny doesn't work anymore. Him and his wife retired and are traveling the coastline.

Oh, I bet that would be super fun. I would love to buy a huge RV and just go, take off, not knowing where we are heading, not knowing where we will stop and camp for the night. Maybe it's something we can do when Juni is done with school for the summer, depending on if Finan can take that amount of time off.

It has been three weeks since we sorted things out and it has been the best time ever. Juni was over the moon when we told her that we were together. She cried and threw herself at me, and then Finan.

With only growing up with a small family, she had my brother as an uncle, Owen's sister, and Joy as an aunt. Now she has the whole Rugged Skulls club. Even gone as far as calling Rookie and Della her grandparents. She knows about Della's cancer, so she said to Finan one night that she would like to call Della her 'Grams' because she treated her like my mother did, and better than Owen's parents have done.

They seem to have backed off some. The press was sent a statement, explaining Juni's disappearance, so they backed off, not bothering to listen to my mother-in-law. But I know she won't let things lie. She will find the perfect opportunity to fire things up again. She was never one to back down.

She has always made things about her. She lost a son; I never lost a husband. He was a man that I trapped. When it came to our wedding, she tried to take over, wanting the perfect wedding, but I put my foot down and we got the wedding we wanted, except for the fact that she wore a black dress with matching hat that even had a small front veil, like a fucking funeral hat.

"Joss?" a sweet voice says my name, pulling me out of my musings.

I look up and see a very pretty woman standing in front of me. I smile and get to my feet.

"Yes, that's me. Have a seat," I say to my client.

We hit the ground running, going through all the sections she wants on her new website and social media platforms. Also, I design her new logo for her small business, which I am sure will grow fairly quickly. She makes these pretty ceramic bowls that come in all sizes and colors.

It takes nearly an hour to get the first rough draft, and she is so easy to work with that time flies.

My phone buzzes next to my laptop, and I see that it's the school calling. That split second of seeing the name, my stomach drops into my shoes.

"Excuse me for a moment. My daughter's school is calling."

I get to my feet and walk out to the back decking, answering the call as I go.

"Hello?"

"Mrs. Abraham. This is Principal Maynard. I noticed that Juni wasn't in school this morning. Is everything okay? Does she need more time off?" His voice comes through the phone, but I have gone numb, like ice water has been poured over me.

Juni's not in school? She has to be.

"I-I dropped her off at the school this morning. I swear I saw her walk inside," I stammer.

"Oh. Um, let me check my computer to see if she was registered in her classes."

I hear him tapping on the phone, but I'm already walking back inside to get my things.

Farrah meets me at my table, recognizing my shaken state.

"What's happened? What do you need?" I shake my head, unable to speak at first.

I close my eyes, taking in a few deep breaths before looking at Farrah.

"Finan," is all I say, and she nods, rushing back to the counter.

"Mrs. Abrahams, I am sorry, but Juni hasn't been in any of her morning classes. Do I need to call the police?"

Shaking my head, I speak into the phone.

"No, I will contact them, but be easy to contact in case they need to see any security footage."

"Of course. I will check with her friends to see if they know anything. I will keep you updated."

"Thank you."

The second I hang up, my phone rings.

"Baby, what's happened?" Finan's voice soothes over me, and I sag, falling into my seat.

I faintly hear Farrah dealing with my client, before I see her packing my things away.

"The school called. Juni isn't in school. I swear, Fin, I dropped her off and saw her walk towards the main buildings door." As my panic rises, Farrah stands close to me, offering her support in silence.

"Okay, I will have Mav track her cell phone. Baby, I need you to not freak out until we know what is happening, okay?"

I nod, even though I know he can't see me through the phone. "I will try, but this all feels too familiar, Finan," I cry softly, trying to keep myself under control.

"I know, baby. We will find her, and I will bring our girl home." His voice takes on a softer tone.

"Okay. I love you; you know that, right?" I say into the device. I notice that Farrah takes a step back, giving me some privacy to talk to my man.

I hear an intake of breath, before his voice comes through the speaker, making my body respond to his tone, the sound of promise.

"I love you too, Joss. No more pain or upset will come to you or Juni after this. You are mine to protect, and I plan on doing just that. Go home. I will come to you when I find something."

"Way to make a woman swoon over you, Finan Price."

He chuckles lightly. "There is only one woman I want to make swoon, or come, baby."

"There go my panties and my heart."

"Later, babe. Let me find Juni. She might have just taken off for some time alone."

"Her phone is off," I hear Maverick in the background.

"Not again, Fin," I cry, my stomach dropping into my shoes. Farrah is back at my side, hugging me to her.

"Let us work, baby. Go home. Love you." With that, he hangs up.

"Come on, let me call the girls and we will sit with you until they find something," Farrah's voice is soft, calming, so I nod.

I can't go through this again, are my thoughts as Farrah drives my car to my house. She must have made the call before we left Coffee Cove, because when we arrive at my house, I see who is here.

Della and all the old ladies are here. Luna, Astrid, Perri and Winnie are also here, along with Ranger and Juliet.

"They're all here?" I question, looking at Farrah.

"Of course they are. When one of us needs something, we all come." She groans, shaking her head. "Do not repeat what I just said in front of Slide. He will have no issues rubbing it in my face." She shakes her head again with a smile on her face. "And I keep saying shit like that. Damn, he is truly rubbing... nope, not going to finish that sentence. Come on, let's go inside."

We both get out of the car, Della coming to me when I step closer. She pulls me in for a hug, leading me into my house. I see Luna holding the door open, so I assume she opened the door, then I see her holding my purse.

"I text Joy, but I know she's out of state right now. She said to keep her posted." I nod to Luna in thanks.

The ladies file into my kitchen. I sit on a stool while they all flit around the room, making coffee and getting snacks.

"The guys will find her. I'm sure she is safe and just wanted some alone time," Astrid speaks up.

"Finan said the same thing," I reply.

A mug of coffee is placed in front of me, so I wrap my hands around it, enjoying the feel of the hot ceramic against my cold hands.

I watch as the ladies make themselves at home in my kitchen, and I have to say that it feels nice. My family and very little amount of friends come here, so seeing all of these ladies makes my heart blossom even more with the friendship and support.

Della comes over to me, slipping her arm around my shoulders, pulling me into her body for a hug.

"I'm sure she is perfectly fine. Finn and the club will bring her home in one piece," she tells me. I offer her a sad smile.

"I hope so. I can't believe we are going through this again."

"I know, honey."

"Fucking kids, I tell you. Nothing but trouble," Risky pipes in, before pushing a slice of turkey into her mouth.

"Gee, thanks, Mom," Perri whines sarcastically, making the girls giggle.

"Oh, shut it, you. You know I love you and the twins just the same, but fuck me, you didn't half help toward running my hair gray," is Risky's reply to her daughter.

Their relationship reminds me so much of me and Juni, even with her at such a young age.

There is a knock on the door, and Luna rushes over to answer it. When she comes back into the room, Tree and Kady follow her. They both step over to me, hugging me tightly.

Tears burn my nose and my eyes water at the support from these women who I haven't known very long.

"Hey, hey, what's with the tears? Miss. J will be fine," Jodie speaks up, her voice holding so much conviction in her statement.

"I hope so. Does this type of thing happen this much? I mean, the same girl being taken twice? What if someone connected with Rolland has taken her? Oh, God. They might hurt her worse because she got away from them the first time."

"You can't think like that, Joss. Stay positive. That is the best thing right now. Think, deep down, does this feel like the first time?" Luna asks me.

I shake my head. "No, I don't feel the dread I did the first time. The feeling I had of her being hurt isn't there."

"See, a mother knows," Risky throws out there, saying the same thing she did to the group when Juni first went missing.

Sagging against the island, I drop my head into my hands, while a hand soothes up and down my back. I know it's Della because she hasn't moved from my side.

"So how are things with you and Finan?" Tree asks. She looks genuinely interested when I look at her. I also know what they are doing.

They are trying to take my mind off what is happening until the time comes to worry and freak out.

"They're going good. Really good actually. He is amazing with Juni; it's good that they share a love for crime TV shows," I explain with a fond smile on my face.

"Oh, do not get me started on the freaky shows that he loves. It used to scare me to hell and back, seeing all those crime videos and photos from crime scenes." Astrid shivers, with a look of disgust on her pretty face.

"Tell me about it. Do you remember when he would always be in the right place, at the right time, to attack one of us, mainly the boys doing something wrong? Then hold that shit over our heads." Luna laughs through her question to the younger girls.

"Oh, my God. Yes," Perri gasps. "He caught me with what's his name and said that he would tell Royal and Jack, so they could kick his ass. I stayed away from boys after that. Well, until college." She winks at me.

"He is an evil mastermind," Winnie throws her two cents in, making everyone laugh.

I look at Della and see the love and adoration she has for the girls in the room that grew up like sisters to her two boys.

"Yes, and creepy like a freaking Ninja," Astrid adds. The older ladies stand back and let the women my age talk and banter about the men in the club.

They are all close in age, all younger then my thirty-one years, but I don't feel out of place with them.

They all tell me stories of Finan and the other men in the club. It shows how close they all are, like real blood brothers and sisters. Well, it was going well until someone brings up Lennox and someone called Silas.

"What is up with you and Lennox?" I look to Astrid. "Who is Silas?"

"Silas is Syn's nephew, her brother River and his wife, Dezi. Syn wanted to come today but was feeling under the weather," Farrah explains.

"I was wondering where that mouthy bitch was," Risky says.

A nervous wave washes over my body, and my legs starts to bounce in time with my elevated heartrate. I bite my thumbnail, looking down at my phone that still has a dark screen.

Shit, what if something bad has happened? Even though I feel it in my bones that it's not. My mom used to always say that she knew if something was wrong with Matt and me, but I never truly believed it until Juni was born.

Like when she was four months old and the doctor at the clinic told me it was just a cold, but I refused to believe that. I called my parents and they met me at the ER. I was glad that I did, because she had a respiratory infection and was in hospital for nearly two weeks.

I stare at my phone like it will magically light up with a call or text, but nothing.

What is taking so long? I have no doubt that the club are doing everything they can to find her, but that doesn't help my worry ease.

No parent wants this to happen to their child, let alone a second time.

"Breathe for me." I hadn't noticed that I was holding my breath.

Turning my head, I see Della smiling at me, her gaze soft and understanding. I nod and let out a long breath, before pulling a steady breath in, and do that three more times to get my lungs under control.

"Did you know that we thought for a time that Finan was gay?"

My head swivels on my shoulders, looking at Luna with wide, shocked eyes, while she nods a smile at me.

"Yeah, we all did, even the boys. Except Calder," Astrid adds.

"Finan and Calder are every bit twins as actual twins are. They are just under eleven months apart. Irish twins. They were inseparable. Hell, they still are. But complete opposites," Della explains with a smile and a look of adoration on her face.

She is proud of her boys.

"Definitely opposites. Finan isn't about screwing his way through the continental US, while Calder is happy diving into every free, willing pussy that's offered to him," Kady spits out.

Her voice is a mixture of disgust and longing. Holy cow, does Kady have feelings for Calder? Well, I never saw that coming. Not that I have spent a lot of time with her, but wow, no wonder she feels the way she does. Calder can be sweet and amazing, especially with Juni. He has taken her on like she is his own niece. But he does like to share is love around, if you know what I mean.

My gaze slides over to Tree, who looks from her sister to me. The little chin dip lets me know that what I'm thinking is right.

Damn, it's like living in a soap opera being around these girls. Kady and Calder. Astrid and Lennox. I'm sure that Winnie's face twitched at the mention of Silas.

Interesting.

I decide to carry on with the conversation, pulling the attention away from Kady, who is looking down at the mug in her hands, avoiding looking at anyone in the room, more so Della.

"Well, Finan is most certainly not gay. He has never given off the gay vibe with me. Why would you think that?"

Before they can answer, I know it in my heart. It's because he never slept around with loads of random women, but hearing it will make me feel good, at ease.

"Oh, we know he's not gay, considering the sounds coming from his room at the clubhouse not so long ago." Astrid winks at me, and heat licks at my face.

Oh, my God. How embarrassing. His mom is sitting right next to me, and they are talking about me banging her son.

Covering my face with my hands, I groan, making the girls giggle.

Della nudges my shoulder, so I peek at her through my fingers.

"We were all young once, Joss. I know what it's like to crave the touch of a biker. Hence why my sons are so close together in age." She winks at me, and I can't stop the smile from appearing on my face.

They keep me company until we hear a car stopping in front of my house. Risky gets there first, her face showing a thundering look as I approach her.

I gasp in shock when I see who it is, but soon, my shock turns to rage, as I swing the door open and storm out.

CHAPTER TWENTY-FIVE

FINAN

Stretching out on the bed in the shitty motel, basking in the quiet, I close my eyes and let the peace settle over me. Maverick is on his laptop, hacking into traffic cams, to give us eyes on the bitch we are tracking.

She is a sneaky little piece of shit. She gets her claws in men, then cons them out of whatever they will hand over. Well, the bitch conned the wrong man, because his daughter is gunning for her.

We got a lead that she is in the area, and she has the routine of staying at this motel. Clearly she isn't that fucking clever if people know where she is after fucking people's lives up.

My stomach grumbles, making Maverick look over his shoulder at me with a grin on his face.

"Pizza?"

"I could go for pizza." I nod to him.

Reaching over to the small bedside table, I pick up my phone, just as a text comes through from Farrah. What the hell? Why is she texting me?

Farrah: Call Joss. Juni is not in school by the sounds of it. Could be missing.

I pull up Joss's contact and hit the call button. It rings once, then she answers.

"Finan." Her voice is small, lost even.

"Baby, what's happened?" I ask, sitting up, gaining the attention of Mav from across the room.

He frowns at me. I hold my hand up, telling him to wait a fucking second.

"The school called. Juni isn't in school. I swear, Fin, I dropped her off and saw her walk towards the main buildings door." I can hear the panic in her voice. Shit, not again.

I scoot off the bed, walking across the room. "Okay, I will have Mav track her cell phone. Baby, I need you to not freak the fuck out until we know what is happening, okay?"

I click my fingers at Mav and mouth, "Track Juni's cell." He nods and gets to it.

"I will try, but this all feels familiar, Finan." I can hear her crying, and it breaks my fucking heart that I'm not there with her.

My fist clenches at my side. I hate being away from them, but I have a job to do. Plus, we didn't think this would happen again.

Watching Maverick tap on the laptop, I pace back and forth, keeping my eye locked on the small screen.

"I know, baby. We will find her, and I will bring our girl home, okay?" I say into the phone.

I step away from Maverick and open the door to the room. Fuck the mark. This is more important.

"Okay. I love you; you know that, right?" she asks me in a quiet tone.

The image of her face, tear-stained, looking sad. I pinch the bridge of my nose, hating that I am not holding her right now.

"I love you too, Joss. No more pain or upset will come to you or Juni after this. You are mine to protect, and I plan on doing just that. Go home. I will come to you when I find something."

"Way to make a woman swoon over you, Finan Price."

I chuckle at her words. Damn fucking right I can make her swoon, and wet all at the same time, but now is not the time to be thinking of sinking into her.

"There is only one woman I want to make swoon, or come, baby."

"There go my panties and my heart," she whispers, and fuck me, my dick twitches in my jeans at the sound of her talking about her panties and her heart.

"Later, babe. Let me find Juni. She might have just taken some time alone," I explain, praying to every fucking God out there that my words are true.

"Her phone is turned off," Maverick says from behind me. Fucking hell, not again. The feeling of déjà vu is fucking strong with this one.

"Not again, Fin," she cries.

"Let us work, baby. Go home. Love you."

I hang up before she can say anything else. I close my eyes tightly, wishing that this shit wasn't happening again.

How can this happen to the same girl twice?

"We'll find her brother," Maverick says from behind me. I nod and storm over to my bed, quickly packing my things back into my duffle.

"Where was her phone switched off?" I call to him.

"A few miles from the school."

Fucking hell on a stick.

"Everyone has been informed. You drive, I will keep looking for any connection to Rolland and his crew." I nod and walk out to the truck, Maverick hot on my heels, his duffle slung over his shoulder, laptop balancing on his forearm, while he taps on the keys.

Thank fuck for my brothers. Always there for each other no matter the cost.

We will lose another job, but fuck it, Juni is more important.

Once we are settled in the truck, I hit the road, and it isn't long until I hear the tailpipes of my brothers behind us on the highway.

The drive to Joss's is filled with regret for not being there, and guilt for not being able to protect Juni again.

Thank fuck we are less than an hour way, but I make it back to Joss's house in less than that. Fuck knows what traffic laws I broke.

I pull up outside her house, parking behind an expensive looking BMW. I barely have time to switch the engine off and rip off the seatbelt before I'm out of the car. The rest of the club is here, the older members, my parents, and the younger generation.

My brothers walk behind me to the huge scene of screaming on the front lawn.

"You had no right to take her. You do not have my permission," Joss yells at the older lady, who looks like she is decked out in Gucci from head to toe.

She waves her hand at Joss, dismissing her statement.

"She is my granddaughter. I have every right to spend time with her. If you wouldn't poison her against me, then she would want to come and see us. All of this is down to you and your spiteful ways, Joss."

"Spiteful? I'm the spiteful one? Ines, you have never been stopped from seeing Juni, even though you have treated me so badly. Juni should know her father's family. Of course she should. But when she sees what you have done and said about me, then she makes up her own mind."

I glance around the lawn, seeing Juni tucked against my mother's side, my father standing close, in a protective stance.

"I do not believe that a fourteen-year-old girl should be able to make those types of decisions. I want to spend time with her, and if you are not going to allow that, then I will have no choice but to take you to court."

Juni gasps, and my mom hugs her tighter.

"That will never happen, Ines. And if you say you love her like you do, then you wouldn't make threats like that.

You wouldn't drag her through the court system just to win one over on me. You have always seen me as competition. When I married Owen, you told me that I took him from you. When I named her Juni, you told me that I did it to get back at you because I didn't use your name. Owen picked her name, Ines, not me. It was his wish to name her Juni."

Joss is crying, but I see the anger that is still simmering there.

I step over to her, not wanting to be away from her anymore. Ines's eyes go wide when she sees me slide my arm round Joss's waist and lean in to kiss the side of her head.

"This—this is who you have around my granddaughter? This will not stand, Joss. I will not have these people influence Juni. I will simply have to take her way from you, as you cannot be a responsible mother to her. Putting her life in danger around these people."

Juni screams, "NO." Then she is at our side, hugging me tightly.

"Juni, come here, dear. We will leave now. You won't have to be around these disgusting bikers again." She waves her skinny hand out, but Juni hugs me tighter.

"You need to leave, lady," I growl.

Usually, I have a moment when I need to gather my thoughts before speaking in a situation like this, with someone I don't know. But all of that is pushed down because she is threatening my girls, my family.

"Lady," someone scoffs, then sniggers break out.

"I am not leaving without my granddaughter. I will phone the police if you won't let me take her," Ines snaps.

"Does it look like she wants to go with you?" I nod to where Juni is holding on to me for dear life. "Besides, I think my grandfather's men would like to know that you took a minor without informing her mother."

She completely ignores me and focuses on Joss again.

"My Owen would be so disappointed in you. You have done wrong by his daughter and his family. You should be ashamed of yourself. I will be contacting my lawyer on getting custody of Juni."

Juni cries against her mother, both my girls shaking but for very different reasons. Juni out of upset and fear, whereas for Joss, it is out of pure rage and the need to spill blood.

I know that feeling all too well. No fucker will take my family from me.

Joss pulls away, and 1 tuck Juni tight to me. My woman steps up to her ex-mother-in-law, making Ines flinch.

"*My Owen* would be fucking proud of the job I have done to raise our daughter. She is bright, strong, and independent. He would want me to love again. To find someone WHO LOVES ME, AND HIS DAUGHTER. And I have found that. *We* have found that in Finan. And not only him, but the entire Rugged Skulls MC. They dropped everything to help find Juni the first time. Lost money from their business all because Finan felt something for me after a brief meeting.

"That, to me, screams loyalty, trust, and fucking respect, which is something you do not possess. They have been there for us, helped us through everything. Where were you? Oh yes, in front of any camera that would look at you, down the golfclub, verbally attacking me, deeming me to be a bad mother. When Juni is my fucking life, I would die for her. Would you?" Joss fumes, but she isn't finished.

"These women took me in. They are my friends. Family." Joss points to my parents, and my brother who has joined them. "Della has been more of a grandmother to Juni in a short few weeks than you have in her entire fourteen years. Rookie sees her like Juni is his own flesh and blood."

"Damn straight she is," my dad yells.

"Juni may have only grown up with my brother, Joy and Olivia, but now she has a new uncle, one who is there for her, listens to her, is so fucking attentive with her."

"We're a team, right, Junes?" Calder calls to her. In a flash, Juni runs from me and to my family, Calder holding her close while my mother rubs her back, my dad standing guard.

I look back to Ines and see she is fuming. Her eyes are narrowed on Juni, her lips thinned, and her chest heaving.

"You are the reason I have lost everything. I lost my Owen because of you. Now I have lost my granddaughter, my only connection to him. I will make you pay for this. You took him from me, made him marry you when he had his whole life ahead of him."

In an instant, Joss's body sags in defeat. She swipes the tears away, stepping back into my front. My arms go around her waist, giving her my strength.

"Ines, Owen died in the army. It was his lifelong dream to enlist, and he did. I was and still am proud of the man he was. I am a proud army wife. It was you who refused to believe that he followed his passion. It was a bomb that killed him, not me. As for Juni, that was all on you. You should be proud of the men and women that serve our country. I know I am. Every last one of them put their lives on the line for this country. They deserve honor and respect."

"Damn fucking straight, darling," Sarge growls, stepping forward. So do the rest of the brothers that have served.

"Yes, we were young when we got married, but we loved each other. Do you know how many people around the world marry young? Many. We were teenagers yes, but love is love, there is no age on the emotion," I add.

"Each of us have served for our country. Proud to do it. We are sorry that Owen lost his life over there as have many before and after him. Their lives won't be in vain. But you, as his mother, should be the proudest," Magnum speaks up.

"It was a foolish mistake on his part. One I know he regretted. He did it for her," Ines snaps, pointing at Joss.

"No, Ines. He did it for him. For his family," Opal adds in a calming voice.

"Just leave, Ines. Juni is safe here with me, with the family. If she wants to contact you, to pay a visit, I will be in touch. Be lucky that I didn't involve the police," Joss says. Her voice is stronger now than it was a little time ago.

"Before you open your mouth, Mrs. Abraham," Maverick pipes up, moving closer, "I suggest you take a look at this before you decide to involve the police and courts against Joss." He shows her the laptop.

Her eyes go wide, and she gasps, covering her mouth with her hand. Then she clutches her pearls. We wait for what feels like forever before she speaks again.

"I will be in touch." She looks at Joss, then Juni one last time, before spinning on her heels and darting to her car.

We all look to a smirking Maverick, who simply closes his laptop, tucking it under his arm.

"What did you show her?" Royal asks. Maverick looks to Juni, then back to me and Joss.

"Why doesn't someone take Juni inside?" he says to the group. Looking over my shoulder, I see my mom and Farrah taking her inside, away from the adult information I assume Mav is about to give us.

Once they ladies are inside, he brings his smirk back.

"I found some information on the family. Your sister-in-law is fucking hot, by the way," he says, looking at Joss. She nods in agreement.

"Any ways, after some digging, I found out that your ex-father-in-law is getting his dick wet by multiple women. Including his partners daughter, who is barely legal." He bounces his eyebrows.

"Oh, my God. He always seemed like a nice guy, besides putting me down. He did treat Juni good but would always let Ines call the shots," Joss explains, leaning into me.

"Well, I don't think they will be a problem from now on. You're welcome," Maverick spouts. "That is me done. I am out. I have to be...somewhere." He winks at me, saluting everyone else, then leaves.

"Do not tell me he is going to pin the badge on the ass," Slide pipes in, and we all laugh, except Joss, who frowns at us.

"Don't worry, baby. Just Slide being Slide. Nothing good ever comes out of his mouth."

"Hey, I resent that statement," Slide pipes in, as he walks into the house, flipping me off.

I sling my arm around Joss's shoulders, pulling her to me for a kiss. Her arm goes around my waist, her fingers slipping under my cut and t-shirt. The feel of her cold hands on me makes me shiver, which causes her to giggle.

"Always with the cold hands," I mutter.

"I know a way for you to warm me up." She wiggles her eyebrows and runs into the house.

"Damn, I love that woman," I mutter to myself, before following her inside.

CHAPTER TWENTY-SIX

JOSS

I sigh, dropping the pizza crust into the now empty box on the coffee table. Finan is next to me, stuffing his face with the last slice, while Juni is on the floor, lying on her stomach while we watch *Ella Enchanted*. It's one of Juni's favorites.

I was surprised when Finan said yes to watching it. He doesn't seem like the type of guy to want to watch some cheesy teen girl movie about princesses and princes, but here we are.

Finishing off my beer, I get to my feet, looking down at him.

"Do you want another one?"

"Yeah, baby. Thanks." The smile he gives me makes my knees weak. Damn this man.

"Juni, you want anything from the kitchen?"

"No, I'm good, Mom." I nod and walk into the kitchen, pulling open the fridge and picking up two beers.

I let out a yelp when arms snake around my waist, pulling me flush against his warm, hard body.

God, I love his arms around me. His body pressed to mine does some serious things to me.

"Damn, you smell good," he says close to my ear.

His hot breath whispers across my bare shoulder. After a day of work, chores and running errands, I wanted to be comfortable, so I changed into cotton shorts and a cami with a built in bra.

It has been two weeks since Ines took Juni without my permission, and we have heard nothing from her, which is not surprising.

His hand splays across my stomach, his fingers slowly slipping beneath the waistband of my shorts, pushing my ass back into him. A low moan escapes my lips at the feel of his fingers moving lower, into my panties, brushing against the small amount of hair I leave there.

"Fin, we can't," is all I say, but I don't push him away or stop him.

He bites my earlobe, before sucking it into his mouth. I close my eyes, relishing in the feel of him touching me. All I want is for him to bend me over and take me from behind, helping me release all the tension from a busy workday, but my daughter is right in the next room.

"Later," I promise, and force myself to pull away.

I turn around to look at Finan, and see he is pouting. His bottom lip is jutting out, and he has lowered his eyelids, giving the puppy dog look. Hell, it's cute, but those puppy dog eyes don't work on me.

"Not going to work, lover boy. Come on, we have more chick-flicks to watch."

"Fine." He sighs and picks up our beers before he walks back to the couch.

We snuggle back up on the couch as the end credits roll on the movie. Juni sits up, picking up the TV remote, and looks for something else for us to watch. Finan looks at me when he sees what she has stopped on. He rolls his eyes, and I giggle.

We are now onto Spiderman movies again. Juni has a huge thing for Tom Holland. He is her first celebrity crush. Bless her. Mine was Paul Walker.

Finan kisses the side of my head, my hand finding its way to his chest. I tilt my head to look up at him. His eyes shine with love, and it makes me swoon for him.

I knew that I loved Owen. I will always love Owen. He will hold a piece of my heart that I will carry with me always. Juni will always carry her father with her. She will never meet him, but I feel that she knows him enough.

Now Finan, he owns my heart too. Joy used to try and get me to date so many times since Owen, but nothing ever felt right. No guys got my heart kicking up a notch, but seeing Finan on that mountain, something sparked in my chest.

"Are you mom's boyfriend?" comes my daughter's voice from the floor.

My gaze snaps to her to see her sitting up, leaning against the chaise chair. She looks between us, waiting for one of us to speak, but it seems that my voice has done a runner, because I can't find it.

I look to Finan, seeing him grinning at me. He kisses my nose before looking back to Juni.

"I am. She's my old lady. I love your mom, Juni, and I love you too. You may not have met your dad, but I know he truly loved you, and I will never want to take his place, but I will be here right alongside you and your mom in every aspect. If that's okay with you."

Holy cow, there goes the whooshing feeling in my heart again.

Damn, this man always knows what to say. It's even more sexy and beautiful because I know he means it.

"Old lady?" she asks him.

"It's what we call our women in MC's. It means that your mom is mine to love and protect. Like a wife, but without the ring. That will come later." He brings his eyes back to me, and I know I look like a fish out of water with how my eyes are wide and my mouth is popping open and closed at a fast pace.

"So it's serious? Between you and Mom, I mean," Juni adds on.

"As a heart attack," he finishes.

Juni looks at him for a little time, but I'm not overly worried because I know how much she loves and respects Finan. She gets to her feet, running and jumping into his lap. Her legs rest over my thighs, while she hugs him tightly round the neck.

"Thank you for making her extra happy. I love you too," she whispers into his neck. I see his eyes close, and his arms tighten around her, holding on to what she said. My heart flutters.

Pulling back, she smiles at us then slips back to the floor like she didn't just make this rugged biker tear up and make his heart swell.

"Fuck," he mutters, pulling me to him. "She knows how to unman a biker, doesn't she? The guys at the club have talked about how she has them wrapped around her finger already. She told Calder a few days ago that some boy from school wants to take her on a date."

I gasp and look up at him, pulling back. He nods. "Yeah. I know. Not fucking happening." He throws out there, and now I giggle.

"What did Calder say?" I have to ask, but I think I already know the answer.

"He told her that she can't date until she is thirty. But he might not be ready then to see it, so she might have to join a nunnery."

"Oh, my God." I laugh, burying my face in his chest.

These men are simply amazing. They have taken Juni under their wings, treated her like she is one of their own. They would die for her, and that makes me love this club even more.

This is a family.

"Fuck, yes. Take it, baby. Let me feel the back of your throat," Finan growls from above me.

We are in my bedroom. Juni went to bed a few hours ago. Finan and I watched some action movies before he started touching me and got me all hot and flustered. I rubbed my hand over his dick, only to find him hard, so I took his hand and lead him to my room.

He's sitting on a chair I have in the corner of the room, and I am on my knees, sucking his cock, tasting him on my tongue. His balls in my hands, I tug on them, making him growl my name.

Knowing that it's me making him growl, putting that flush of pink in his cheeks, making his chest heave with each breath, makes me feel empowered and sexy.

"Harder," he grinds out. I look up at him from under my lashes.

He's looking down at me, biting his bottom lip, nostrils flaring with desire for me, but I know he's also holding back. He is giving this to me, before he takes complete control.

Pulling my mouth off him, I hold his cock at an angle, licking him from root to top. I suck the head into my mouth, running my tongue over the slit that is leaking his desire for me.

"Fuck. Shit, baby," he croaks.

Moving my mouth lower, I lick my way down, dragging my tongue over the vein on the underside of his shaft.

When I reach his balls, I lick them, making sure to pay the same amount of attention to them both before sucking each one into my mouth.

His hips come off the chair when I do this, so I smile against him.

"You like that?" I ask, then kiss his thigh, keeping my gaze locked on him.

"You know I do."

I smile at his reply, sucking on his balls as I jerk my hand up and down his length.

He pants and growls my name, until I feel his balls tighten. Then I am being picked up off the floor.

My ass touches his thighs, his cock nestled between us, as he feasts on my breasts. Sucking, licking, pushing them together while he plays. I rest my hands on his shoulders, loving the feel of his mouth on me.

"Suck," I demand, and thank fuck he listens.

My nipples feel raw from all the sucking, licking, and biting that he does.

My hips rock back and forth at a sweet pace, his cock rubbing against my clit. I know I'm coating his cock with my arousal, adding a more sensual feel to it.

"I need to be in you, baby. Lift." His voice is a command, deep and strong.

I do as he says, getting up onto my knees, while he grips his cock in one hand, directing the head to my pussy. His other hand grips my hip, guiding me down, until I filled full of him.

My fingers dig into his shoulder, no doubt leaving my marks on him.

"Move, baby. You take us there," is all·he says.

My feet are braced on his thighs behind me, and I use the leverage to roll my hips, dragging my clit over his pubic bone as I do.

I gasp and breathe his name, my tits bouncing with each thrust.

Sucking his dick turned me on, so much so I'm already close. The idea of pleasing him, pleasuring Finan, turns me on. I am dripping all over him, and I know he loves that.

Over and over, I roll my hips, taking him deep in me, as I slide up and down.

My gaze connects with his. Eyes stare back at me, dark, full of lust, but I can tell by the look on his face that he is close. But he wants to hold off.

"Let go," I tell him. I want him to explode inside of me. I want him to fill me up.

Finan sits forward, not dislodging me from his cock. His hands roam my back, gripping me as he slams his mouth onto mine. His tongue dances with mine as I pick up the pace. Rocking back and forth, pushing down to make him go deeper. He growls into my mouth, and holy cow that is hot as hell.

He holds me close, my chest pressed against his. Our bodies are slick with sweat, but I don't care. I just want to come all over him and have him finish inside me.

Finan pulls his mouth away from mine, then he is kissing my neck, my collarbone. My hips faulter when he sucks on the skin below my ear, no doubt leaving a red mark he will be proud of.

Looking up at me as my pussy starts to flutter, we stare into each other's eyes, and my climax washes over me. I cry out his name and try to throw my head back, but Finan holds me in place, keeping eye contact throughout the sudden rush.

His hips move under me, fucking me through my rush, just as he takes his.

I know the second he comes. His nostrils flare, he grinds his teeth, and he holds me down on his cock as he pulses inside of me.

My body goes lax against his chest, and his arms flex and tighten around me. We both breathe each other in, letting the intense moment wash over us.

"I have never come that hard before," I say against his neck, making his chest puff out.

"Tell me about it. I think a few brain cells got sucked out through my dick," he chuckles, and I smile, before licking the sweat off his skin.

"Not yet, woman. Give me a few minutes and we can go again."

And go again we do. Three more times before we fall asleep wrapped up in each other's arms, where I dream of a baby with Finan's coloring and Juni's sweetness.

CHAPTER TWENTY-SEVEN

FINAN

"But you are wrong. Tom Holland is the better Spiderman, because one, he is really good looking. Two, he is more flexible, he did all his own stunts, and he acts way better than Tobey Maguire," Juni argues back at me, making me smile.

"That is where you are wrong though, because Toby did his own stunts until he threw his back out. Tobey Maguire is a versatile actor. He can play other roles, more mature roles. Tom Holland is a pretty face; he is a baby. So he can't play hardened characters with depth," I argue back, just to rile her up.

"Of course he is a baby. He is only young. His career is just taking off. You watch, Mr." Juni throws a fry at me. I catch it and pop it into my mouth.

We're at Crossroads, having lunch. I decided to treat my girl since Juni is finished for the summer, and going away for two weeks with her grandparents traveling in an RV. She is so fucking excited, and I'm not going to lie, but so am I. I get Joss around the clock, twenty-four seven, and I plan to have her naked as much of that time as possible.

"Will you two give it a rest. Geez, you have been at this fight for days," Joss pipes in, before sipping at her iced tea.

My gaze drops to her mouth as it wraps around the straw. Fucking lucky piece of plastic. My dick stirs in my jeans, so I internally push those naughty thoughts of her away.

"It's fun to push her buttons, *Mom*," I joke, winking at her.

Juni giggles from her seat across from us, and I wink at her as well.

"Well, look how cozy this is. This seat taken, Sparkles?" Royal says to Juni, using the nickname the brothers have given her. She shakes her head as he sits his ass down, not caring if it was.

The guys said that her eyes sparkle when she is happy, so the name stuck. Calder has his own nickname for her, and only he can call her that. He calls her 'Junes.'

"Duchess, bring me my usual, please, baby," he calls out to his wife, who rolls her eyes at him.

"Lazy runt," Tree calls back to him. He winks at her, and I don't miss the smile she has on her face when she goes into the kitchen.

This is the way these two are. Some find it strange with their banter, but that's Royal and Tree. He worships the ground she walks on.

"So, Sparkles." He steals one of Juni's fries when he says this.

"Hey! Get your own, runt," Juni replies, making Royal's eyes go wide.

Joss covers her mouth with her hand to cover her laughter. I don't give a fuck. I laugh at them. Royal bursts out laughing, and Juni follows. We are still laughing when Tree comes over with his food and drinks.

"What did I miss?" she asks, leaning on Royal's shoulder.

He wraps his arm around her waist, tilting his head back for a kiss, which Tree gives him. I smile at them. Seeing how they got together is one for the story books, but it was perfect for them, and it's good to see my brother happy.

"This little shit called me a 'runt.' Clearly she is hanging round the wrong kind of people," he tells his wife, who laughs, reaching over to high-five Juni.

"Hey, wife. What the hell? You do know that I can withhold my di—" Tree covers his mouth with her hand, stopping him from finishing his sentence, and for that I am grateful.

"Enough out of you. Eat your food," she scolds him. "Call me if you need me." With one more kiss, she leaves.

"Damn, my woman is fine," Royal mutters, watching Tree walk away.

I click my fingers, getting his attention, nodding in Juni's direction. He gives me a little nod of understanding. I need him to reel his mouth in. Looking at Juni, I see her cheeks are red and she is smiling. She knows exactly what Royal was going to say and what he is insinuating about Tree.

See, she is a clever kid.

"When do you and the oldies leave?" Royal asks Juni, before he takes a huge bite out of his burger.

"Monday. Mom and Finan said we could come here for some food and dessert." She beams at him.

"Do not let my dad hear you calling him old," Joss tells Royal, pointing her fork at him.

He grins. "I'm used to being slapped around the head for that shit. Have you met the older members of the club?"

"But they're all silver foxes, so I would slap you too," Juni comments without looking up from her phone.

My gaze snaps to hers, then to Joss, show shrugs with a smile on her face.

"What can I say, my girl has taste." She grins at me.

"Hell to the fucking no," I reply, looking between my girls with a shocked expression on my face. "We talked about this. You can date when you are thirty, or when Tom Holland wants to date you," I throw out there.

Royal holds his fist out for me to bump. "What Fin said, kid."

"But that is forever away. My body is changing, Finan. I am becoming a woman. My period will come soon. I can feel it. My boobs are growing."

"Fuck." I cover my ears with my hands, not wanting to hear this shit. "Nope. You will be my baby girl forever. Simple," I snap, looking at a giggling Joss. She winks at Juni, who simply smiles wide. To say that I am grateful for that smile can't be put into words. Us finding her the way we did could have ended far fucking worse.

"Brother, we need to lock her away. The pervy boys will come around sniffing. Not happening on my watch," Royal bitches, shaking his head.

"Oh, behave, you two. She is fine. I was twelve getting my period. Juni is a little late, but it's normal." She looks at me. "Baby, you need to get over it. She is growing up."

"You do know that Dominic will grow up too, yeah?" Juni says, looking between Royal and me, frowning.

"But he's a boy," I state.

"And?" I get the *if looks could kill* look from her.

"Ummm," I stammer, looking at Royal and Joss for help. Joss holds her hand up leaving me to my own devices.

"Listen, boys can't get pregnant, so they get it easier than girls," Royal starts. "They don't have all the cramps, and blood, and PMSing to deal with. They deal with boners, and raging hormones, that's it. Plus, he can handle himself when he starts to date. You are a girl, so you need the club to protect you." He shrugs at the end.

Juni looks at him with a gaping mouth, like he didn't just say all of that.

Royal goes back to eating his food, the table completely silent. Juni is looking at her new uncle, then looks at me, then back to Royal. I can see the wheels turning in her head.

Oh shit, she is running through her memory bank, looking for ideas on how to get away with murder. Crime shows is a me and Juni thing. Even Joss knows not to interrupt us when we are watching them.

We like to pick apart the episode and plan it better.

317

He looks up after a few minutes, glancing between the three of us. "What?"

"While you were enjoying your food, Juni here was plotting your murder and thinking of the quickest way to dispose of your body." I smirk at him.

His eyes go wide as he looks to Juni.

"Why? You love me," he whines.

She simply shrugs. "I love you all, but I can take care of myself. Being the new kid at the Rugged Skulls MC, I need to prove my place so no one will mess with me." She leans into him and lowers her voice. "But I will call on you if needed."

A huge smile covers Royal's face, then he bumps his shoulder with hers.

"You came here without me?" Calder's voice floats through the room.

"Finan made me," Juni calls out.

"Nark." I throw a fry at her, making her giggle.

I see my parents walk in behind my brother, my father and brother standing out in their jeans, boots and cut, whereas my mom is dressed in a floral summer dress. Juni looks over her shoulder at my family, and her eyes sparkle, hence the name.

"Grams, Grandpa," she calls to them. I swear I feel my mom's eyes fill with tears before she blinks them away. My father and brother drag a table closer to ours. I notice Tree rolling her eyes at the antics, but she says nothing. She knows we will put it back.

My mom kisses Juni on the head, taking the seat next to her, while my dad ruffles her hair, before taking a seat next to me.

"Are you excited to be going on vacation with your grandparents?" my mom asks Juni.

"You bet. We have so much planned. Tours of museums, going to watch a movie on the beach... I can't wait." Her smile is wide as she bounces in her seat with excitement.

"I bet Finan is more excited than you." Calder pipes in, earning a fist pump from Royal but a glare from Rookie.

"Watch it," Dad says with a deep, warning tone.

"What? She is just as interested in the opposite sex as we are. She's fourteen." Calder shrugs, stealing one of her onion rings.

Juni slaps the back of his hand. He scowls at her, pulling said hand away, rubbing it.

"Fucking brute." He frowns at her.

"Big baby." She tilts her head at him, before looking at Joss, who gives her a little nod.

I know what they're doing, and I know that Juni has been scared and nervous about letting family know.

My hand goes to Joss's thigh, rubbing up and down in support. This is a huge step for both of my girls, but one I will stand by, and I know that the club and family will.

"It's not the opposite sex I'm interested in," Juni says to the table.

The table goes silent. Joss tenses up, but I stay calm as fuck because I know my family.

My mom gasps, putting her hand over her heart, smiling at Juni. My dad leans over the table, placing his hand on hers in support. Juni looks down at Rookie's hand covering hers, before she brings her eyes up to meet his aging ones.

"Fucking proud of you, kid. Love you just as much."

Joss cries next to me as Juni runs around the table and throws herself at my father. Damn, I swallow the thickening lump in my throat at the sight.

"Oh, Juni, that was a brave thing you just did, but you need to know that we always love you. Always support you. Being gay does not define you as a person. You are simply you, baby girl," my mom adds, then Juni is hugging her.

I look over to Calder and Royal, who are staring at her. Juni stands at the end of the table, looking at each of them, but her gaze stops on Calder. I know the pair have formed a solid connection, and he would do anything for her.

Royal sinks back into his seat, nodding.

"You do you, kid. Don't love you less," is all he says as he opens his arms to her for a hug, which she goes and does.

Calder still hasn't said anything, but I know he will support her, he is just looking for the right things to say.

Finally my brother opens his mouth, and yeah, it is inappropriate as fuck.

"Oh, thank fuck. I don't need to go chasing horny, pervy little shits away from you," he says dramatically. "But let me tell you this: the chick you decide to bang had better be fit. I mean big as hell tits, legs that go all the way up and an ass for days. You have good taste, my darling niece. Stick with me and you will hook a beauty." He winks at Juni, who goes bright red but bursts out laughing.

I shake my head at him, and Royal high-fives both Calder and Juni. My mom covers her eyes with her hand, shaking her head, while Rookie smiles, watching everything play out in front of him.

He looks to me, catching me watching him.

"You did good, son." The pride in his voice matches the look on his face as he takes in my family. "You need to take them over to Ireland for a visit. Your family over there would want to meet your girls."

I nod. "I will one day."

"I love you," comes Joss's voice. I turn my head to look at her, seeing her eyes filled with tears, but a wide, happy smile on her face.

"I love you, always, baby. Never expected you, but so dammed happy that I got you."

"Ditto, Fin. Ditto."

Us adults talk, while Juni, Calder, and Royal talk about celebrity crushes, and by that I mean female celebrities.

We discuss plans for R.O.E. Mom wants Perri to take on a more active role in the office. She has been doing great over there, bringing in new ideas on how to expand the company. Perri even updated the sex packs that you can order online from us.

They always sell well.

Sitting back, I place my arm across the back of Joss's chair and watch as my family bond. We are a group of mismatched people. We don't ever want to be like the Hallmark perfect family.

We are who we are, and if you don't like us, then no skin off our noses.

Go about your day, do not interfere with us, and we will leave you alone.

CHAPTER TWENTY-EIGHT

JOSS

Hitting save on my computer, I sit back in my office chair, happy that the workload I had today is done. I get to spend the day with Juni before she heads out tomorrow with my parents for two weeks.

She is packed and ready to go.

To say she is excited is an understatement. She packed and unpacked a few times before I took over. My parents have told her that they will do laundry, so she doesn't need to pack so much. Her tech bag is filled with her chargers, her laptop, and Kindle, which she also uses as a tablet.

To my surprise, she even packed some make-up and some hair products. Juni told my parents that she is gay, and they embraced her in a second.

Some people say that teenagers can't know if they are gay or not, but who says it's for them to decide who someone is or isn't. We have sat and talked about the way she feels, and I believe that she has a sensible head on her shoulders and can make her own choices.

We talked about all the different variants of sexual preference in the world, but right now, Juni is happy being a girl liking other girls. Will that change in the future? Who knows. If it does, I believe that when she makes that decision, she will have all the love and support she needs.

Pushing back from my desk, I make my way to the front of the house and up the stairs, to Juni's room. When I get close to her door, I hear her on the phone, clearly Facetiming or on speaker because I can hear the other girl's voice.

"You are so lucky you get to go away with your grandparents for two whole weeks. I'm stuck helping my dad at the store. God, I hate handling soil and seeds all day."

I smile, and it hits me that it is Nicole, her friend from school.

I step away and let the girls talk. Going to my bedroom, I strip out of my work clothes, and dress in a pair of jeans with some rips in them and a short, black shirt that ties at the waist. Going barefoot, I make my way downstairs.

Pulling open the fridge door, I collect items to make some lunch for Juni and me. Finan is out on a hunt today, working some case for another MC, so he couldn't talk about it. Club business, I was told.

The other old ladies have told me all about how the club works, something the ladies just aren't allowed to be involved in, and I get that. From the little snippets I have heard from being around Finan and the club, they do protection runs for other MC's. I'm not sure what they are protecting when they go on runs, but I'm not gutsy enough to ask Finan.

In my heart, I know that if something impacts Juni and I, Finan will let me know. He would never put either of us at risk. He did warn me that sometimes the darker side of the Rugged Hunters spill into the club life, but they do their best to neutralize it ASAP.

One time, they hunted for a guy who stole money from the man he was working for. They caught him, handed him over, but his girlfriend hunted the club down and almost attacked Travis, but they got to her in time.

Opening the drawer, I pull out a knife to cut up some vegetables for a salad to go with our chicken, when my phone rings from my back pocket.

I smile when I see Rookie's name, then answer it.

"Hey."

"Joss. Are you at home?"

"I am, why? Juni is finishing packing."

"There has been an accident. Finan has been hurt. I have one of the prospects coming to get you and Juni. He should be there any second," comes his calm voice through the phone.

If he is calm, he's not hurt that bad, right?

"How bad, Rookie?"

"He's okay. Banged up, but he wants you both here."

I go to reply when I hear a truck pulling into my drive.

"Rookie, I think the prospect is here."

"Good. Listen to him. He will get you here safe." I hang up and call for Juni. She comes running down the stairs, thankfully dressed.

"Put your shoes on. We are going to the hospital. Finan has been hurt."

I see the pain and worry flash in her eyes, but she nods and runs back upstairs to get her shoes. I slip into my flats, before collecting my purse and slinging it over my body with my phone tightly in my hand.

The feeling of waiting for the next call to come to say something has gone wrong and Finan is more hurt then they initially thought, swirls around my head making me think things that might not happen. Losing one man I have loved almost killed me, I am not sure I could survive it again.

Once we are seated in the truck, the prospect makes sure we are strapped in before he pulls away from my house.

I look out the front window, watching the scenery rush past as we speed toward the hospital. My legs bounce, my hands are knotting on my lap. I can't lose him. I know that Rookie assured me that he is not badly hurt, but I can't help but go back to the day I was informed that Owen was hurt, then a few hours later I was told that he didn't make it.

Life can end in the blink of an eye and there is no stopping it.

Before I know it, the car comes to a stop and the prospect is climbing out. He opens the door for Juni while I get myself out.

"I will walk you to the door. Prez is just inside with everyone. Then I'll park the car." With a nod, he leads both Juni and I over to the large glass doors that lead into the Emergency Room.

I nod to the prospect in thanks when I see Magnum and Opal.

"Joss." Tears flow down my face as Magnum opens his arms for me.

I run to him, crying while he holds me.

"Hey, come on now. He's fine. A little banged up, but good." Magnum's deep, smooth voice echoes through my head.

My head snaps back, looking at him with wide eyes.

"Come on," Opal says from behind me, with his arm around Juni.

We walk down the hall that has white walls, some machines off to the side, people walking past, giving the two men with us side glances. I know they may look imposing, and they can be if you get on their wrong side, but for the most part, the club are amazing.

Kind, respectful, and fiercely loyal.

When we turn the corner, we see more of the club. The older generation and the younger generation all looking like magazine and romance book cover models leaning against the walls in a variety of poses.

"Joss." My gaze lands on Rookie. He offers me a smile and nods toward the room. "Della is in with him, so is Calder. He is fine." His hands come to rest on my shoulders, as he looks me in the eyes.

Juni runs into the room, pushing the door open with so much force the door swings and hits the wall behind it, no doubt leaving a mark.

"DAD," comes Juni's panicked voice.

Dad? Why does my heart swell at the sound of that?

I run in after her, and my feet come to a screeching halt when I see Finan lying in the hospital bed, shirtless, his leg propped up on a pile of pillows, in a bright white cast. Juni is on the bed with him, tucked into his side while she cries.

This is new for us, seeing him looking so vulnerable. He has always been the strong one around us.

My eyes scan over his body. I see blood on his jaw, but it looks like a scratch. Another one is on his bicep, running down his forearm to his wrist. Bringing my gaze back up to his handsome face, I see him smiling at me, albeit it is a small one, but it is there.

My heart is racing, pounding so hard I'm surprised no one can hear it.

A ray of emotions rush over my body.

Fear, anguish. Relief, love.

Tears still flow down my face. My heart and air are on that bed together, giving each other support, because even though it's Fin who is hurt, he is holding Juni together with his strong arms that I should be wrapped in also, but I can't make my feet move.

"Joss?"

I blink, bringing my gaze back to his face. He looks at me with pleading eyes, hopeful that I go to him.

"Come here, baby." He holds his free hand out to me, a woosh of air leaves my lungs hearing him say my name.

It is like I needed that little confirmation of his voice that he is really okay.

I rush over to him, throwing myself into his arms as much as I can. I bury my head in his neck, breathing in his scent that is mixed with soap. They must have washed him. A flare of jealousy hits me in the chest at some random woman touching his body, cleaning his skin, when that is my job.

I pull back, my brow dipped. Finan watches me with a knowing smile on his face.

"Baby, my mom gave me a quick clean. No other woman touched me." His voice holds an amused tone.

"How did you know?"

He tilts his head, smirking. "Because I know you, baby," is all he says.

I shrug. Damn, he can read me like a book. Why can't I have that superpower? I look down his body to the large, imposing white cast, then back up to meet his gaze.

"Are you sure you're okay?"

He nods. "I am. Just some scratches and the broken leg. It was a clean break, so no surgery."

"How?"

"Some crazy chick ran me down. She didn't want us to take her sister. That's all I can tell you, babe." I nod in understanding.

He tells me very little about the hunts the Rugged Hunters go on, but it still gets to me sometimes that I don't know everything. But that is a 'Joss thing,' not a Finan thing.

"It takes a lot to take my brother down. The crazy bitch used a fucking Dodge Ram to stop him. Even hit her own sister too," Calder explains with a chuckle.

"Oh, my gosh, is the sister okay?" I ask. I know that she must have done something bad because they were hunting her, but I still don't like the idea of people getting hurt.

"She's fine. A broken arm, and a gash on her head," he finishes off explaining.

"Travis called the local police. She was arrested for trying to take Fin out," Calder explains.

"Finan needs to get some rest," Magnum says to the room.

"I'm not leaving him," I state firmly, looking at the aging club President. One side of his mouth tips up in smirk, then he nods.

"Joss is staying. Someone arrange a cot for her," Rookie says to the room. Royal and Jack leave, no doubt to arrange something for me.

"I want to stay too, Dad," Juni whispers, and everyone stops moving.

"Dad? Where is all of this coming from, Juni?" Finan asks her, using his finger to lift her chin so he can see her eyes.

"I love you. Mom loves you, and I know that you love us." Finan nods. "I never had a dad, only Grandad, and Uncle Matt. I love them too. You're different from them. All my friends have a dad, and I know that Daddy Owen died in the army, but I want you to be my dad."

The room has gone completely silent. Everyone is looking between the three of us. Juni and I are sitting on the edge of the bed, mirroring each other's positions.

Finan takes her hand in his, his other hand finding mine close to his hip.

"I would be honored if you called me 'dad,' but I want you to be completely sure on this, baby girl. Once you say yes, you are mine. You belong to the Rugged Skulls MC. Your family will triple in size, and sometimes that is not a good thing." He winks at her, making her giggle.

"Hey, I resent that, fuckface," Calder pipes in, but with a smile on his face.

The smile on Juni's face gets wider and brighter, and holy cow, it makes my heart melt.

"I want in. Does that make me a club brat now?" Juni looks from Finan, to Rookie to Magnum, who nods his head, smiling.

"Can never have too many Rugged Brats running around, Sparkles."

"See, you even have your own club name," Slide calls to her, making her jump off the bed and hug all the members one by one.

"I love you, Joss." Finan's words pull me from watching my daughter with the burly bikers in the room.

Seeing them in leather and denim, looking imposing and rugged, yet welcoming this teenage girl into their lives that I know they will protect her with everything they are.

"I love you too, Fin. So freaking much. You came into my life, our lives, when we needed you, and you have implanted yourself deep in our hearts."

"Not just your heart, though, right?" He wriggles his eyebrows, and I smile before kissing him.

"Holy fuck, did my brother just make a joke? A sex joke that that?" Calder says loudly to the room.

"And that is my cue to leave with Grams and Grampa." Juni says before coming around the bed and hugging Finan and me.

"I will see you in the morning, okay. Be a good girl for me," I tell her, cupping her face. "I love you."

"Love you too. Both of you. Do I still have to go on vacation now that Dad is hurt"?

"Yes, it's all planned out. I will take care of Finan. He will be here when you get back."

"Good. Love you both," she says, running from the bed and jumping on Calder's back.

"Peace out, brother. Try not to make the nurses blush when they walk in on something." He throws me a wink, before leaving.

Everyone says their goodbye to him, leaving Rookie and Della in the room with us.

"Boy, you gave us a scare. My heart fucking stopped getting that call from your brother," Rookie reveals.

"I'm sorry, Pop."

"Nothing to be sorry for. You may be an adult, a patched member of this club, have a woman and kid, but you are still our boy, and we still worry about you and your brother. Fuck, all the kids in the club. I'm getting gray before my time here, lad," Rookie carries on.

"Bullshit. That was Calder. He turned you gray years ago. Got fuck all to do with me."

I laugh at the banter between them, then look to Della, who has tears in her eyes as she watches her two guys talk.

"You okay?" I step over to her, touching her arm.

She gives me a sweet, wide smile; some tears spill free.

"Every hunt they go on, I pray that they come home in one piece. Not just my two, but all the guys," she says.

"I know. We haven't been together long, and I hate it when he leaves for a hunt, but it is his job, his priority. So is the club. I understand that. I knew what I was signing up for."

"You are good for him, ya know." I smile.

"He's good for me too. The best thing, besides Juni. I believe that Owen sent him to me when I needed him the most. That day we met on the trail, it was the anniversary of Owen's death. I needed some space and time to myself, so I went hiking, which is something that Owen and I liked to do together.

336

"Just as I passed Finan, the sun broke through the clouds and touched the rock he was sitting on. As cheesy and corny as it might sound, I felt Owen beside me. It was like he was pointing Finan out, but I pushed it down and carried on to the top. When I was coming back down, the same thing happened, but this time Finan jumped down into my path and we collided. I believe it was fate."

New tears blur my vision, thinking of that day. It was unreal how much I could feel Owen with me. I believe with all my heart that he sent Finan to me.

He knew what I needed when he was alive, and he knows what I need even though he has passed.

You know what they say: 'There is no accidental meetings between souls."

CHAPTER TWENTY-NINE

FINAN

Holy fucking shit, never did I think the last ten weeks would drag so much. I have just had my cruddy cast taken off, but I am now in a black temporary boot to support my leg for the next two weeks. Thankfully, I can take it off for bed or get in the bath with my woman.

Joss has played nurse with me the past few weeks. She made me move into her house, with her and Juni, so they could take care of me. The first two weeks, it was just the two of us, as Juni went on her vacation.

It was fucking beyond bliss. The first few days, Joss wouldn't let me touch her, because I was still having some pain, but then all bets were off when I was feeling better. Every time we fucked, she rode me to orgasm.

Facing me, reverse cowgirl—that was hot as fuck, seeing my cock slide into and out of her, covered with her slick juices.

Not only was the sex off the charts, but so was the simple times with her. We got to talk about anything and everything, since I was off work for the near future. I still worked but it was in the office at the clubhouse, or here at home, because Joss made room for me in her office.

Maverick took more field jobs and left the techy shit to me. I'm happy to be spending time with Joss, but I am missing my time out there with my brothers, watching people getting the information we need.

I love deducing shit down.

Love seeing someone's face when I tell them they are lying or give them information just by spending time with them.

Sitting next to my brother on our way home from the hospital, my leg feels so much fucking lighter. The black boot I'm wearing will do for now, but I can't wait to get back out there. The thrill of catching some sick fucks, or someone who has big enough balls to rip off an MC.

"I bet you are happy as fuck to get that shit off," Calder asks.

"Hell yeah. Do you know how hard it is to fuck my woman with this thing on? Or to have a fucking shower? The things we take for granted."

"I'm pretty sure that I will *never* know what it is like to fuck your woman, brother." Calder grins at me. I slug him in the shoulder as he drives me home.

"Prick," I say, grinning.

"Do you want to stop for something to eat? I'm fucking starving." He rubs his flat stomach.

"Man, you are always hungry."

"Yeah, and?" He smiles at me.

Shaking my head, I pull out my phone and send a text to Joss.

Me: Cast off. Juni still with my mom?

She doesn't leave me waiting.

Joss: She is. They will be home around four.

I look at my watch, noting the time is only ten-thirty, and smile. Fuck yes.

Me: Good. I'm on my way. Be in bed and naked.

Joss: What do you plan on doing to me, Mr. Price?

Me: Oh, baby, I plan on doing lots of things to you. I plan on making you writhe beneath me. I plan on making you shiver at my touch. Make you wet, soft, and hot. I plan on watching you come apart beneath my fingers, then my tongue, then my fat cock.

My cock thickens in my jeans at the thought of everything I want to do to her. I smirk down at my phone because she takes longer to reply this time. Looking up, I see that we are only a few minutes away from her house.

My phone dings, bringing my attention back to the device. I see that she has sent me a photo. Clicking on the attachment, I nearly swallow my tongue.

Holy motherfucking hell.

The image is of Joss in a maroon, lace cropped top that hugs her tits perfectly, and matching panties.

"Fuck," I growl. My cock goes rock hard behind my zipper.

"What? What is it?" Before I can tilt my phone away, my brother sees the photo. "Holy fucking shit. You lucky bastard." He grins.

"Fuck off." I push him away as he pulls into the drive.

"Do you need help getting out of the truck? I mean, your cock has to be solid steel right now and that is going to make limping impossible, brother." He winks at me.

"Little shit," I grind out and push the door open.

"Give Joss a kiss from me," he calls as I push the door shut and walk away.

He waits until I'm through the door before driving off, and I can't help but feel a sense of brotherhood when he does that. I'm vulnerable right now, still, so I know they have my back.

Locking the front door, I limp across the room, up the stairs, and down the hall to Joss's bedroom.

Sucking in a deep breath, my fist wraps around the handle, and I pull down, opening the door. The sight before me makes my heart fucking roar and my cock scream in pure agony at not being free to play.

Lying on the bright white bedding is my woman in the outfit she sent me. Her hair is partially pulled up, out of her face, and her make-up seems darker than it did this morning.

"All of this for me?" I ask her.

She nods, her eyes taking me in. I pull my cut off, placing it on the chair. Tugging the back of my t-shirt, the material drops to the floor. Knowing that I have to remove my boots before my jeans, I sit on the chair where my cut lays and unclip each strap.

"You okay?" Joss asks from the bed.

"Yeah, baby. Just need to be buried inside of you," I growl. Without taking my eyes off her, I remove the boots, get to my feet, and remove my jeans with little pressure on my healing leg.

She watches me like a hawk. No doubt waiting to see if I need her, and I do, just not in the way she thinks.

Once I'm naked, I step over to the bed with my cock in hand. Pre-cum leaks from the tip, and I use that to slick up my cock.

Joss licks her lips, so I nod down to where my hand is and smirk. Thank fuck she gets what I want. With no hesitation, Joss gets to her hands and knees and crawls slowly toward me. And fuck me, what a sight. Her ass is up in the air, her tits hanging perfectly, her eyes dark with desire.

She reaches me and parts her lips, keeping her gaze locked on mine.

"Do you know how sexy you look right now?" I ask her, as I direct my cock to her mouth.

Shaking her head at my question, I grip her jaw firmly with my free hand.

"You are the most stunning and sexy as fuck woman I have ever seen, Joss. No woman compares to you. Over the years, I have struggled to talk to women. I have been taken the wrong way because of the way I think and say things, but with you, everything seems to click into place," I tell her honestly. Her eyes fill with tears as she looks at me.

"I know what you mean. Fate stepped in that day on the mountain. I was meant to find you, Finan Price."

I nod because I think she's right.

"Good, I'm glad that we have all that soppy shit cleared up. Suck my cock." I grin down at her.

"Ever the romantic, baby," she says with a sexy smile on her face.

Opening her mouth, I push my cock through her parted lips, and my eyes roll into the back of my head at the feel of her wet mouth surrounding me.

"Oh, shit," I moan.

Tilting my head back, I savor her mouth on me. Her tongue dragging along my shaft, pressing against the vein, making my balls draw up. She licks and nips at the head of my cock, her hand going to my balls and giving a gentle tug, but hell it feels good.

Not wanting to come in her mouth, I tilt my hips back, making my cock slide out of her mouth.

"Why did you stop?" she whines, and it makes me laugh.

"You are a greedy little woman, aren't you? I want to come in your pussy, baby, not your mouth. Get on the bed."

She gives me a smile that makes my heart skip a beat, then she darts across the small distance to the bed, climbing on, giving me the perfect view of her tight ass.

"I am going to fuck that one day," I growl, moving toward her.

She looks at me and smirks. "I would love to feel you in my ass, baby."

"Fuck me."

"That is the plan," she purrs.

I kneel on the bed and move closer. Knowing she is ready for me, I kiss my way up her toned legs, her calves, her knee, then her thighs. Leaving her panties on, I slip a finger between the material, and her flesh, loving seeing the shiver that I caused.

Her breath hitches at the contact, her clit pulsing against my knuckle.

Looking up at her, I grin, seeing the blissed look on her face. Her eyes are wide and dark. Her lips plump and red from sucking my cock.

Lowering my head, I suck her little nub into my mouth at the same time I push a finger into her slick pussy. I watch in fascination as she arches off the bed, gasps leaving her mouth.

"Make me come with your dirty mouth, baby." Have I said how much I fucking love her calling me 'baby'?

I used to hate it when random women called me that. For me, it was a sense of commitment, unlike my brothers who call most women baby because of the time old tale of they forget the names of the chicks they are fucking.

No way in hell am I not giving my woman want she wants. Dropping my head again, I suck on her clit, hard, loving hearing her scream my name. Her thighs clamp around my ears, blocking out some of the sounds she's making.

Not liking that, I pull my fingers from her drenched pussy, using both hands to push her thighs wide, giving me more room to eat her.

"Oh, fuck. Yes," she cries out as she comes. Her juices flood my tongue, and I growl, loving the taste of her.

Lapping at her pussy, I drink down her climax. Seeing what I have done to her makes my cock leak just as much and my ego inflate big time.

Crawling up the bed, I am mindful of my leg, making sure not to add too much pressure on it. Her legs are still wide, her arms are out to the sides, and her eyes are closed while her chest heaves in heavy pants.

"Fuck, you look sexy after you come."

"You look hot all the time." This time, she winks, lifting her head to look at me.

"So do you baby. So fucking much. My dick is hard all the time around you."

Still on my hands and knees, braced above her, I stare down at the woman who holds my heart. My breath hitches at the new contact, and my cock in the palm of my hand.

"I know what you mean. I will need a whole new drawer of panties because you make them burst into flames by just touching me. I cream them when you look at me."

A throaty growl emanates from my body. My cock has never been so fucking hard for her. I love her dirty mouth. She surprised me when she first did it, and fuck me, I love hearing what she has to say when we are in bed.

"Fuck," I mutter to her. "Feed my cock to your pussy, baby."

Her eyes go wide with excitement, as she does what I tell her.

With her hand wrapped around me, she directs me to the one place I could live forever.

I feel the heat of her pussy on the head of my cock as I slip inside of her. Damn, she is fucking hot.

"Oh, Finan. You feel so good, honey," Joss pants. Her hands grip my forearms, her nails digging into my flesh.

"Ditto, baby." Fucking hell, she does.

I snap my hips, slamming my dick into her in short, fast movements. Her breath hitches, her chest rises and falls, and her tits bounce.

My gaze is fixated on the way her trim body moves beneath mine. She fits me perfectly. Never have I ever wanted to please a woman as much as I want to please her. Before Joss, it was all about getting in, getting off, and fucking off, but with her I want it all.

I have from the get-go.

"Yes. Keep going. Don't stop. Do not stop," she cries out as I pick up the pace.

I grunt.

She pants.

The sound of skin slapping against skin fills the room.

I hitch my leg up, hooking her calf over my shoulder, which opens her pussy up more for me.

"Oh shit. Finan, yes, baby, make me come," she screeches.

"Yes. Gush, baby. Come all over me," I grind out as her pussy starts to flutter around me.

"FUCK," she bellows as she finally clamps down, sucking my cock, needing more of him.

My hips stutter because the force of her climax is making it difficult to move. Pulling her body up a fraction, my eyes roll into the back of my head as the rush of sensation races through me like a mac truck.

My balls burst, filling my woman up in seconds.

My body stills over her. My leg aches, but I push the pain down as I settle next to my woman, pulling her to me. Her thigh comes up over my body, crushing her against my cock.

"Ewww, your dick is sticky," she whines, before jumping off the bed.

She is gone for a minute or two, before coming back to the bed with a wet washcloth, which she uses to clean my dick up. I smile as she tosses it back into the bathroom and settles back into my body.

"Always looking out for me, babe," I say against her head, kissing her hair.

"That's what I'm here for, Finan. You take care of us, and we take care of you. That is family."

"Couldn't agree more." I smile.

We lay in her bed in silence for what seems forever. I can feel myself dropping off to sleep. It's close to noon, so a nap sounds like a good plan right about now.

I breathe out, letting out a content sigh, letting myself relax and drift off.

"Move in with us." Joss's voice startles me.

Keeping my arms around her, I wrench my head back to look down at her.

"What did you just say?" I question her.

She giggles at me, leaning up to peck a kiss on my lips.

I know I must look stupid as fuck right now, with the shocked look on my face.

"You have been here while you were healing up. Juni and I have loved having you here, even though you were Mr. Grumpy pants for a while there. We still love you."

She kisses me again, her hand cupping my jaw.

"I like having you here. Going to sleep next to you, waking up next to you. It makes my heart full, having both you and Juni under one roof. So what do you say?"

"Fuck yes." I slam my mouth on hers, taking her mouth in a rough, hard kiss, showing how much I fucking love her through this one kiss.

My dick turns to steel with her body rubbing all over mine, her lips kissing me back with as much need as I give her.

"Need you again, baby."

"Then have me," she whispers as her mouth is still pressed to mine.

And fuck me do I have her. Three more times before Juni comes home. After we're freshly showered, we head to the clubhouse, chill with the club, and spend some quality time with the family before the guys get called out again. Thank fuck I only have two more weeks before I can go hunting again.

EPILOGUE

FINAN

Leaning back in my chair, I watch as Joss laughs with the ladies of the club, her gaze drifting over to Juni, then to me from time to time. I wink at her, making her smile. Damn, I am one lucky fucker to catch her.

Astrid leans forward, touching Joss's collarbone. A week ago, I took Joss to Rugged Ink so we could get our tattoos. Looking down at mine, I can't help but touch it.

Mine is a picture image of the same trail that I met Joss on; the trees, the path, that one rock I sat on and watched her pass me by. The words *'Your feet will bring you where your heart is.'* The words were fucking perfect because it needed that hike that day, because we got the news of my mom's cancer.

She's doing great. The docs cut out the lump and they are waiting for some test results to see if she needs chemo or any other treatment.

Joss needed that day because it was the anniversary of Owen's death. It was like fate stepped in and gave us a little nudge, then gave us both a huge shove when Juni was taken.

Looking back up, I see the ladies each take a look at Joss's tattoo. She has a simple delicate outlining of mountains, with some little trees, a stream, with a moon and stars. There are two faint geometrical circles that are almost complete, that Joss says she will have completed when we have another baby.

The best part of the tattoo is the words 'Property of Finan' running along the bottom of the stream.

"Damn, brother, keep looking at her like that and your cock will bust out of your jeans." I look to my side to see Lennox smirking at me.

I flip him off. "Fuck off, brother. At least my woman is letting my dick touch her." I wink.

The guys burst out laughing, but Lennox punches me in the thigh.

"Still not talking to her, huh?" Jack edges.

"I don't want to talk to her," Lennox says, shrugging.

"Yeah, you do, man. You have been pining over her for fucking years but refuse to make the move. What, you got a pencil cock or something?" Travis jests.

"Fuck you, man." Lennox sits up in his seat. "No, I don't. Nothing can happen. She isn't the girl for me, brother."

I watch as he nods a fraction when he says 'No, I don't.' Then he looks to the left when he says she is not the girl for him. People tend to look to the left when they are lying about something.

"You called it, man," Royal reminds him.

"I know," he growls. "This is fucked up."

"Can't be more fucked up than me, brother. I can't get fucking hard because my cock only seems to want one chick. Fuck knows where she is." Travis sinks down in his seat in a defeated action. His gaze goes all hazy, like he's remembering something.

Damn, that has to suck balls.

"Sucks to be you, man." Calder chuckles and Trav flips him off.

"At least I don't know where my girl is, brother. You do and are too pussy to do anything about it."

My gaze snaps to my brother. He looks at me with regret in his eyes. He never fucking told me he was pining after someone.

Want to fill me the fuck in, brother?"

"Fucking shit." Calder throws an empty bottle at Travis, who catches it and drops it to the side of his chair.

"Speak," I command, but the fucker shakes his head. "You will fucking talk to me." With a nod from him, I let it go for now.

I look around my brothers, my gaze landing on Royal, who is watching Travis. Cocking my head, he picks up on the action, looking at me. We sit in a stare off, I see his eyes narrow ever so fucking slightly, so I know he's hiding something.

With a little shake of his head telling me to leave it, I nod and mouth 'For now.' He returns a chin dip, and we change the subject.

"Have you been to Wicked Sugar yet, brother," Maverick asks Jack.

"Nope." He shrugs and looks over to where Dom is playing baseball with some of the older brothers.

"Why not?" Calder asks, while I watch him closely.

"Been busy, is all."

"With what?"

"Dom; I do have a kid you know. It's summer. Who wants to be busy all the fucking time?" he tells me.

"So? I have a kid. Albeit she is older than Dom and can go out with friends, but we still plan shit." I love the fact that I get to call Juni mine.

She is perfect, just like her mom, but I want to do the whole pregnancy thing, the diapers and middle of the night bottles. Damn, I need to knock my woman up quick.

"Fucking hell, you guys are worse than old ladies at a bingo game. Gossiping all the damn time," Jack groans.

We laugh at his reaction. Looking around at each of my brothers, I see what is going to happen in the future.

Lennox is going to go down a path that will lead to heartache, then a solid place.

Jack will man the hell up and take a path that will put him in a sugar rush.

Then there is Maverick, who will have to fight for what his heart wants. It will be torn to Hell and back, but he will win the badge in the end.

Now Travis, his path is something that will cause him to take a step back, look and listen before he sets his path in stone.

Calder will need to push his cocksure attitude down if he is to make someone his, but by the looks on him, he will have a fight on his hands.

"Baby." I look up and see Joss standing over me.

I pull her into my lap. She lets out a yelp but kisses me.

"It's time, handsome." With a nod, I get to my feet, settling Joss on hers before pulling her over to the middle of the yard.

A whistle comes from behind me, and I look over my shoulder to see Travis pulling his fingers out of his mouth with a wink. I give him a chin dip, before turning back to my club.

"I know some of you never thought I was in the right mind to find an old lady, and I get that. Knowing what plays out in my head, I know how I project shit sometimes, but fuck me, the day I met Joss, it was like some sort of switch was flicked and things seemed to settle in place. She makes me a better person, as cheesy as that is."

"Totally fucking cheesy, brother, but cheese tastes so fucking good," Slide calls out.

"Anyway. I'm claiming Joss Abrahams as mine. She is my old lady, and soon to be wife." Joss gasps as I drop to my knee, catching the white box Calder tosses to me.

"Get her, brother," he calls to me.

I look up at Joss, seeing her eyes swim with tears.

"We were both on that mountain for different reasons. Reasons that I think brought us together. Meeting you has been the best thing that has happened to me, but I not only got you, but I got a daughter out of it also. You and

Juni are mine, and there is no way I am letting either of you go."

Joss looks over to where Juni is standing with both of our parents. With a wide-ass smile on her face. Joy is close by, and I see Luna eyeing her, with a slight frown.

"You knew?" Joss asks Juni.

"He asked my permission," Juni replies.

Joss snaps her gaze to mine. "You did?"

"I did. And Owen's."

"Oh, Finan." She covers her mouth with her hand, looking down at me.

"Will you marry me, Joss?"

"YES. A MILLION TIMES YES," she screams.

Everyone cheers, clapping and calling out our names with congratulations.

The club is with us on this day, because in the words of the Rugged Skulls MC.

No one stands alone.

Pulling her to me I kiss her, delving my tongue in her mouth, savoring what she tastes like on the day I make her mine.

Against her lips, I grin. "You know what else I have to do?"

She nods, giving me a brilliant smile that lights up her face.

"Do it."

"DIBS!"

THE END

ACKNOWLEDGMENTS

Again, I have to thank you, boss man, my King. Thank you for always supporting me and at my side through it all. I love you, baby.

My 3 babies, even though you aren't babies anymore. Always be you.

Thank you to my girls for always supporting me through my writing process.

Huge thanks to Steph for making Finan more readable.

Thank you to the amazing readers for the support and kind words.

BOOKS BY AUTHOR

Standalones

Let Me Love You

What Are The Chances

This Time Around

Defeating The Odds

Christmas at Paradise Meadow

The Phoenix Boys

Rafe

Ryder

Reeve

Castle Ink

Dex

Jay

Ivy

Unforgiven Riders MC

Claiming Mine

Protecting Mine

Taking Mine

Getting Mine

Keeping Mine

Reckless Angels MC

Part 1 - Twisted Tales of Mayhem

Part 2 - Twisted Steel

Santa's Naughty Helpers – Unwrapping Mine

Twisted Steel Second Edition: NOMAD

Twisted Steel Third Edition: Preacher

Rebel Hype

Creed - Heart Beats Anthology

Rugged Skulls MC

Magnum

Opal

Slide

Sarge

Rookie

Edge

Rugged Ink

Zeb

Lee

Rugged Skulls MC – Next generation

Royal

Riot: Road Wreckers MC #4

Fighting for Una: Royal Bastards MC

ABOUT THE AUTHOR

Amy lives in South Wales with her husband and 3 children. Their family dogs and musk turtle. Besides writing Amy is very fond of photography and a lover of music. She is also a big fan of Supernatural, Sons of Anarchy, plus The Medici. Amy is also a huge ice hockey fan, mainly the Cardiff Devils. She loves spending time with her family and friends, plus meeting new people. From bad boys to rock stars and bikers, Amy's books cover them all.

Facebook Author Page
Amy's Awesome Nerds
Goodreads
Twitter
Instagram
Bookbub
Newsletter
Amazon

Printed in Great Britain
by Amazon